© Sigrid Estrada

ANDRÉ ACIMAN is the author of *Eight White Nights, Call Me by Your Name* (now a major motion picture), *Out of Egypt, False Papers, Alibis,* and *Harvard Square,* and the editor of *The Proust Project.* He teaches comparative literature at the Graduate Center of the City University of New York and lives with his wife in Manhattan.

Additional Praise for

ENIGMA VARIATIONS

"An enormously intelligent and captivating novel, filled with surprising twists and psychological acuity."
—Toby Lichtig, *The Wall Street Journal*

"A gorgeous, albeit devastating, journey through the life of Paul . . . With an uncanny knowledge of the human heart, Aciman's ability to create a universe of woe in a single line catapults Paul's story out of the ubiquitous mendacity of a cosmopolitan narrative to a profound meditation on love."
—Michael Raver, *The Huffington Post*

"Aciman's description of [Paul's] love is devastatingly, excruciatingly real. He exquisitely puts into language what we know of first love, whether we experience it early in life or later."
—Hooman Majd, *Los Angeles Review of Books*

"A worthy successor to *Call Me by Your Name*. [*Enigma Variations*] is a thing of beauty, with sentences that suck the breath out of the reader. . . . André Aciman is a writer of such skill that he is incapable of writing anything less than thrilling."
—*New York Journal of Books*

"[Aciman's] poetic novel charts rich emotional terrain. . . . *Enigma Variations* is a rewarding excavation about one man's inner life, mapping out the way our emotional and romantic ties can shape our self-knowledge for the rest of our lives."
—*Lambda Literary Review*

"The minute mapping of Paul's shifting emotions convinces and compels. . . . Depth, not breadth, is the treasure, and grasping after the ungraspable present along with Paul becomes the point of the quest itself." —Jeff P. Jones, *The Millions*

"Always searching for more, for something that isn't there, and wondering if finding true love happens only once—these are the twin themes upon which Aciman artfully constructs his latest deeply felt novel. . . . Aciman's sensuous, subtle language supports not only his marvelous descriptive power but also how deeply and resonantly he constructs his fondly and fully conceived characters." —*Booklist*

"A breathless, sketched rendering of one man's life in love, Aciman's novel speaks earnestly not only of longing and lust, but also of more complicated emotions. . . . [Aciman] portrays Paul convincingly as a sensuous and self-aware figure, forever treading the border between melodrama and tragedy." —*Publishers Weekly*

"As often in his fiction, Aciman immerses readers in a milieu that is achingly sensuous—and sensual, too. . . . An eminently adult look at desire and attachment, with all the usual regrets and then some—but also with the knowledge that such regret 'is easy enough to live down.' " —*Kirkus Reviews*

ENIGMA VARIATIONS

ENIGMA VARIATIONS

ANDRÉ ACIMAN

PICADOR   FARRAR, STRAUS AND GIROUX   NEW YORK

ENIGMA VARIATIONS. Copyright © 2017 André Aciman. All rights reserved. Printed in the United States of America. For information, address Picador, 175 Fifth Avenue, New York, N.Y. 10010.

picadorusa.com • picadorbookroom.tumblr.com
twitter.com/picadorusa • facebook.com/picadorusa

Picador® is a U.S. registered trademark and is used by Macmillan Publishing Group, LLC, under license from Pan Books Limited.

For book club information, please visit facebook.com/picadorbookclub or email marketing@picadorusa.com.

Designed by Jo Anne Metsch

The Library of Congress has cataloged the Farrar, Straus and Giroux edition as follows:

Names: Aciman, André, author.
Title: Enigma variations: a novel / André Aciman.
Description: New York : Farrar, Straus and Giroux, 2017.
Identifiers: LCCN 2016020262 | ISBN 9780374148430 (hardcover) | ISBN 9780374714772 (ebook)
Subjects: LCSH: Desire (Philosophy)—Fiction. | Self-realization—Fiction. | BISAC: FICTION / Literary. | GSAFD: Didactic fiction.
Classification: LCC PS3601.C25 E55 2017 | DDC 813'.6—dc23
LC record available at https://lccn.loc.gov/2016020262

Picador Paperback ISBN 978-1-250-15997-7

Our books may be purchased in bulk for promotional, educational, or business use. Please contact your local bookseller or the Macmillan Corporate and Premium Sales Department at 1-800-221-7945, extension 5442, or by email at MacmillanSpecialMarkets@macmillan.com.

First published by Farrar, Straus and Giroux

First Picador Edition: January 2018

10 9 8 7 6 5 4 3

For Susan,

Amor che nella mente mi ragiona

CONTENTS

FIRST
LOVE

I '*ve come back for him.*

These are the words I wrote down in my notebook when I finally spotted San Giustiniano from the deck of the ferryboat. Just for him. Not for our house, or the island, or my father, or for the view of the mainland when I used to sit alone in the abandoned Norman chapel in the last weeks of our last summer here, wondering why I was the unhappiest person on earth.

I was traveling alone that summer and had started my month-long trip on the coast by going back to a place where I'd spent all my childhood summers. The trip had been a long-standing wish of mine, and now that I had just graduated, there was no better time to pay a short visit to the island. Our house had burned down years earlier, and after we'd moved to the north, no one in the family was ever keen on revisiting the place, or selling the property, or finding out what had really happened. We simply abandoned it, especially on hearing that, after the fire, the locals had pillaged what they could and laid waste to the rest. Some even held that the fire was no accident. But these were mere speculations, my father said, and there was no way of knowing anything but by going there. So the first thing I promised I'd do on stepping off the ferryboat was to make a right turn, walk down the familiar esplanade, past the imposing Grand Hotel and the guesthouses lining the waterfront, and head straight to our house to see the damage myself. This is what I'd promised my father. He himself had no wish to set foot on the island again. I was a man now, and it was up to me to see what needed to be done.

But perhaps I wasn't coming back just for Nanni. I was coming back for the boy of twelve I'd been ten years earlier—though I knew I'd find neither one. The boy now was tall and sported a bushy reddish beard, and as for Nanni, he'd disappeared altogether and was never heard from again.

I still remembered the island. I remembered how it looked the last time I'd seen it on our last day, scarcely a week before school started, when my father had taken us to the ferry station and then stood on the dock waving at us as the anchor chain clamored and the boat screeched its way backward while he stayed there motionless, growing smaller and smaller until we were no longer able to see him. As had been his habit each fall, he would stay behind for a week to ten days to make sure the house was locked down properly, the electricity, water, and gas turned off, the furniture protected, and all the local help on the island paid. I am sure he was not displeased to see his mother-in-law and her sister leave on the ferryboat that would take them back to the mainland.

But what I did as soon as I set foot on the ground after the old *traghetto* clanged and pulled out of the same exact spot a decade later was to turn left instead of right and head straight up the stone-paved path that led to the ancient hilltop town of San

Giustiniano Alta. I loved its narrow alleys, sunken gutters, and old lanes, loved the cooling scent of coffee from the roasting mill that seemed to welcome me no differently now than when I ran errands with my mother, or when, after seeing my Greek and Latin tutor that last summer, I would take the long way home every afternoon. Unlike the more modern San Giustiniano Bassa, San Giustiniano Alta always rested in the shade even when it grew unbearably sunny along the marina. In the evenings oftentimes, when the heat and humidity on the seafront became intolerable, I'd go back up with my father for an ice cream at the Caffè dell'Ulivo, where he sat facing me with a glass of wine and chatted with the townspeople. Everyone knew and liked my father and deemed him *un uomo molto colto*, a very learned man. His hobbling Italian was laced with Spanish words that sought to sound Italian. But everyone understood, and when they couldn't help but correct and laugh at some of his strangely macaronic words, he was happy to join in the laughter himself. They called him Dottore, and though everyone knew he was not a medical doctor, it was not uncommon for someone to ask him for medical advice, especially since everyone trusted his opinion on health matters more than they did the local pharmacist, who liked to pass for the town physician. Signor Arnaldo, the owner of the caffè, had a chronic cough, the barber suffered from eczema, Professore Sermoneta, my tutor, who frequently ended up in the caffè at night, always feared they'd have to remove his gallbladder one day—everyone confided in my father, including the baker, who liked to show my father the bruises on his arms and shoulders caused by his ill-tempered wife, who, some said, started cheating on him on their very wedding night. Sometimes, my father would even step outside the caffè with someone to dispense an opinion in private, then push aside the beaded curtain and come back in, and return to his seat with both his elbows spread on the table, his emptied glass of wine in the middle, and stare at me, always telling me there was no need to rush with my ice cream, we might still find time to walk up to the abandoned castle if I wished. The castle by night overlooking the faraway lights on the mainland was our favorite spot, and there both of us would sit silent along the ruined ramparts to watch the stars. He called this making memories, for *the day when*, he'd say. *What day?* I'd ask, to tease him. *For the day you know when.* Mother said we were made from the same mold. My thoughts were his thoughts, and his thought my thoughts. Sometimes I feared he might read my mind if he so much as touched me on the shoulder. We were the same person, she said. Gog and Magog, our two Dobermans, loved only my father and me, not my mother or my elder brother, who had stopped spending his summers with us a few years earlier. The dogs turned away from everyone else and growled if you got too close. The townsfolk knew to keep their distance, but the dogs were trained not to bother anyone. We could tie them to the leg of a table outside the Caffè dell'Ulivo, and so long as they could see us, they lay down as meekly as ewes.

On special occasions, rather than head down to the marina after stopping at the castle, my father and I would go back into town, and because we thought alike, we'd stop for another ice cream. "She'll say I'm spoiling you." "Another ice cream, another glass of wine," I'd say. He'd nod, knowing there was no point denying it.

Our nightwalks, as we called them, were our only times alone together. Entire days would go by without him. He was in the habit of going for a swim very early in the morning, then heading for the mainland after breakfast, and coming back in the evening, sometimes late at night on the very last ferry. Even when I was asleep, I loved hearing his footsteps crunching the gravel leading to our house. It meant he was back, and the world was whole again.

My poor final grade in Latin and Greek that spring had put a cruel wedge between my mother and me. My report card had arrived in late May just days before we boarded the ferry to San Giustiniano. The whole boat ride was one loud, unending rant, the reprimands came in buffets, while my father leaned quietly against the railing as though waiting to intervene at the right moment. But there was no stopping her, and the more she yelled, the more she found fault with everything else about me, from the way I sat down to read a book, to my penmanship, to my total inability to give a straight answer whenever anyone asked what I thought about this or that—shifty, always shifty—and, come to think of it, why didn't I have a single friend in the world, not at school, not at the beach, not anywhere, not interested in any-thing, or anyone, for the love of God—what was wrong with me, she said as she kept trying to scratch off a drop of dried chocolate ice cream that had dripped on my shirt when I'd gone with my father to buy a cone before boarding the boat. I was convinced that her disapproval had been waiting for who knows how long and needed my botched Latin and Greek exam to burst into the open.

To soothe her, I promised I'd work harder during the summer. Work? Everything about me needed work, she said. There was so much wrath in her voice that day that it verged on palpable contempt, especially when she laced her fury with snarks of irony, finally exploding at my father, "And you wanted to buy him a Pelikan pen!"

My grandmother and her sister, who were with us on the ferry that day, sided with my mother, of course. My father didn't say a word. He hated both women—the shrew and the über-shrew, he called them. He knew that the moment he asked my mother to lower her voice or to temper her reprimands, they'd immediately chime in as well, which would easily push him over the edge and make him blow up at the two, if not all three, of them, at which point they'd quietly let him know they'd rather head straight back to the mainland on the ferry than spend the summer in our house. I'd seen him explode once or twice over the years and could tell he was trying to keep a lid on things and not ruin the trip. He'd simply nod a few times in token agreement when she criticized me for wasting so much time on my stupid stamp collection. But when he finally said something to change the subject and cheer me up a bit, she turned to him and yelled that she wasn't quite done with me yet. "Some of the passengers are beginning to stare," he finally said. "Let them stare all they want, I'll stop when I'm good and ready." I don't know why, but it suddenly occurred to me that, while yelling at me so vehemently, she was really venting her pent-up rage against him, though without drawing him into her line of fire. Like the Greek gods who were constantly feuding with one another using mortals as their pawns, she was haranguing me to beat up on him. He must have realized what she was doing, which is why he smiled at me when she wasn't looking, meaning, *Put up with it for now. Tonight, you and I will head out for ice cream and make memories by the castle.*

That day, after we landed, my mother desperately tried to make it up to me, speaking to me so sweetly and so amicably that we made peace soon enough. Yet the real damage was not in the cutting words she wished she hadn't spoken and that I would never forget. The damage was to our love: it had lost its warmth, its spontaneity, and become a willed, conscious, rueful love. She was pleased to see I still loved her; I was pleased to see how readily both she and I were fooled. The two of us were aware of being pleased, which intensified our truce. But we must have sensed that being so easily reassured was nothing more than a dilution of our love. She hugged me more often, and I wanted to be hugged. But I didn't trust my love, and I could tell, from the way she looked at me when she thought I wasn't looking, that she didn't trust it either.

With my father it was different. On our long nightwalks we spoke of everything. Of the great poets, of parents and children and why friction between them was unavoidable, of his father, who had died in a car accident weeks before my birth and whose name I bore, of love, which happens only once in life, and thereafter is never quite spontaneous or impulsive, and finally, as if by miracle, because it didn't bear on Latin and Greek or on my mother or on the shrew and übershrew, of Beethoven's *Diabelli Variations*, which he'd just discovered that spring and shared with no one but me. My father played Schnabel's recording every evening, so that Schnabel's piano resonated throughout the house and became the sound track of that year. I liked the sixth variation, he the nineteenth, but the twentieth was all about mind, and the twenty-third, well, the twenty-third was probably the liveliest, funniest thing Beethoven ever composed, he said. We replayed the twenty-third so often that my mother begged us to stop. So I'd tease her and hum it to her instead, which made my father and me laugh, but not her. On our way into the caffè on those summer nights, we'd simply throw out a number between one and thirty-four, and each would have to say what he thought of that variation, including Diabelli's theme. Sometimes on our way up to the castle we would sing the words to the twenty-second variation on a theme from *Don Giovanni*, the words of which he'd taught me long before. But when we reached the top and watched the stars, we'd stand quietly and always agree that the thirty-first variation was the most beautiful of them all.

I was thinking of Beethoven on my way up the alley and of

the yelling on the boat. None of it had gone away. I immediately recognized the old pharmacy, the cobbler's, the locksmith's, and the barbershop with its two tattered reclining chairs still patched with leather strips that had been stitched in place who knows how long before I came into the world. As I kept climbing uphill that morning and could already spot a slice of the abandoned castle, I began to have a strong presage of the scent of resin wafting toward me before I'd even reached the cabinetmaker's shop around the bend of vicolo Sant'Eusebio. That feeling hadn't changed, would never change. His shop, with his home right above it, stood two steps past the lumpish curbstone jutting out of the corner building. The memory of the scent stirred a trace of fear and discomfort that I found as thrilling now as I did then, though I was still unable to name that unsettling inflection of fear, shame, and excitement any better a decade later. Nothing had changed. Perhaps I hadn't changed. I didn't know whether I was disappointed or pleased that I hadn't outgrown any of this. The rolling shutter of the cabinetmaker's shop was locked down, and though I stood there trying to gather how much was lost since I'd last been there, I found myself unable to string together a single thought. All I could focus on were the rumors we'd been hearing since the burning of the house.

I walked back to the barbershop, and sticking half my body through the beaded curtain, asked one of the two barbers whether he knew what had happened to the *ebanista* next door.

The bald barber, who was seated on one of the two large chairs in his shop, lowered his newspaper and spoke one word before returning to his reading: "*Sparito*, vanished." That said it all.

Did he know where? Or how? Or why? I asked.

The answer was a summary shrug of the shoulders suggesting he didn't know, couldn't care less, wasn't about to tell some

twentysomething kid who wandered into his shop asking too
many questions.

I thanked the barber, turned around, and proceeded uphill.
What surprised me was that Signor Alessi had not greeted or
recognized me, though God knows the number of times he'd
cut my hair all through my summers here. Perhaps there was no
point in saying anything.

It took me a while to realize that no one seemed to recognize
me on the island. Obviously I must have changed a great deal
since I was twelve, or perhaps my long raincoat, my beard, and
the dark-green knapsack fastened to my back gave me an entirely
different look from that of the clean-cut boy they all remembered.
The grocer, the owners of the two caffès on the tiny piazza by
the church, the butcher, and above all the baker, whose scent of
freshly baked bread hovered like a benison on the side alley when
I left my Latin and Greek tutor in the afternoons and couldn't
have been more famished—no one knew me or gave me a second
glance. Even the old one-legged beggar who had lost his limb in
a boating accident during the war and was back to his usual spot
by the main fountain in the square failed to know who I was when
I gave him something. Hadn't even thanked me, which was truly
unlike him. Part of me felt rising contempt for San Giustiniano
and its people, while another was not entirely saddened to see I
no longer cared for it. Perhaps I had put it behind me and not
realized it. Perhaps I was like my parents and my brother in this.
No point going back.

On my way downhill, I resolved to reach what I assumed
was going to be the hollowed-out base of our house, assess
what I could, speak to neighbors who had watched me grow up,
and then head out on the evening ferry. I had a mind to drop in
on my old tutor but kept putting off the meeting. I still remembered him as a soured, prickly fellow who seldom had a kind

word for anyone, least of all his pupils. My father had suggested I book a room in a pension by the harbor in case I wished to stay the night. But I already sensed, just by my hasty amble up and down the old town, that my visit wouldn't last longer than a couple of hours. The question was where to spend the rest of the day until boarding the ferry back.

And yet I had always loved it here, from the soundless mornings when you woke up to face a clear and quiet sky that hadn't changed since the Greeks had settled here, to the sound of my father's footsteps when, contrary to his usual practice on weekdays, he would suddenly come back from the mainland unannounced in the afternoon and something of a feast erupted in our hearts. Not a ruffle, in those days. From my bed, you saw the hills, from the living room the sea, and when the dining room shutters were flung open on cooler days, you could step out on the terrace and take in the valley and beyond the valley the hazy outline of the hills on the mainland across the sea.

On leaving the old town, I was struck by the blinding spill of light sweeping through the fields, onto the esplanade, down to the glinting sea beyond. I loved the silence. I'd been dreaming of coming back for so long. Everything felt familiar, nothing had changed. And yet everything felt distant, frayed, unreachable, as though something in me were unable to register that all this was real, that so much of it had once belonged to me. The path to our house, including the shortcut I'd "invented" as a boy and wasn't for anything going to miss taking today, was exactly as I'd left it. I remembered the walk through the deserted scented grove of limes, which they call *lumie* here, followed by a field of poppies, and finally the quiet, gutted ancient Norman chapel that had more of me in it than any other place in the world, with its huge plinth thrown in among thistles and growth that were as parched now as they'd been then, and as always the dried remnants of wild dog poop and pigeon droppings on its grounds.

What stung me was knowing that our house was no longer there, that all those living in it were gone, that early summer life here was never going to be the same. I felt like a timid ghost who knows his way around town but is no longer wanted or paid attention to. My parents wouldn't be waiting for me, no one would have set aside goodies for when I'd rush back home famished after swimming. All our rituals were disbanded and void. Summer didn't belong to me here.

The closer I neared our house, the more I began dreading the sight of what they'd done to it. The thought of the fire and of the looting, the looting especially, was enough to stoke a demon of sorrow, anger, and spite aimed not only at everyone living here but also against ourselves, as though the inability to prevent plunder and vandalism by alleged friends and neighbors sat on our conscience more than on theirs. "Don't rush to conclusions," my father had warned, "and above all don't argue." This was my father's way. I cared for none of it. I would gladly have dragged each one to court, rich, poor, orphans, widows, cripples, and war disabled.

And yet, of all the people here, there was only one I wished to see, and he was gone, *sparito*. I knew this already. So why even bother asking after him? To see how they'd react? To remind myself that I hadn't invented him? That he'd truly lived here once? That all I had to do was ask about him in the barbershop, and after inquiries were shouted out by so many up and down the narrow, cobbled lanes of San Giustiniano Alta, he would finally turn up just because people had called his name?

Why should he even remember me? He had known me as a twelve-year-old, now I was twenty-two and sported a beard. Yet the years had done nothing to make me forget the rising anxiety that seized me each time I both dreaded and hoped to bump into him at the beach or around town. Wasn't this what I really hoped to feel as I made my way up to his shop this morning? The fear, the panic, the old tightness in my throat, which only a sob could release and which might erupt of its own if he so much as stared at me longer than I could stand. He stares at you, you get worked up, and all you want is to find a quiet spot to let yourself cry the moment you're alone, because nothing, not even failing a Latin and Greek exam or getting badly yelled at, could leave you feeling so beaten and undone. I remembered everything. The wanting to cry, especially, and the waiting to see him because the waiting and hoping were unbearable, the wish to hate everything about him because one short glance from him and suddenly you felt totally distraught and couldn't smile or laugh or find joy in anything.

I WAS WITH my mother the first time I met him. He did not wait to be introduced but right away, "You're Paolo," he said, tousling my hair.

When I gave him a startled look to mean how did he know, his answer was a jaunty "Everyone knows." Then, seeming to remember, "Maybe from the beach," he said.

I knew that his name was Giovanni, just as I knew that everyone called him Nanni. I had seen him at the beach, in the outdoor movie theater by the church, and many times around Caffè dell'Ulivo at night. I had to control myself from showing how thrilled I was to discover that the man before whom I could have sworn being a complete nonentity not only knew my name but was actually standing under my own roof.

Unlike him, though, I did not show that I knew him. My

mother introduced him to me with a note of irony in her voice, meaning, *But surely you do know Signor Giovanni.*

I shook my head and even managed to pretend being embarrassed for being rude at not knowing his name.

"But everyone knows Signor Giovanni," she insisted, as though urging me to find it in me to be polite. But I did not bend.

He gave me his hand. I shook it. He looked younger, and his skin was less dark than I remembered. He was tall, slender, in his late twenties. I'd never seen him up close before. Eyes, lips, cheeks, jaw. It would take me years to know what exactly about each feature had struck me.

On my father's suggestion, my mother had asked him to come by to restore an antique folding desk and two picture frames dating back to the previous century.

He arrived one morning in June, and contrary to custom, he accepted the lemonade she offered. Everyone else who came to our house—the seamstress, the delivery boys, the upholsterer—always asked for water. It was their way of earning their salary plus the inevitable gratuity by showing they owed us nothing and hadn't asked for anything more than the glass of water we'd put before them on a scorching summer day.

That morning in our house, because he stood so very close to me, something undefined in his face left me as shaken and flustered as when I was asked once to recite a poem in front of the entire school, teachers, parents, distant relatives, friends of the family, visiting dignitaries, the world. I couldn't even look at him. I needed to look away. His eyes were too clear. I didn't know whether I wanted to touch them or swim in them.

As he spoke to my mother and occasionally looked in my direction, as though eager to draw my opinion, I would try to stare back at him. But looking into his eyes was like looking down a steep, craggy cliff leading to a billowing green ocean below—you were pulled in and were told not to fight back but warned not to stare, so that you could never look long enough to know why you kept wanting to stare. His gaze didn't just scare me. It troubled me, as if in staring into it I'd risk not only offending him but also exposing some sinister, shameful secret about myself that I did not wish to disclose. Even when I tried to return his glance to reassure myself that he wasn't as threatening as I feared, I still had to look away. He had the most beautiful face I'd ever seen, and I wasn't brave enough to look at it.

And yet each time he turned his gaze away from my mother to look at me, he was also telling me that although he was much older and could see right through me, he and I could be equals, that he wasn't judging me, held no scorn, was interested in what I might have to say about the furniture even if I was just standing quietly, trying to hide how thoroughly unworthy I felt.

So I would look away.

Though I couldn't do that either.

The last thing I wanted was to seem shifty, especially with my mother in the room.

His face was the picture of health, and there was a flush about it, as though he'd just come from swimming. His even-tempered and accommodating smile when it quivered to express his thoughts or his doubts about the desk told me of the very person I wished to be someday. What a pleasure to look at his face and hope to be just like him. If only he could be my friend and teach me things. I had no other concept to draw on.

My mother had meant to show him into the living room, but he had already guessed where it was and had immediately spotted the desk, opened it, and without asking permission hastily proceeded to remove its two slim, squeaky, but unusually long drawers. Before you knew it, he was reaching behind the empty

drawer slots and palming his way inside the hump of the bombe-
form cylinder desk, groping around until he found the hidden
recess, and after some exertion, he fished out a small hidden
box with curved corners that matched the design of the rounded
desk itself. It caught my mother's breath. How did he know this
box existed? she asked. Great carpenters, usually from the north,
possibly French, he said, always liked to show they could create
hidden spaces in the most impenetrable spots; the smaller the
piece of furniture, the more arcane and ingenious the hiding
place. And there was something else he needed to show her,
which she most likely also knew nothing about. "What is it,
Signor Giovanni?" He lifted the desk a bit and showed her hidden
hinges.

"What are they for?" she asked. The desk, he explained, was
totally collapsible so that one could carry it elsewhere very
easily. But he didn't want to task the hinges right now because
he didn't trust the condition of the wood. He handed my mother
the tiny wooden box.

"But this desk has been in my husband's family for at least a
hundred and fifty years," she said, "and yet no one had any idea
this box existed."

"Then the Signora will discover either hidden jewels or letters
some great-grandparent would rather she knew nothing about,"
he said, stifling the quiver of mirth and mischief that I'd seen
rippling on his features a few times already that morning and
that made me want to learn to smile just like that.

The box was locked.

"I don't have a key," she said.

"*Mi lasci fare, Signora*, allow me," he said, every word under-
written with both deference and authority. So saying, he removed from his jacket a ring of tiny tools that looked less like
awls, gouges, and screwdrivers than a collection of sardine-can

openers of all sizes. He then took his eyeglasses from his breast pocket, unfolded both temples, and cautiously slipped the tip of each behind an ear. He reminded me of a boy in kindergarten who had started wearing glasses and was still awkward when putting them on. Then, using his extended middle finger, he pushed the bridge of his glasses ever so delicately over his nose. He might as well have been placing a priceless Cremonese violin under his chin. There was fluency and dexterity in every one of his gestures that stirred not just trust but admiration. What surprised me was his hands. They were neither calloused nor marred by labor or by the products of his trade. The hands of a musician. I wanted to touch his hands, not just because I wanted to see if the pink of his palms was as smooth to the touch as his hands promised, but because, suddenly, I wanted to place my palms under the care of each of his. Unlike his eyes, his hands did not intimidate—instead they welcomed. I wanted his long knuckles and almondine fingernails to slip in between each of my fingers and hold them down in a warm and lasting display of good fellowship, and with this gesture alone repeat the promise that one day, perhaps sooner than I hoped, I too would be a grown man with hands like his, wearing glasses like his, letting a glint of mirth and mischief radiate through my features to tell the world I was an expert at something and a very, very good man.

He saw us watching him trying to pry open the box, and without looking in either my direction or my mother's, he kept smiling to himself, conscious of our suspense, all the while trying to dispel it without suggesting he was aware of it. He knew what he was doing, had done it many times, he said, all the while staring straight into the keyhole. "Signor Giovanni," my mother said as he was still fiddling with the lock, trying not to distract him. "Yes, Signora," he replied without looking up. "You have a beautiful voice." He was so deeply engrossed with the lock that he didn't seem to hear her, but seconds later, "Don't be fooled, Signora, I can't carry a tune." "With that voice?" "Everyone laughs when I sing." "Because they're jealous." "Trust me, I can't even sing 'Happy Birthday.'" All three of us laughed. There was a moment of silence. Without rushing or forcing things or scratching the bronze inlay area around the old lock, he picked at it some more, then *"Eccoci!"* he exclaimed, "here we are," and a few seconds later, as though all that was needed was a bit of persistent, gentle coaxing before even hearing the telltale click of the lock, which had finally yielded, the box opened. I wanted to kiss his hands. What he revealed when he opened it was a gold pocket watch, a pair of gold cuff links, and a fountain pen lying on a lining of thick verdigris felt. On the side of the pen, in gold lettering, was my grandfather's full name, my name as well.

"Who would have known!" exclaimed my mother. These were her father-in-law's cuff links bearing his initials and dating back most probably to his student days in Paris. He was very attached to them. She also remembered seeing the vest watch, though long ago. He must have left the three of them there, but when he never came back after the accident, no one even noticed they were gone. "And now they're suddenly here—but he is not." My mother seemed deep in thought. "I was very fond of him, and he of me."

The cabinetmaker bit his lower lip and nodded quietly.

"This is the cruel thing about the dead. They come back in ways that always catch us off guard, don't they, Signor Giovanni?" Mother said.

"Yes," he agreed. "Sometimes, just wanting to tell them something that would have mattered to them, or to ask about people and places only they would have known about, reminds us that they'll never hear us, won't answer, don't care. But perhaps it's much worse for them: maybe they are the ones calling out to us and it is we who can't listen and don't seem to care."

Nanni had obviously known sorrow in his life. You could tell by how solemn and quiet he'd grown within seconds of smiling. I liked him solemn too.

"You're a philosopher, Signor Giovanni," said my mother with a docile smile on her face as she held the open box in her hands.

"Not a philosopher, Signora. I lost my mother a few years ago when she tripped down the stairs, and within months I lost my father too. Both were in perfect health. But before I knew it I became an orphan, the boss, and a parent to my younger brother. Still, there is so much I need to ask them, so much I could have learned from my father. All he left behind is barely traces."

An awkward silence followed. Nanni continued to examine the desk, and after observing the hinges, he said that someone must have worked on this desk before. Which explained why it still had such a strong sheen. "It was probably my grandfather," he said. My mother was about to give the crown of my grandfather's watch a few twists to wind it. But the *ebanista* told her not to. "It might ruin the spring mechanism. Better have someone look at it."

"The watchmaker?" she asked naïvely.

"The watchmaker is an idiot. Maybe someone on the mainland," he said.

Did he know of one?

Yes.

He could bring it to the watchmaker himself the next time he took the ferry across.

She thought for a moment, then said she'd ask my father to take it in.

"*Capisco*, I understand," he said, with the retiring gesture of a person seemingly guilty of an infraction he knows he hasn't committed but is graceful enough to accept the implied suspicion of those who distrust his motives.

I did not like this about my mother. But there was nothing I could say to mend her allegation without drawing further attention to it.

But with this one word, the *ebanista* said he was happy to have been of help. She was still thinking of the contents of the box and remained silent. Signor Giovanni did not intrude on her silence, and probably not knowing what else to say, he looked around the room for a moment, and finally, coming back to the purpose of his visit, said he would take the desk and restore it to what it must have looked like when it was first built. He recognized the style, he said, but wouldn't pronounce himself as to its builder yet, as the signature under the desk was smudged with age. What he particularly admired, he said as he lifted the desk over his shoulders, was that the designer seemed to have avoided using nails anywhere other than on the hinges. But he wasn't sure about this either, he'd let us know. He said he would come back another day to pick up the frames and walked out of our house while the two of us stood at the doorway.

"Here, take it, it's yours now," said my mother, handing me the pen, which, as luck would have it, turned out to be a Pelikan. The pen looked exactly like the ones sold in the stationery store outside my school. But I found no joy in the pen. It had come like an afterthought, a chance concession, not a gift, and yet on it was inscribed my name, and this pleased me. As we watched Signor Giovanni leave, she told me a strange tale she had heard from her father-in-law: while writing one day during his time in Paris, he had dropped his pen from his desk, and in his rush to catch it, the nib punctured his skin.

"And?" I asked, not seeing her point.

"It left a small tattoo on the palm of his hand. He was quite proud of it. He liked to tell the story of how it had happened."

Why had she told me this?

"No reason," she said. "Maybe because we all wished he had seen you. Your father loved him more than he loved anyone else, I think. In any event, I'm sure he would have wanted you to have his pen. It might help you with the exam coming up."

Later that fall when I retook my Latin and Greek exam, the pen helped.

WITHIN A FEW afternoons, Nanni returned to pick up the frames. My father had taken an earlier ferry and was already home by then.

When we heard the doorbell, my father stood up and opened the door himself. Gog and Magog stood up as they always did when he left the room and followed him.

"*Stai bene?* Are you all right?" he asked as soon as he saw Nanni standing outside.

"*Benone, e tu?* Well enough, and you?" asked Nanni.

Nanni explained he had come for the frames and could stay only a minute. He patted the dogs on the head.

"How is the elbow?" my father asked.

"Much better."

"Did you do what I told you?"

"I always do—you know that—"

"Yes, but did you do it for thirty seconds each time?

"Ye-es!"

"Show me how."

Nanni was about to show how he performed the particular extension of the arm that my father had recommended, but seeing me at the door, he blurted out, "*Ciao, Paolo,*" totally surprised by my presence, as though he'd forgotten I existed or lived here.

He brought down his arm and headed straight for the living room and picked up the two frames leaning against the wall. He managed to exchange a few pleasantries with my mother, who was sitting on the sofa reading a novel. Had she done anything with the watch?

Not yet, unfortunately. She sounded peeved. My mother did not like to be reminded of things she had overlooked.

There was an awkward moment when all four of us stood speechless.

"Did you know that he's the fastest swimmer in San Giustiniano?" said my father to my mother.

"*Ma che cosa stai a dire?* What are you saying?" protested Nanni.

Of course I knew that my father liked to swim every morning before coming back home and catching the ferry to the mainland, but I didn't know that Nanni was a swimmer as well.

"We call him Tarzan."

"Tarzan, what a pretty name," said my mother with a dash of irony in her voice, as though she had never heard the word before and was determined not to participate in the inane banter between the small-town cabinetmaker and the world-famous scholar. My father's camaraderie with Nanni vexed her, I could tell.

"You should hear him imitate Tarzan's yell." And turning to Nanni, he said, "Show them."

"Absolutely not."

"He yells and then he swims. The other day he crossed the bay in four and a half minutes. I do it in eight."

"When you don't give up, you mean," scoffed Nanni. "Actually, ten to eleven is more like it." Then, feeling the sense of pressure in the room, he did a quick pivot and, informal as ever, said, *"Alla prossima,* until next time." My father uttered a compliant *"Sì."*

I liked their fellowship and the way they gibed with each other. I had seldom seen my father like this, sprightly, impish, boyish, even. "What do you think of him?" he asked my mother.

"He seems like a nice chap," she said, almost trying to sound cordially indifferent. There was even a note of suppressed hostility toward the cabinetmaker that might not have been entirely genuine but that was her typical way of dangling her veto on anything or anyone she had not brought into our fold. But then, noticing my father's exasperated shrug, which was his way of saying she could still have said something nice about the poor fellow, she added that he had the most beautiful eyelashes. "Women notice these things."

I hadn't noticed his eyelashes. But then, maybe this is why I was never able to hold his gaze. He had the most beautiful eyes I'd ever seen, certainly the only ones I'd ever paid any attention to. "Still, I find him a bit too bold, too forward. He doesn't really know his place, does he?"

I was sure that what had irked her and why her mood changed as soon as Nanni walked into our house and made a beeline to the frames was that he had used the familiar *tu* with the man who had hired him.

A WEEK LATER my mother decided to pay the cabinetmaker a visit. Did I want to go with her? "Why not," I answered, adding a casual "I wouldn't mind." Perhaps she picked up an inflection in the studied nonchalance of my *Why not* that alerted her to something, because a few minutes later, as though from nowhere, she said she was glad to hear that I was interested in the ordinary

things of our planet. What things of our planet? I asked, trying
to gauge what she had really inferred from my hasty reply. "Oh,
I don't know—furniture, for example." I could just picture her
adding "friends, people, life," always a bit arch and suspicious in
the way she took in my seemingly offhand remarks. Or perhaps
she wasn't aware of anything, any more than I really was myself,
though I felt, and perhaps she felt so as well, that there was something too deliberate in my carefree reply.

But as we ambled to the old town to Signor Giovanni's shop
early that afternoon, I didn't know why but her cryptic silence
reminded me of what she had told me a year or so earlier during a
similar walk: I was never to let a man or a grown boy touch me
there. I was so thrown off by her remark that it never occurred to
me to ask why anyone would want to touch me there in the first
place. But that afternoon on our walk up the hill to San Giustiniano Alta, I remembered her warning.

The shop reeked of turpentine. I recognized the smell from
art class. But here it spoke to me of quiet afternoons when just a
few shops stayed open while everyone else was closed for hours
after lunch. The barber, the grocer, the coffee mill, the baker—
all closed. Signor Giovanni was quietly carving away at some
ornate woodwork with his doors wide open to let out the fumes.
He was not surprised to see us, and right away stood up and
with his left hand lifted the hem of his apron to wipe the sweat
off his brow. He excused himself and disappeared into another
room to bring out the desk.

Left alone together on this quiet afternoon, my mother and
I felt entirely out of place. I looked around. Too many tools, too
much junk, too much wood dust everywhere. On a brick wall,
a coarse brown sweater hung on a nail. You could tell it was
bristly, but when I reached up to touch it, it felt less like wool

than it did something between burlap and male stubble. A look from my mother said *Don't touch.*

The desk, when he finally carried it in and stood it on the ground before us, had lost its sheen and looked dulled and blanched, as if it had been skinned alive. "This is work in progress," he said, to assuage what was clearly a horrified look trying to pass for restrained concern on my mother's face. He knew what she was thinking and reminded her that in a few weeks she wouldn't believe how the desk would glow under candlelight, more luminous and translucent than polished marble, he said. To move away from his awkward and perhaps futile attempts to comfort her, I asked Signor Giovanni how he had known about the box. "After a while of doing this, one just knows," he said, repeating *one just knows* as though mulling the answer himself, because difficult admissions about hard work and experience gathered over years of exacting labor could be justified only with a sigh. Suddenly he seemed older than his looks, work-weary, muted, even sad. He showed my mother the repairs he was doing on the desk. It was a masterpiece of smoothed and sanded curves, but the legs were grayed out with a protective temporary coat. He touched the exaggeratedly rounded corners of the desk, let his hand rest there, as on the rump of a docile pony. Then he placed a hand on my back as I pretended to peer into the cavity where my grandfather's box had lain hidden for so long. To prevent him from changing the subject or from removing his hand if my mother was to speak, I kept looking in and stringing one question after the next about the wood, the design, the products he used to remove the layers of grime to bring back to life the shabby object that had always languished in a corner of our house. How did he know when to change from thick sandpaper to thin? When was turpentine bad for wood? What other products did he use, where had he learned all this, why did it take so long? I loved hearing him speak, especially when I pointed at something and he'd lean next to me to explain. My mother was right. I loved his voice, especially when he was so close that he seemed to breathe on me and speak in whispers. He knew so much and yet, when he'd sigh before answering, he sounded so vulnerable and so wary of the unexpected turns things took sometimes. Things didn't always cooperate, he said. What things? I asked. He seemed amused by this. Then, turning to my mother: "It could be life or it could be a strip of wood that refuses to bend as it should."

I remembered how upon ending his inspection of the desk the first time in our house, he had tied up and secured the movable parts that might have opened or dropped on the floor and then hoisted the whole thing on one shoulder and walked away with it. He reminded me of Aeneas fleeing Troy balancing his elderly father on his shoulder and holding his young son Ascanius by the hand. I wanted to be Ascanius. I wanted him to be my father, I wanted to leave and walk away with him. I wanted his tiny shop to be our home, grime, wood shavings, dust, turpentine, the lot. The father I had was a wonderful man. But Signor Giovanni would be better, more than a father to me.

When we left, my mother stopped by the baker's and bought me a small pastry. She bought one for herself as well. We ate them as we walked. Neither of us spoke.

I knew that what I'd felt in the shop was unusual and stealthy, possibly unwholesome. I felt it yet more keenly on the day I decided to take the long way home after seeing my tutor and, while circling through the old town at least twice, ended up knocking at the glass door of his shop. He was giving instructions to his assistant, a boy slightly older than I, who I later found out was his brother Ruggiero.

When he saw me, he gave a quick nod, and all the while

greeting me, he continued to wipe oil stains off his hands with a rag, which I later realized was soaked in paint thinner. "I already told your mother that it's not ready yet," he said, clearly annoyed by my impromptu visit, which he probably took as a sly, nudging intrusion spurred by my mother's impatience to see the job done. I was passing by after seeing my tutor, I said, and just wanted to say hello. I could take only hasty peeks at his face.

"Well, well then, hello, come in anyway," he said, opening up. And suddenly, because of his expansive welcome, I hugged him as I'd hug all my parents' friends when they visited. The last thing I wanted to be was a boss's son dropping in on an unsuspecting hireling caught slouching on the job. But I was interrupting, and he was halting everything and setting time aside for me, because I was, there was no hiding it, the boss's son. I should never have come, I thought, feeling unbearably awkward as he produced a small, rickety wooden chair for me to sit on. I should have gone straight home and helped the gardener prune herbs instead. But he broke my silence. Did I want lemonade? he asked. I did not weigh my answer. I nodded. He stepped over to a very thick, sagging worker's table littered with tools, lifted a porcelain pitcher whose top was covered with a faded doily, and poured a glass. It's not cold, he said—meaning not like the lemonade they serve in your house—but it will quench your thirst. He handed me the glass and then stood there and stared like a nurse making sure the patient downed his medicine to the last drop. It smelled not just of strong lemon or of those midsummer afternoons when the heat weighs you down and you're just seconds away from dropping on your bed and are grateful that someone invented lemonade; it smelled of the turpentine on his hands. I loved that it smelled of his hands. I grew to love the scent of his shop, his little bric-a-brac world made of wood and sagging tables and ragged sweaters and rickety chairs that you could rest on during scorching afternoons when your entire being seemed intoxicated by the tart, sweet, overpowering scent of lime and linseed oil.

A few days after my visit, I decided to drop in on the cabinet-maker a second time, and then a few days later again, each time immediately following my tutorial. Along the way I was so starved that I was in the habit of buying the same pastry as soon as the baker reopened. But thinking twice about it, I decided to purchase two more, one for him and one for his brother. I would wait to eat mine until I sat with him in his dingy shop for five minutes. Had I been slightly older, I would have right away known that I was disturbing him. But I was convinced he was happy to see me and that our friendship had indeed blossomed. He offered me lemonade, pulled up a chair to sit beside me, and talked as he ate the pastry, one adult speaking to another adult. I loved it. He talked about his father and grandfather, who had been cabinetmakers as well. They went back generations, he said, throwing a hand behind his shoulder to mime the passage of time. And was his son going to be a cabinetmaker too? He did not have children, he said. But didn't he want children? I asked, feeling that this was grown-up talk. Who knows, he mused, he hadn't found the right wife yet. I wanted to tell him that I would gladly fill in the role of a son and serve as his apprentice every summer and learn everything there was to learn until his son would replace me. "I want to work with you," I said. He smiled, then stood up and poured himself a glass as well. "Don't you have friends?" he asked. He might have meant, *Don't people your age have better things to do?*

"I don't have friends here. But I don't have many at home either."

So what did I do all day these days?

The beach, reading, the daily homework for my Greek and Latin tutor.

He recited the opening verses of *The Aeneid*.

"You studied Latin?" I asked, thrilled by the news.

"*Poco*, hardly, but then I had to abandon it."

To tease him, I asked him to recite the opening verses again.

He started reciting them but then burst out laughing mid-verse. Which made me laugh as well.

"The things you make me say, *Arma virumque cano*, really, Paolo!"

He was making fun of himself. I loved when he did this. It drew us closer.

"So why don't you have friends?" Were we being serious again? He was starting to sound like my mother. Yet I didn't mind it coming from him.

"I don't know. I want friends. Maybe not everyone likes me."

"Maybe you think they don't. Everyone makes friends."

"Not everyone."

"But you've made friends here."

"That's because I like coming here."

"Don't you like people your age?"

I hunched my shoulders. "I don't know."

And, as though to punctuate what I was saying to him, I caught myself exhaling something like a mini-sigh, which was the younger version of the weary sigh he himself had emitted when speaking about his years growing up as a cabinetmaker. What I liked was not only having to put my cards on the table and disclosing a very private fact about myself but, for the first time, I had spoken with someone about things I thought troubled me and no one but me. I liked speaking like this.

When my father or my relatives asked why I had no friends, I would find a way to avoid the subject or claim that I had very good friends, but only at school. At school I'd say that I might not have classmates as friends but that I had many friends in San Giustiniano. Yet I had never had a friend with whom I could talk about not having friends. Here it felt so easy that I had to hold myself back from sharing too much for fear of boring him.

"I want to learn everything from you."

He smiled wistfully. "Wood is impossible to learn quickly." And so saying, he walked over to a shelf and brought down a long-ish object wrapped in what looked like a blanket. "This," he said, cautiously unwrapping the object, "is a very, very old violin." It had no strings at all. "My grandfather made it. I've never built a violin, and I wouldn't even try, but I know wood, I've grown up with wood, and I know what needs to be done to keep the sound alive." He had me slide my hand on the base of the instrument. "Wood is unforgiving. A painter, even a great painter, can change his mind midway or paint over a serious mistake. But you can't undo a mistake on wood. You need to understand how wood thinks, how woods speaks, and what each sound it makes means. Wood, like very, very few living things, never dies."

One might have thought he was Michelangelo speaking about marble.

"So, do you still want to work in my stinking shop?" he finally asked after I said I didn't care how long it took to learn. More than ever, I wished to say, adding, I want to be with you, I want to be your son, I want to open the shop for you before you arrive and close it after you leave, I want to bring you coffee and warm bread in the morning, squeeze lemons for you, sweep and mop the floor, and, should you ask, forswear my parents, my home, everything. I want to be you.

I knew my answer would have made him laugh. So to re-strain my fervor, I said, no, I didn't want to work in his stinking shop. The wording became a source of humor between us.

I dropped by twice a week, then more frequently.

One day, as I was coming with pastries for the three of us, I froze on the spot. My mother was leaving his shop. She was wearing a large straw hat and sunglasses. I spotted her right away and immediately dashed inside the barbershop and kept watch behind the beaded curtain until I saw her pass by on her way down vicolo Sant'Eusebio. She hadn't seen me. But it gave me a shock and I promised never to walk in on him unless I'd made certain she wasn't visiting. I was sure that they had spoken about me. But I never asked myself what impulse had driven me to hide from her. Perhaps I didn't want her to think I idled around town after my tutorial. But I knew this wasn't the reason.

Nanni was always working whenever I walked in. Sometimes it would be so hot in his shop that he would not be wearing a shirt. My father was right. I had no idea he had an athlete's frame.

"*Che sorpresa*, what a surprise, two days in a row!" he said when I decided not to space my visits. "Today I will let you help me."

So he brought down a large picture frame. Even though I'd been staring at it during my previous visits, it took me a few moments to recognize it was ours. It looked so clean, so new, so bleached of color that it made me think of a tanned man whose naked butt is as white as talcum.

The frame was far from finished, he said. We needed to remove the grime that had accumulated over the years from its carved floral molding and in the ridges at the corners.

"And how does one do this?"

"I'll show you. Just do as you're told."

"And if I don't?"

"It will be the end of you."

We smiled at each other.

He bit off a piece of the pastry I had brought and left the rest of it on that day's newspaper that lay wide open on the sagging table. It had most likely served as a makeshift tablecloth during today's lunch with his brother.

He handed me a simple gouger the likes of which I'd never seen before and said that I should do exactly what he told me.

He brought two chairs out to the sidewalk where it was cooler and then handed me an apron.

"Because I don't want you to dirty your clothes."

"I'll be careful."

"Put the apron on."

I smiled at the mock command. He was smiling too.

After we both sat down with our aprons on facing each other, he let the frame rest on our knees and showed me how to scrape off the impacted grit, but not too aggressively, because I might be removing not just dirt but also the wood underneath it. He said he had already sanded the frame and just this morning treated it with a very weak acid to remove some stains. He also pointed out spots I needed to avoid touching with my gouge because he'd rebuilt some of the damaged or rotten sections of the frame with gesso.

Wouldn't it have been wiser to use the gesso after the acid, not before? I asked.

He looked at me. *"Ma senti quello*, listen to this one. Doesn't think I know what I'm doing. Just do as you're told."

He was making fun of me. I liked it.

And so I did all I was asked to do, and for about two hours late that afternoon we sat there on the *vicolo*, a step away from the gutter that runs down its middle, digging into the frame, clearing the dirt that had caked into its carved crevices. Tomorrow

he was going to treat it with clear oil. No stain, just oil. "You'll
see how beautiful wood can be once I'm done with it. A work
of art. In a few days I'll bring it over to let your parents see."

"I can't wait to see it, Nanni."

I wanted to come back on the morrow and work with him, sit
face-to-face with him as we'd done today, and occasionally draw
closer to him to get a whiff of his underarms, which smelled like
mine but much, much stronger. I liked that he wasn't wearing a
shirt, just an apron, with his chest ever so visible. I could look at
the rest of him all I wanted now without worrying about his eyes
or not being able to hold his gaze. I just didn't want him to know
I was staring.

Neither of us stopped working until it got dark that day. His
eyes were tired, the two of us had worked really well, he said. Let
me see your hands, he added. Tentatively, I put out my two hands,
palms up. He held both my hands and, squinting, inspected them.
Did it burn? he asked, wondering if the light coat of acid had
touched my hand. "I don't think so," I said, almost breathless from
knowing that at this very moment my two hands were now resting in both of his, exactly as I'd wished a few weeks before. Maybe
here, I said, pointing to two fingers on my left hand, but I knew I
was making it up. He held the fingers to the poor light in the shop,
inspected them, and said it was nothing, just dirt. Here, use this,
he said, producing a rag which he dunked in some paint thinner. I
looked at the rag. What was I to do with it, I motioned, as though
I had no idea what one did with a rag dunked in paint thinner.

"You scrub the stain off with it, for God's sake. You patricians
are all alike! Here, let me show you." He took the rag in his right
hand and grabbed my two hands in his left hand as a grown-up
would do with a child's, and scrubbed them clean. I loved the
smell. From now on I would smell of my friend's shop, of his
world, of his body, of his life.

"Now, go home."

I rushed downhill and watched the town grow dark after sunset. I was happy. It was the first time that I watched the view without my father, and I loved it both for itself and for being alone so late. It was on one of those early evenings that I discovered my "shortcut" by the abandoned Norman chapel and the lime shrubs. The chapel had no roof, no altar, nothing, just a plinth sitting on wild, abundant yellow growth. Here, I decided, I'd sit every evening and think of Nanni and me.

When I got home, I did not tell my mother where I'd been, nor did she ask. I took off my clothes and washed my hands and my arms with Mother's scented soap to remove or, at best, cover up the smell of turpentine.

But in case my parents asked, I had already rehearsed an excuse: I'd spent the afternoon with another student I'd met at my tutor's. No, not bright at all, I'd add, trying to look bored by the subject. The only thing we had in common was failing our Latin and Greek exam. But should they bring up the desk, the frames, the living room, the inhabitants of the island, or Nanni himself, I'd mention something about him that might throw them off the scent. "What was that?" asked my father, when indeed the three of us were having dinner and the conversation drifted to Nanni's work on the desk. "Has either of you noticed how his hand shakes?" And to push the point, I made light of the tremor by mimicking the way he'd pointed at the keyhole with a trembling forefinger the first time I'd met him. "Maybe he drinks too much coffee or smokes a lot, or just drinks," added my mother. "Who knows what his sort does."

"Who, Tarzan? Never," threw in my father.

"How about alcohol?"

"Of course he drinks, but he is no alcoholic."

I could easily have told my parents that I'd never seen him

drink coffee or touch a cigarette, but they'd ask how I could possibly know, and then I'd have to spill everything. The irony is that Nanni's hands did not tremble at all; I had made the whole thing up. Perhaps I had spoken about his hands, hoping Mother would have something good to say about him, because when it came to him, I had run out of new things to think about.

I RETURNED TO his shop two days later, and rather than wait for him to tell me what to do, I placed my books under the table, put on the apron, and helped myself to some lemonade. He asked me to take a good look at the frame we'd cleaned the other day. I saw, once he lifted it from the wall and brought it to the light, that it was a masterpiece. "Nanni!" I gasped.

"It's not finished," meaning, *no need to get too excited yet.*

He was going to add another layer of oil, he said. I thought he'd do it with a brush. He shook his head. If I wanted, he said, I could help. He knew I'd ask for nothing better. He took out a rag, folded it into a thick wad, dunked it in a thick, clear liquid, and proceeded to dab it lightly on the frame and then to daub the wood with long, measured, fluid sweeps. Here, you try, he said, handing me the cloth. But my gestures were too jerky and brusque. "Look at me." He extended his arm in slow, deliberate, confident motions, putting his whole heart in each sweep no differently and no less devotedly than if he were sliding a long, slow bow across violin strings or washing the back of a wounded soldier lying on a gurney, washing and scrubbing, gently and softly. His hand followed the grain in the wood, and the smell of his shop and of his underarms was, like incense, wholesome and good, because one had to be selfless and unsparing in one's work, he said, and there was piety in his gesture, and everything about him told you he was honest, humble, and good. We could not oil the wood sitting down. Instead, the two of us stood around the frame, I dabbing then sliding the cloth at one end, as he had shown me, he at the other. When he caught me working too hastily, he asked me to slow down. *Con calma*, calmly. It was hot in the shop, we sweated. I was happy.

"Let's let it dry for now," he said afterward.

He said he would show me how to work on the desk. Meanwhile, I would be the one to work on the box, he said, *tutto da solo*, all by yourself.

As some point, a fly landed on my face and was crawling on my cheek. It itched and I wanted to scratch the spot, but then in an effort to flick it away I ended up damping my cheek with the rag dunked in linseed oil. Not to worry, he said. He folded another rag, added the slightest drop of thinner on it, brought it to my face, and with one finger pressing under the rag itself, dabbed the spot on my cheek with cautious, tentative, timid taps that told me he was trying not to let the thinner burn. I loved how he touched my face, cared for my face; there was far more friendship and kindness in this man's tiny gesture than in anyone related to me by blood. I wished it had been his whole palm that had touched my face and had made the burning go away. "Don't move," he said as he dabbed the spot again. "I said don't move." I didn't move. I could now feel his breath, he was going to kiss me. He brought his finger to his mouth, put some spit on its tip, and applied it to the spot of my cheek. I would have done anything he asked at that moment. "Just another touch, be patient, it won't burn," he had said, and I trusted him, and I liked trusting him, and my mother's warning didn't for a second matter to me, because what coursed through my mind at that very moment was that instead of rubbing my cheek with that rag he should have rubbed my cock ever so gently with it, and if it burned, as I knew it would, so be it, so long as I let him hold it in the palm of his hand as he'd done with both my hands the other day. I could feel the burning begin to spread on my cheek and intensify, and it hurt, but I didn't mind, because he had said it wouldn't hurt, and I wanted him to know that I trusted him, trusted everything, that I didn't mind when he dabbed his spit again on my face, because I didn't mind, didn't mind, because it was my fault if it burned, not his, not ever his. When he patted my cheek with the palm of his hand, without thinking I leaned into it and let the side of my face rest on it. But I did it discreetly. He didn't notice.

"Wasn't so bad now, was it?" he said, tapping my cheek again and smiling. An old pockmarked mirror with multiple tain stains revealed a reddish blotch on my cheek.

"Back to work," he said.

Nearing sundown, he threw me a rag to clean my hands with. He threw it the way our swimming instructor at school used to fling towels at each of us as soon as we got out of the pool.

There was peace and such longevity in those afternoon hours after my tutorial. Pastry, lemonade, and the small box, which had become my project and mine only, while he looked over my shoulders and kept an eye on my progress. You could keep doing this as his forefathers had done, day in and day out, hour after hour, year after year. We make assumptions about how our lives are being charted without knowing that we're even making these assumptions—which is the beauty of assumptions: they anchor us without the slightest clue that what we're doing is trusting that nothing changes. We believe that the street we live on will remain the same and bear its name forever. We believe that our friends will stay our friends, and that those we love we'll love forever. We trust and, by dint of trusting, forget we trusted.

A few days later, I almost ran into my mother as she was walking down Sant'Eusebio. I immediately ducked into the tiny bookstore, hoping that if she walked in, she'd see me trying to decide what novel to purchase. No sooner had I made certain that she was farther down the street than I headed to Nanni's. He was busy putting back our desk in its corner. She had dropped in for another one of her spot inspections.

He told me right away to come in. *"Oggi non si scherza,* no joking today," he said. I put on my dirty apron as I was in the habit of doing and waited for my orders. But then I saw that the small box, which I'd thought was entirely mine to work on, had been resanded, presumably by his younger brother. Obviously he didn't like the way I'd primed it and had asked his brother to undo my work. But I was wrong. "Today you'll watch what I do with the desk. Then you'll do exactly the same with the box. First we need to find some stain. I like to start with the corner, so you'll start with a corner too."

I did everything he asked and copied every move he performed on the desk, using the same products.

I stained and kept staining as he showed me, slowly, smoothly, sedulously. We seldom talked when we worked, although occasionally we'd discuss soccer teams. I don't think we even thought about anything while working. We just worked. When we were finished for the day, he had me stand facing him, placed a hand on my shoulder, and inspected my face. I was fine. No blotches anywhere. "You worked well."

"And you too worked well," I said, sensing that this was something said among workers after a long day's work.

He nodded. A moment of silence followed. "So, tell me, was my hand shaking today?"

I must have given him the most petrified look while attempting a blank, baffled, uncomprehending stare. I'm sure he noticed.

"Paolo, *scherzavo*, I was joking," he said, obviously trying to remedy my shock. I believed him. But the ground had shaken under me.

On my way home, I stopped by the Norman chapel and sat on my plinth and looked out to the sea toward the lights on the mainland as I liked to do just before twilight after work. Except that this time I felt as though I'd been carved open in one of those old anatomical theaters while my heart was still pounding and my lungs still breathing and every organ in my abdomen laid bare to a multitude of snickering young medical students.

I had filched a piece of a damp rag from Nanni's shop and had snuck it into the paper bag I'd brought from the baker's that day. I took it out and then unbuttoned and pulled down my shorts. I liked being stripped and exposed, as though this is what I'd been meaning to do for hours. I wanted him to see me naked. With the rag in one hand I dabbed my cock once with it. But feeling nothing save a mild tingling, I dabbed it a second time. Then I began to feel it. It was hot at first, and it thrilled me, because I felt as though something other than my hand was touching me, but then it began to burn, and to burn more and, without relenting, even more. I began to panic, because it hurt, and though part of me wanted it to hurt and liked that it hurt, I feared that the burning might never go away, that my cock would always burn, in my sleep, or when I bathed, or when I sat in our dining room with my parents, or when I dropped into Nanni's shop. I began to be horrified by what I had done to myself. *Perché, ma perché*, I groaned out, thinking that this was his voice speaking to me and that if he knew what I'd just done to myself, he would have shown up in this vacant little chapel within seconds and held me in the palm of his hand to make the burning go away. And I thought of his spit, and how the spit had eased the burning, and, because I didn't know anything else, all I could do was break down and say, *Ma che cosa ti sei fatto?* What did you do to yourself? And just hearing his voice say these words as I spoke them out loud tightened my throat and made it impossible to breathe until I burst out sobbing. I had never felt so sorry for myself.

I thought I was crying because of the pain or because I was starting to panic. But I knew that there was another reason, though I couldn't fathom the reason or why it had brought me to tears. There was sorrow in the chapel and in my heart and across the water toward the mainland and more sorrow in my body, because I didn't know my body and the very simple thing I needed at the moment. And I thought of the years ahead of me and knew that this was never going to go away, that even if the burning subsided and wore itself off, I would never live down the shame or ever forgive myself or him for making me do this. I would sit on this very same spot in the years to come and re-member that never in my life had I known the sort of loneliness that you can actually touch on your body. I threw the rag on the ground and before entering the house made sure to wash my hand, arms, and knees, using the gardener's faucet and his dirty bar of soap.

AFTER MY TUTORIAL a few days later, I went to his shop and for the first time found the door shut. When I knocked, all I heard was the glass panels rattling against the old wooden door. He was never not there, I thought, so he had to be inside. I began to pull the bell. Its hollow chime told me that it was pointless to insist, but I pulled and made more noise, heedless of what those in the vicinity might say, totally persuaded that he'd materialize at some point. It was Alessi, the barber, who finally stepped out of his shop, and standing on the lane, he shouted, "Can't you see no one's there?" I was angry, crushed, humiliated. I could still hear the tinnitus of the bell in my head as I stomped down the cobbled lane on my way home. Why had he let me down, why had I trusted, why had I even gone there in the first place? I had no idea what had happened to him, or where he was, or why he wouldn't open the door. I should never have allowed myself to take his friendship for granted—what friendship?

I fell prey to the same paralyzing sense of panic I had known earlier that year on parents' day at school when I knew that my teachers' report was not going to go over well. I should never have trusted him so blindly. He wasn't my friend, was never going to be. I should have known, should have found friends my age.

To make matters worse, it started to rain, the water pelting my head as I saw the lights of our home in the distance and knew that by the time I reached our porch, I would be soaking. No Norman chapel today. Serves me right. I must never trust anyone, won't ever seek anyone out again, never. I had only one friend on this planet, my father, and even then, I wouldn't know what to tell him. Tell him what? That I felt totally awkward, that I was hurt, that I wished to hate Nanni, that we should never hire him again, that Nanni was no better than the ruffians who hung outside Caffè dell'Ulivo at night and talked dirty or made obscene sounds when a woman passed by?

But before pushing open our door all the way, I spotted our cylinder desk sitting in the entrance and next to it the two picture frames leaning half wrapped against the wall. Then I heard Nanni's voice. I was in heaven. He was standing with my mother, trying to help her find an appropriate spot for the desk. They had turned on the lights, which made it seem far later in the day than it actually was. He was discussing the damage done to furniture by sunlight, which is why, he said, she should keep the desk away from the large balcony window. She listened, quietly and softly caressing the wood as though she needed to touch it to believe it but also feared she'd disturb it. I too was startled by the desk's brilliance. What made me happier yet was the thought that while I was pulling his bell ever so feverishly that afternoon, all he was doing was standing in our living room talking to my parents, showing off his work.

I told them that I was running upstairs to change, took everything off, left all my wet clothes on the floor, and came right downstairs in my bathrobe and stood in the doorway, thinking, *I worship this man.*

"I also took the liberty of using a new product on the bronze to bring out its gloss," he explained. He had never told me that he'd done this. My mother said she hadn't noticed the bronze, but, yes, he was right, even the bronze keyholes he had tinkered with that very first time had acquired an unmistakable gloss. He explained how he had replaced the keyhole on one of the drawers, because at some point, who knows when, someone had replaced it with one that did not match the design, which meant he had to replace the key as well. "Probably my crazy great-uncle Federico," he said. Then he described the design on the keyhole on the desk and pointed at its quatrefoil pattern. I saw his hands as I'd seen them the first time weeks earlier in this very room. They hadn't changed. Even with sandpaper and who knows how many years of resin, paint thinner, lacquer, and acid, they were kind and ever so smooth to the touch, as I'd felt when he helped remove the stain from my cheek, when he rubbed my hair with his palm when I said I didn't need an apron, when he held both my hands in one of his and began to clean them. I remembered his bare chest under the apron.

Then my mother asked, "And the small box?"

"The small box," repeated Nanni, suddenly taking his time. "That's a real gem." He removed the drawers as he'd done that first day, but this time the drawers slipped out smoothly, without friction or sound. He reached into the desk and pulled out the box. I hadn't seen it in days and had no idea it would look so finished, so radiant.

"Beautiful, isn't it?" he asked.

"You're a miracle worker."

She inspected the key and the lock. I had never seen either the new key or the new lock before, because while I was working on the box in the shop, Nanni had already removed the lock.

My mother couldn't help herself and complimented him again. He made a nodding gesture that was meant both to acknowledge yet play down her compliment. He lifted his face and looked over in my direction and cast something that might almost have been the flicker of a complicit smile, and then looked down at the box he held in his hand before setting it upon the refurbished desk, saying nothing. It meant, *Let it be our secret.*

So we had a secret.

But the real secret was not that I had gone to see him almost every afternoon but that he sensed I didn't want my parents to know. *This* was the secret.

It never occurred to me to wonder why he hadn't brought up my visits, or why he hadn't acknowledged my role in polishing the box.

I nursed that secret all through my Latin homework that evening. An hour or so later, I went downstairs again, thinking that Nanni had already left, and was surprised to see that he was still there, helping my parents put the two paintings back into their frames. I kept hoping he'd speak to me. But he didn't. When I walked out to get some water in the kitchen, I could hear him explaining to my parents precisely what he had done to the frames. Then my father, who always managed to make people want to confide in him, asked him what other work awaited him in the shop. There was a moment's silence. Nanni said he wished to move his shop to the mainland, because though he'd inherited the craft and the shop and the apartment above the shop, he wanted to be more than a cabinetmaker. He was a creator, he said, he was an artist, not just a *falegname*, a carpenter.

I liked the way he had spoken these last words. They came like the admission of something irreducibly truthful. He was speaking with the most guileless humility and something verging on apology, as though asking for my father's blessing and friendship. "I am speaking to you as to a father," he finally said. Why had I never opened up to Nanni as truthfully as he was doing now with my father? Would I ever be able to tell him what I'd done to myself in the chapel while hoping he'd pass by to rescue me? Not in ten years, not in a lifetime. And yet I wanted to, and the thought of telling him aroused me.

Nanni was telling my father that there was also the matter of his younger brother. "I promised my father that I would take care of my brother and set him up in business here. So I have to wait until he grows up. But my dream was always to become a journeyman, a *compagnon*, as they still have in France, to travel and learn from others. Instead, I worked with my father and grandfather, and that served me well enough—still, I need to go away."

What I loved seeing was the ease with which he spoke to my father, as so many others did in San Giustiniano. I had never confided in anyone this way, not even my father. What it also told me was that this way of baring one's soul with people was itself the very essence of friendship, which was something I knew nothing about and was precisely what I craved from Nanni, except that I wanted it with his face, from his hands, his smell. Perhaps I wasn't capable of such trust or of eliciting it in others. Besides,

I was just a kid, and I knew it. Did others even think about friendship as much as I did, or did they simply trust you and become your friend naturally? What had ever come naturally to me?

"But why leave San Giustiniano?" asked my mother.

"I can't go on here. I've grown up here. I know everyone. Plus, there's so much talk in this town. I want to get away."

I was so intrigued by this person whom I was hearing for the first time that I stood on the threshold of the living room without walking in, fearing that the least step would interrupt the conversation. I wanted him to keep talking. Why didn't he speak like this when he was with me? He was drinking something with my parents and was sitting in an armchair leaning forward toward my father, both elbows resting on his thighs, as though he hadn't finished his admission and was still imploring my parents' leave to hear him out. When he put down his glass, I had the impression that he was just about to reach out and clasp one of my father's hands. "I am the last person to give advice," my father finally said. "Besides, who knows of what value my words are, Nanni. But if you really must go away, maybe Europe is not the place. There's Canada, for instance. Or New Zealand, Australia, and America, of course. But the world is filled with crooks and hooligans."

"Oh, crooks and hooligans there are plenty around us, more than you know. It's not because you don't see them knocking at your door that they're not here," he said, eying my father. Then, turning to my mother: "Things are not easy for me here, Signora."

"For a moment I was sure he was going to ask us for a loan," said my mother after Nanni had left. "He's just the type to."

"But he didn't. He would never."

"He will the next time he comes around—you watch. They're all the same, these people."

Many people used to come to visit in the evening only to end up trying to borrow funds at the end of their visit. By then I'd usually be asked to leave the room. But I loved to overhear the labored blandishments preceding their request.

Here nothing of the sort was happening.

"Stay in Europe, Nanni, stay here," said my mother. "You have no idea what taking the first ferry of the year does to me when I cross the water and leave the world behind and finally walk along the esplanade and make out the scent of the fishing boats along the marina. This is heaven."

Why was my mother saying this, when none of us could forget that our first ride on the ferry this summer had been an unmitigated hell?

"I have some friends at the Canadian embassy who might be able to help," said my father.

"My husband and I disagree. Which isn't surprising. You belong here, Signor Giovanni." But to show there was no significant rift in our household, she moved toward my father's armchair and sat on its armrest, placing her hand on his shoulder. It suggested warmth, youth, and solidarity, even if her gesture struck me as a touch mannered and too demonstrative for the occasion. It must have seemed so to my father as well, because he simply sat there, rigid, uneasy, letting my mother do the talking, allowing her hand to rest there until she'd tire. "Ironically," she said, smiling, "we too may be thinking of moving, especially for Paolo's schooling."

Nanni turned and looked at me. "Yes, especially for Paolo."

The way he spoke these words broke my heart. Yet anything having to do with my school could easily devolve into talk about my Latin and Greek exam, my tutor, and ultimately my visits. I panicked. He must have read my mind and stayed clear of the subject.

"We do everything for our children, Nanni. But then one day they leave us and we lose them," said my father. It was coming out of nowhere.

"I'm not going to leave you," I said.

My father mused a moment. "I know, I know," he finally replied. But I could read him well enough to sense he did not believe what I'd just said, for what he really meant with that pensive inflection in his voice was, *You may not want to leave now, but one day you will.* He looked at Nanni as though to draw a nodding agreement from him, when suddenly, as happened almost every evening, the lights went out. We waited all of us in the dark. My father lit the three long tapers standing on the candle holder on the living room piano and approached the desk in the middle of the room. He wanted to see it in a different light. It looked more stunning by candlelight. It belonged in a museum. "You are an artist," said my father as soon we saw the cylinder beam like the most polished Stradivarius. *"Anzi,* a great artist," my mother added. I was so happy that I wished we'd stay all four of us in this room forever under the intimate, spare glow of the candles. I wanted it to be dark again. I wanted to hug him in the dark.

When the lights came on, Nanni looked at his watch. "Perhaps it's time I should get back," he said.

My father walked him to the door while my mother stayed in the living room staring at the desk. I was sure my father had stepped aside to pay Nanni's fee, which is why I didn't accompany him. As my father did with everyone, he walked Nanni to the end of the garden, opened the gate for him, and then stood there, courteous as ever, watching his guest make his way back toward the marina. Nanni turned back and waved a second time. No one had extinguished the candles yet. It made me think he was still in the room with us.

"A great talent, but a strange one, this Nanni, a bit creepy, if you ask me, don't you think?" asked my mother once my father shut our main door behind him.

"Yes, very talented." He didn't care to sit in judgment.

"Still, something very louche about him. Can you imagine in what seedy digs he must live? What I think he should do is find a nice girl and settle down in San Giustiniano. This is where he belongs."

"Maybe," said my father, "but he's too complicated to settle down with one of those beefy, unshorn town girls. He's too polished and too handsome for them. He belongs in the great wide world, in Paris, Rome, London, not a fishing hamlet."

My father's admiration, unlike mine, was devoid of equivocation. I envied the absence of smokescreens and double-talk in what he'd said. Nothing stealthy or dissimulated about voicing one's admiration for another man. Indeed, his praise of Nanni was so unhindered that it made me realize I had never said nor would ever be able to say anything of the sort. I'd have made up something crass about him or pointed to a birth defect here, a tremor there, if only to censor anything that betrayed what I felt each time I found the courage to look in his eyes.

That night, in midsleep, I thought of something I'd overheard my mother say and hadn't wanted to focus on until I could devote myself entirely to it. I thought—or was it dreamt?—of what she called his seedy living quarters above his shop. I knew there was a stairway leading upstairs, but I had never seen where he lived, how he lived. I wanted to see his room, his things, his shoes, his clothes, touch his bed, his bathrobe, his towel. What if, instead of going to school one winter morning, I took the ferry from the mainland and dropped in on him? Would he put me up, help me dry my feet if it rained that day, lend me something to wear until my clothes were dry? I'd work with him, have lunch with him, and take a long nap on his bed in that ratty brown sweater of his that felt of him and smelled of him and spoke of him in the coarse, sacred tongue of things.

WHAT I FAILED to realize after he had brought the refurbished frames and desk is that I no longer had a reason to visit him in the afternoon. As I drank my usual lemonade in his shop the next day and asked if there was anything else for me to do, he shook his head and said we were done with the work on my parents' furniture. He looked awkward, tense. Part of me felt he was struggling to find the right words. "With your parents' desk finished, maybe it's time you stopped being a manual laborer," he said, finally landing on the right words with the right inflection of both humor and apology to soften the blow. His brother Ruggiero was busy sandpapering a drawer, but even though he wasn't turning around, I could tell he wasn't missing a syllable.

"So I've been allowed here so long as I worked for my parents?" I was so shocked by what he'd just said that I couldn't phrase my disappointment more delicately.

"You helped a great deal," he replied, deflecting my question, "and you did a fabulous job, they even said so in your home."

The startled look on my face must have screamed that he should not have told my mother about me. So it had never been *our* secret.

I tried not to show how totally rattled I felt. What shocked me even more was not just that my mother had known about my visits to the shop, but that she had decided not to breathe a word of them to me. Her silence suddenly cast a cloud on my visits and confirmed that there was always a troubling and furtive character to what I'd been doing in his shop that justified her silence. Earlier, I had thought of asking my parents to have

Nanni come over and look at our dining room table and its chairs, as these too looked so old and beaten that they clearly needed restoring. But now my mother would probably see through this and know that it was only a ploy for me to continue visiting his shop.

When I got home, not a word, not a look, nothing. At dinner, I looked over to my father. He too was inscrutably quiet. Something was bound to come out. It was just a question of when.

But the more days that passed with neither one mentioning my visits, the more difficult it became to even speak his name at home. When my mother did speak it once, while asking me to help her move the desk from one corner of the living room to the other—because we still couldn't find a spot for it—I pretended I hadn't heard it. But I caught my entire body shaking. Say his name and I froze. Say "Nanni" and all the bulwarks I'd put around this one word suddenly came crashing down. Say his name in the winter when we were back in the city, and I would suddenly feel a thousand pinpricks tickling the crown of my head. I loved his name. It meant far, far more to me than it did to anyone else. No one would understand, much less explain why it filled me with stealthy pleasure, with anguish and shame.

On one of my last afternoons before leaving San Giustiniano, after my tutorial I dropped by Nanni's shop. He was there, shirtless, working with Ruggiero on a large drawer that was squatting on its hind side on the cobbled alley. I envied him the peace, the heat, the work, the ancient, timeless ritual of it all. And then, as if something were being torn out of my lungs and needed to be said, I finally found a moment when he was alone to tell him. "I've never had friends, you've been my only friend," I said, speaking these words without even realizing I had said them. What I'd meant to say was, *I was your friend, I wish you'd stayed mine.* Instead we hugged as we always did, except that he said, *"Scusa il sudore,* pardon the sweat." But that was exactly what I wanted on my face.

I wouldn't tell my parents about this. They wouldn't understand. No one would.

The closest I got to understand anything came much later that winter when I walked into our kitchen and made out the scent of turpentine wafting from the open door of one of the adjoining kitchens in the building. Our neighbors were having their kitchen painted. Suddenly, without thinking, I was on that cobblestone lane in San Giustiniano, headed uphill in the scorching late-July afternoon heat, the shoemaker, the locksmith, the barber, every step marked by what the presage of that scent promised once I'd passed the giant cornerstone where the alley took a turn farther uphill toward the caffè and then up to the castle. The turpentine, I realized that day, was the cover, the cloaking device. What I really wanted was his sweat, his smile, the way he'd speak to me, and the smell of his underarms under exertion on those sweltering summer days. And then, in our kitchen and to my undying shame, I remembered what had occurred between us exactly a day after the episode with turpentine in the Norman chapel.

We were going to work on the frames again. We had brought two chairs out in the alley and sat facing each other with the wooden frame placed on all four of our knees, both of us with our tools on the pavement—the large gouge, the smaller gouge, the tiny awls for digging into the florid patterns to remove the encrusted dirt. Sometimes, when he made an effort with his arm, his knee would bump mine and stay in place until he released the pressure on his hand and began working on another spot on the frame. At first, I'd pull back my knee, but soon I learned to keep mine in place and never pulled back. Sometimes our knees

stayed so close you'd think they were like twins who'd grown
up together and were happy only when they touched. Once, my
knee touched his and made a point of pressing against it. His
withdrew. So, to punish him and demean him in my mind, I began to think of him naked under his apron, and I liked thinking
of him naked. I knew it was wrong, even cruel, but I couldn't
stop myself, I liked looking at his crotch.

While nursing these disturbing images, I suddenly caught
him staring at me. Had he watched my eyes roaming all over
his body when he stood up? Was he going to be upset that I had
stared?

He had stopped speaking. I began to wonder why. Then I
saw him still staring at me. And his eyes were so beautiful and,
as it hit me for the first time, so thoroughly green, that I had to
look at them some more. My impulse had always been to look
away to avoid his eyes, but they held me, and I wanted to be held
by them, for they were ordering me not to turn away this time,
for this was why adults stared each other in the eye: you looked
straight back and there was no running away for cover, because
you were invited to stare too, because it was no longer a breach
of any kind, it was a breach not to stare—which is when I realized
that what I'd been craving all this time was his eyes, not his
hands, not his voice, not his knees, or even his friendship, just
his eyes, for I wanted his eyes to rest forever on me the way they
were doing just now, because I loved the way they hovered over
my face and eventually landed on my eyes like the hand of a holy
man who is about to touch your eyelids, your forehead, your
whole face, because his eyes kept swearing I was the dearest thing
in the world, because there was piety, grace, and beneficence in
his gaze that favored me with its beauty and told me there was
no less piety, beauty, and grace in mine. And this, on one of my
last afternoons in his shop and in that distant part of the globe,

was a wellspring of happiness, hope, and friendship. He had looked at me with sorrow because I was leaving soon. I was his friend. There was nothing more to want. But something broke the moment he said, "You shouldn't stare at people like this."

His words cut me. All at once our delicate exchange of glances was out in the open and dashed to pieces, exposed by the very person who should never have been so thoroughly aware of it.

"What do you mean?"

"You're old enough to know," he chided. "Or aren't you?"

Something cold, curt, almost ill-tempered in this short snub couldn't begin to chime with the grace and tenderness of a moment earlier. Had I made the whole thing up?

I immediately averted my eyes and kept looking away, as if to prove him wrong and to show that something to my left had caught my attention and had nothing to do with him. But I had begun to shake. I had violated something. But what? All I knew was that he had put me in my place—and in the process left me feeling totally numbed. Never had I been scolded without anger in someone's voice, or felt so easily unraveled by words that were neither hostile nor harsh, which was why they hurt so much—because he might have meant them kindly, because I knew he was right, because he could see right through me, and I disliked this so much yet liked it so much. I had hoped to cross a line while staring and get away with it without his knowing or calling me on it. This was worse than being scolded by a schoolteacher, or caught lying or stealing, worse than when I'd made an obscene gesture at a fruit vendor only to see the old man turn to me and say, *Svergognato,* shameless. Nanni might as well have said *Svergognato.* He had seen who I was, construed every filthy bend in my heart and read my foulest thoughts—he knew, knew everything, knew what I'd been looking at the moment he had stood up to fetch sandpaper, knew what I was doing when I touched his knee. I felt so trounced by the implied reprimand in his quiet words that I was about to ask him please not to tell my parents.

"Did I offend you, Nanni?" I finally had the courage to ask, perhaps as a way of allaying his reaction. Unable to stand the sudden chill between us, I asked, "Are you angry with me?" I could tell my voice was failing. He too could tell.

He nodded ever so slightly five or six times, pensive as I'd never seen him before. Then he gave me a patronizing smile.

"*Sta' buono, Paolo, e va' a casa,* behave, Paolo, and go home. I'll see you in a few days," he said.

But there was still that dark, unwavering glare in his eyes, as though he was holding something back. "But I don't want to leave yet," I mumbled, before even thinking, already resigned to leave, which is why I drew closer for the usual goodbye hug.

"*Devi,* you must."

He said it without the slightest rebuke in his voice, like a dismissal that could easily be mistaken for a plea. He was stepping back from me.

I didn't understand what *devi* meant that day. But thinking back now to that one word and to the way he'd spoken it, I must have sensed somewhere that this was the first time in my life that someone had treated me not as the child I still was or as a child who'd stayed out playing with friends one evening without letting his parents know he'd be late for supper, but as someone who on that very hour had strayed from being just a boy to becoming a desirable young man, who had tempted, maybe even threatened, someone quite older. On that day, without knowing the first thing, I'd been let into someone's life as surely as I'd drawn him into mine. It took years to suspect he had struggled.

I had seen my father bid my brother farewell a year earlier at the train station, and the two had hugged before my father released himself from his son's embrace and asked him to just go now, *for both our sakes*.

I didn't hug Nanni again. I walked out of his shop, already planning my return in a day or so. After that, perhaps I might come back in the winter sometime. But I was also aware—and it came to me for the first time as I was heading back home that evening—that this, however unreal and unthinkable, might be my last time in his shop.

For the next few years, what that *devi* meant kept changing like the colors on a mood stone. Sometimes it was like a slap and a warning; sometimes like the shrug of a friend who chooses to overlook a slip and pretends to forget; and sometimes, it burned through me like muted, imperiled consent. *Go away* is what one said to the devil, when the devil is already in us, and what he meant with that look in his eyes as he watched me walk away was, *If you don't leave now, I won't fight you.*

On leaving his shop that day, I couldn't have been more furious. I stomped along my shortcut, stopped at the Norman chapel, sat on the plinth to look out to the sea toward the mainland, but couldn't gather my thoughts. All I was aware of was that I'd been chastised and then dismissed. I was livid. Because I knew he was right. He knew me more than I knew myself, and there was nowhere to hide from his words. *Behave, Paolo, and go home.* And as I was sitting there, I don't know what seized me, but I tore off all my clothes, removed my sandals, even, and sat naked inside the chapel, trying to imagine that Nanni had told me to undress and stay naked until he'd come. And I sat there on the chipped limestone and saw us talking together, both naked, and I could tell he was going to touch me, but instead he looked down on my body and, smiling, started to spit on my thighs, my groin, my erection, and on my chest, as if to put out a fire, and I loved how I had come up with the idea of his saliva dripping on my body, because it told me that after doing this to me there was no way he wouldn't come by now. I waited forever, aroused and naked, hoping he'd come, because he had to. I didn't know what else to do.

It was nighttime when I got home. In the mirror before bathing, I looked awful, but no one asked why I was home so late, or what had happened to make me look so gaunt and disheveled. But I knew that day that if I was ever going to come back as an adult to the island it would be to build my home in that chapel. It had seen me suffer and cry as I'd never wept before. I knew every one of its exposed stones, every inch, every weed, every crawling lizard, down to the feel of the chipped stones and pebbles under my bare feet. I belonged here the way I belonged to this planet and its people, but on one condition: alone, always alone.

And as I stood inside the abandoned chapel that I had sworn someday to rebuild and make my home, I also knew then that if I had to wait ten years to see Nanni again, I would rather die now. Take me now, I asked, just take me now. I didn't have such a decade in me. But what I also began to sense after sundown that evening, as I'd already sensed on the evening I stood burning in my nakedness in this old sanctuary, was the certainty that I was lying, that I would indeed be willing to wait and still wait, as those who stop their lives to expiate forgotten crimes are told to wait, because their true punishment is no longer to know whether they're actually waiting for pardon and grace, or whether what they've waited for has long been granted unbeknownst to them, and that they'd lived out the term of their life without ever holding what was theirs to have and theirs alone. This was my first encounter with time. I became a person that evening, and I had him to thank. And blame.

NOW, ON THAT same shortcut years later, past the Norman chapel and the lime grove, I had the feeling that I should never have come. I had come for nothing. All that remained of our house was the blackened stump of what seemed a far, far smaller house than I remembered. For a moment I thought that some-one had tampered with the layout, but the walls told me that this indeed had been the size of our house. The windows, the doors, the roof, all gone, and as I stepped into what had once been our living room, I thought of those Gothic abbeys that are com-pletely hollow and all that stands between heaven and earth is a gutted hull and grass in the middle. But there was no grass here. Just metal scraps everywhere, peeling shreds of what I for-got had been the dark lime-green wallpaper in our living room, and in the middle a dead cat teeming with maggots. This was the carcass of our house. All I could think of was the silverware. Silverware doesn't burn, doesn't melt. Some of it bore my grand-father's initials, and therefore mine as well. Where was the silverware? They'd most likely say it disappeared with the house. Everything disappeared. *Sparito*. That one word was supposed to explain everything, because what else could one say about honor and friendship and loyalty, except that time undoes them all, erases debts, forgives plunder, overlooks larceny and be-trayal? Civilization would never be jump-started here unless all was whitewashed and forgotten. My room was upstairs—but of upstairs not even a trace. Something in me had died here. The night the lights went out and I wished to be held in the dark, not a trace of that either. The day he walked out with the desk and I thought of Aeneas and how I wanted to be his son. The evening I stood on the threshold to our living room and thought why can't I be him instead of me. The evening I sat naked before God and couldn't even begin to know what I wanted. So much had happened since that last summer—schools, lovers, my mother's death, more travels, and above all the loss of people I didn't even know I had yet to meet and love but then lost track of and never saw again.

Looking around me, I began to suspect that many of the locals were observing me survey the grounds but that none would come out to say hello. The more I thought of them, the more I lingered over what had once been our home. I was touching and groping its debris, less to see if I recognized anything than to show those spying from behind their lace curtains that I had every claim to what I was doing. And yet as I continued wishing to prove that I belonged here and that what I was touching was mine, I was growing uncomfortable, sensing that I should perhaps avoid picking things up for fear anyone might mistake me for a thief. All I needed now was to be arrested for trespassing in my own home.

Suddenly it hit me that what I'd lost was not only our house but also the right to think it would be mine someday. I owned nothing here. I remembered my grandfather's pen. Should I even bother to look for it, or had it melted too?

A stray dog who had been watching me from a distance finally nuzzled up to me. I did not know him, nor did he know me. But we shared one thing—we belonged to no one here. From where I now stood, rebuilding seemed so pointless. I never wanted to come back here. The mere thought of rebuilding and of hiring architects, builders, masons, carpenters, plumbers, electricians, painters, and of walking up and down the glistening empty lanes past sundown in the rainy winter months here horrified me.

And yet my life started here and stopped here one summer long ago, in this house, which no longer exists, in this decade, which slipped away so fast, with this never love that altered everything but went nowhere. *You made me who I am today, Nanni.*

Wherever I go, everyone I see and crave is ultimately measured by the glow of your light. If my life were a boat, you were the one who stepped on board, turned on its running lights, and was never heard from again. All this might as well be in my head, and in my head it stays. But I've lived and loved by your light alone. In a bus, on a busy street, in class, in a crowded concert hall, once or twice a year, whether for a man or a woman, my heart still jolts when I spot your look-alike. We love only once in our lives, my father had said, sometimes too early, sometimes too late; the other times are always a touch deliberate.

A FEW YEARS earlier a classmate in college had shown me an article about San Giustiniano and asked if this was the same San Giustiniano I'd mentioned once. I wasn't sure, I said. Even when I looked at the picture of the bay I continued to say I wasn't sure—as if something in me no longer wanted to believe that the place could still exist without me there. It was the first and only time I'd ever seen a picture of the island in print. The article didn't refer to anyone in particular, just to a significant police presence in this little-known fishing community in Italy. There had been no murders, the article said, but there were a few incidents involving the Mob where groups of young men were rounded up, stripped, questioned, beaten, and later released. The article spoke of local mobsters. I had an image of naked young men covering their genitals with both hands; it was the only other time in my life when I'd allowed myself to imagine Nanni standing stark naked. It felt like a taboo. All I imagined was Nanni trying to comfort his panicked younger brother. This was all hearsay, I figured, but until that very day in school, with the magazine in my hand showing an ancient stock photograph of the marina of San Giustiniano, I'd seldom allowed myself to linger on the thought of him without clothes. Something like

deference and simple decency toward the young man whom I
venerated and who had stepped into our living room and confided
in my parents with such unguarded candor had always stood in
the way. But the magazine stirred images I could no longer sup-
press. What was even more disturbing was that the article made
a veiled suggestion of vile acts committed by the carabinieri. I
read in these vile acts what had long been on my mind. I knew I
was feeling a lingering, insidious joy in thinking of what the police could have done to him, as though their crime had freed my
imagination and allowed it to roam into secret chambers I had
so cautiously locked and lost the keys to. Had I stayed in San
Giustiniano, I might have been one of these young men standing naked next to him.

I lingered awhile longer, then decided to move toward a
house adjoining ours. My father had heard that the other houses
had suffered no damage and stayed intact despite their proximity
to the fire. I knocked at the door, but no one was home. I walked
behind the house and knocked at the back door in case they hadn't
heard my knock at the front door. But no one answered there
either. I waited, then knocked once more. Someone must be home,
I thought, because the garden hose was running. *"C'è nessuno? Is
anyone there?"* I cried out. I heard one door bang shut inside.
Someone was coming to open. But then I heard another door
shut. I could even hear the patter of hasty footsteps. They weren't
coming to the door, they were scrambling to the other side of
the house. Possibly children who were warned never to open the
door to strangers. Or children playing a prank. Or just people
avoiding strangers.

I had no better luck with the house next to that one.

On my way to try the fourth and last house along our stretch,
I eventually ran into someone I thought I recognized because of
his limp: it was our old gardener. He, it turned out, now owned

a house much farther down on the same road. Had he seen me
first, he would probably have skittered away like everyone else.
He remembered my father, he said. He remembered my older
brother and my mother—and with great affection, he added. He
remembered the two Dobermans that accompanied my father
wherever he went. I don't think the gardener remembered me at
all. I told him that my brother had settled elsewhere but that
we all missed San Giustiniano still. I lied, perhaps to make conversation, or to draw him out, or just to show we bore no hard
feelings for the locals. My father was aging and was sad he couldn't
come in the summer. I understand him, said the gardener. And
your mother? *È mancata*, I said, she's no longer with us.

"There was a huge fire," he said after a while. "Everyone came
to see, but the flames ate everything. The firemen arrived from
the adjoining town and were a band of incompetent *sciagurati*,
wretches. They expected the fire to wait for them, but by the time
they came everything was already up in smoke. The conflagration was brutal and so fast."

He kept quiet for a moment.

"So you came to see."

"So I came to see," I echoed. "It's always so quiet and so peace-
ful," I said, trying to show I had come with no agenda whatsoever.
But then, after chatting mostly about nothing, I was not able
to hold back. "Was anything salvaged—anything?"

"*Purtroppo, no*, unfortunately, no. It hurts me to say it. Yours
was the most beautiful house—and all that lovely furniture. I
remember it well. At least you weren't here to witness what we
all saw. *Indimenticabile*, unforgettable."

There was a touch of high drama in his narrative. He must
have sensed it too. "And now look at this cat," he said in an attempt to change the subject and bring things down to a lower

key. "I'll have to go and find something to wrap it in and bury it now."

"Tell me about Nanni."

"Nanni the carpenter?"

As if there were another.

"Yes."

"*Quello è stato veramente sfortunato*, now, he was truly unlucky. The police suspected him, since he knew the house. They suspected his brother as well."

"Why?" I asked, looking up at the scenery and the surrounding trees and affecting fatigue and nonchalant admiration verging on apathy so as not to show I was actually grilling him.

"Why, why. Is there ever a why? Everyone knew he came to restore the furniture. He was always restoring this, repairing that. Your father trusted him."

"And what do you think?"

"The only one who had a key to the house was Nanni. Even I didn't have a key. So it was natural to suspect him, but they arrested a whole group of them, not because of the fire but because some robbers used the house for smuggling and hoarding stolen goods. The carabinieri beat everyone. Then they had them strip and continued to search and beat them. So one sick officer came up with a twisted idea, singled out two young men and I don't have to tell you what this officer wanted the two of them to do. I was there and witnessed everything. Nanni refused. He said he couldn't. 'Why?' yelled the officer, slapping him twice in the face and then with his belt. 'Because he is my brother.' I heard those very words from his mouth and it broke my heart, because everyone knew that the two were inseparable, especially after their parents died. But then another officer stepped in and let the younger brother go. The poor boy opened the gate as fast as he could and dashed off naked, crying Nanni's name as he ran out into the night. They beat Nanni more, of course. There was going to be an inquest, but Ruggiero was a smart lad. He packed all he could, stole into the office where Nanni was being kept that night, and the two ran away."

"And?"

"He and his brother hid in the hills for a few days, then at night they took a boat and rowed to the mainland. And from there, Canada, Australia, South America, *chissà dove*, who knows where."

Again I looked around the scene where our old house stood.

"So who really burned the house?"

"Who'll ever know. Many had their eyes on the house. But why would anyone burn it? Maybe an accident. Or it could be the Mob."

"And Nanni? Do you think he had anything to do with it?"

"Not Nanni. Your father was like a father to him. We all knew that the house was stocked with contraband that year, but no one dared to say anything. Nanni, however, was the easiest one to blame. The police knew it was the Mob, but they blamed him."

The gardener squatted down to pick up the cat, and with the dead animal in one arm, he hugged me with the other.

We were on the point of saying goodbye when I asked him one last question. "Why are people avoiding me?"

He chuckled. "Because they're afraid you've come to repossess the land. Everyone has an eye on abandoned land these days."

I smiled. "Are you eyeing abandoned land these days?" I asked.

"I wouldn't be human if I weren't."

Then, to test his reaction, I told him we were probably going to rebuild the house. Part of me was almost ready to swear I wasn't lying.

"So I will be your gardener again."

"So you will be our gardener again."

He gave me another hug, and without thinking, I caught myself embracing him as well.

I never wanted to see his face again. He knew, as I knew, that he had no intention of being a gardener. One day I'll come back and find he owns all the adjoining properties, including ours.

ON MY WAY back to the harbor, I crossed the tiny piazza and decided to knock at the small door that opened to the mayor's one-room office. There, an old lady who had pulled open her desk drawer and was busy rummaging for something in its rickety, cluttered space, told me that her son wasn't in the office. "Come back tomorrow" was her peremptory reply when I asked when he'd be back. But I was leaving this afternoon, I said, and then introduced myself. She interrupted whatever she was doing in her drawer, seemed to recognize the family name, and gradually remembered that our villa had burned down. Years ago, wasn't it? she asked. Then, suddenly, she was cordial, deferential, almost diffident. In a year or so we were going to rebuild, I said, not so much to convey a fait accompli or to project a sense of ownership and authority but more to test her reaction. She couldn't have looked more disappointed. *"Mi dica allora,* so tell me," she said, already anticipating worse news. There was nothing to say. I just wanted the mayor to know we were going to hire builders from the mainland. I knew she would have preferred local workers. There was spite in my heart, and I liked watching discontent limn itself on her features. "Please tell your son that

I came by today." And as I opened the door, I pivoted and performed what I hoped was one of those accomplished inspectors' *by the way* exit lines seen in so many movies: Did she happen to know how one could reach Giovanni, the cabinetmaker?

The old lady thought for a moment. No, she didn't. *"Quello è sparito tempo fa!* He disappeared long ago." "Any idea where?" She hunched her shoulders. "Perhaps your father knows." Why would my father know? I asked. But she didn't hear me or pretended not to and was back rifling through her wide-open desk drawer. Finally, with a barely concealed dismissive glance, she said, "Good luck finding workers."

I headed out into the blazing sun, where I looked for a caffè. I wanted to sit somewhere and jot down thoughts about my return visit. I thought of seeking my Norman chapel, but I'd already seen it on my way to our grounds and, strangely, it hadn't spoken to me.

Nothing spoke to me. Even jotting a few thoughts in my notebook failed to mean anything. I wanted something and could not begin to know what it was. The last thing I'd written was *I've come back for him.* And that was hours ago. I closed my notebook and looked around. I was seeing the place for the first time. I was seeing it for the last time. The caffè faced the harbor, with a view of the town uphill, while fishermen were at work with their cordage and nets. At this hour of the morning, I was the only customer. None of the umbrellas had been opened yet, and I knew that sitting under direct sunlight would inevitably give me a headache. So after finishing my coffee I decided to walk back up into town and amble about in the shade. I remembered where the bookseller was and hoped to drop by and buy something to while away the time until the ferry docked. But I also thought I should visit my old tutor and get this personal errand out of the way.

I had forgotten absolutely nothing and was able to find his building right away. At the entrance, by the portico, sat the same lopsided, dilapidated mailboxes I had seen a decade before. His name was written in large capitals that betrayed an old man's tremor as well as his determined will to proclaim his name. He had written each letter three times, once in purple, twice in blue, on square math paper that had been folded over to fit in the name slot. *Prof. Sermoneta*. Interno 34. I hadn't forgotten that either.

After climbing the spiral stairway, I stopped on the fourth floor and rang his doorbell. I felt nothing. From behind the door, I could hear the clumsy chink of dishes and silverware, then the slow shuffle of feet, and a tremulous, ill-tempered, jerky hand opening the locks on the door. The same three locks, and as always the same struggle to remember which lock went which way, which invariably put him in a foul mood before even opening his door to you. This also made you want to crawl in and apologize for troubling him to teach you Latin and Greek.

He was wearing slippers, as usual. *Chi è?* he asked with the door still shut. But before I could make up my mind how to let him know who I was, he had already flung the door open, almost with a rage. *"Ah, sei tu?* Oh, it's you?" he said on seeing me. "So come in." I stepped inside. The place smelled as it always did: of camphor for his joints and of Tuscan mini-cigars, which had always made my clothes stink. "I was just washing some dishes, come in, come in," he said impatiently as he led me straight into the kitchen. "And give me a hand, will you." He handed me a towel and a teacup, which were immediately followed by a saucer and a plate. "Dry them well." This too hadn't changed. You became his apprentice, his disciple, his servant. "So you've come for a lesson?" I stared at him in disbelief. Did he really remember me, or was he just trying to hide that he had absolutely no idea?

"No, no lessons for today," I said, almost catching myself saying it the way one might turn down a strong dose of grappa on an empty stomach for breakfast.

"Why not? A bit of Latin never hurt," he insisted. We might as well have been arguing about grappa. "Have you studied?"

These were strange questions. He hadn't seen me in a decade and he was picking up a conversation from scarcely the other day.

"Why haven't you studied? Are you not well?" he asked.

"I've been quite well," I said, changing my mind about telling him what I'd studied in college, how, despite failing my Latin and Greek exam ten years earlier, I had majored in classical literature. I was even going to allege that it was because of him that I had developed a fondness for Greek literature. For all he knew, it seemed, I was just late for class again and, as usual, had been playing marbles with the local boys before coming upstairs for my tutorial.

"*Allora?* So?"

"*Allora* nothing, really. My father asked me to say hello," I lied. I was not going to mention my mother.

"And promise to say hello back. Promise?"

I promised.

"Do you still read one canto a day?" I asked, trying to break the strain in our conversation, only to realize I had given it a further torsion.

"A canto a day it still is."

Silence, again.

"And do you still teach?"

"And do I still eat?" he snapped back, parodying my question.

He looked at me as if I was meant to provide an answer to his question. But in this strange conversation, I had nothing to add. I had not expected such erratic small talk.

"Of course I teach," he went on, seeing I had failed to supply an answer in the allotted time. "Not as much as before. I need to sleep more, but I have some very gifted students."

"Like me?" I asked, trying to liven the conversation with a dash of irony.

"If it pleases you to think so, why not. Like you."

As he was lighting his cigar I couldn't help but ask, "Do you remember me?"

"Do I remember you? Of course I remember you. What kind of a question is that?"

"Because I remember everything," I added, swiftly trying to cover up my tracks by throwing in the first thing that came to mind.

"And why shouldn't you remember everything? I'm not going to ask you to decline words today. But don't tempt me."

I'd been expecting an expression of utter surprise at the door, even an embrace and a warm welcome once we sat down in his musty old study, not this sputter of jolts and darts.

"These have not been easy times, let me tell you."

"How so?"

"How so? You ask the most fatuous questions. Everyone is getting wealthy these days, thievery everywhere, except for teachers, to say nothing of penniless tutors in their late seventies. Difficult enough not to afford a new winter coat. Need to hear more? No."

I apologized.

"Plus there are other issues."

"Other issues? What other issues?"

"Called old age. May the good Lord spare you that craggy abyss."

I could do no more than nod.

"You nodded. Why, because you know so much about old age?"

"My father."

"Your father?" He breathed deeply. "Your father was a genius."

"My father, a genius?"

"A genius, and don't disrespect! He knew more than any doctor both here and on the mainland. But he also saw where things were headed here so he decided to move. Not all of us were as *prévoyant*," he said, using French to prove he was still in possession of his marbles. "But as a result, this town was left without a single man who had read a book, any book. Except for the pharmacist—and what does the poor clueless soul know about aches and gallstones and enlarged prostates?"

As a joke, I was going to recommend our barber Signor Alessi but held myself back. Still, the comic thought brought a smile to my lips that I couldn't quite contain.

"This is no laughing matter. You've always been a bit of a blockhead, Paolo, haven't you?"

This was the first time he had used my name. So he did know who I was.

"Explain," I asked.

"Only a blockhead would need to have things spelled out. To see a real doctor I have to catch the ferry, and a ferry ride in mid-winter is no funny business. I see no reason for smiling."

I apologized.

Was this the lost world I had come looking for—all bile inside his small apartment and rank looting outside? No wonder Nanni couldn't wait to get out of this medieval gutter that had once been home to pirates and Saracens.

"So your father is well?" he said.

"My father is well."

"I am happy for you." As always, bitterness and humanity,

like kindness dipped in venom. All I wanted was to get as far away from him as I could. I told him about my visit to what had once been our villa.

"The house did not catch fire. They burned it down, the animals. Everyone came to see. I came to see." He made a huge gesture with his arms and hands to imitate the conflagration. "They blamed a young cabinetmaker. But everyone knows he had caught the bandits using your parents' house as a storage space for their loot. Our lovely police were in on it too, I am sure. They arrested him, beat him, then they burned the house."

"Why?"

"Because everyone in this wretched little town has larceny and treachery seared into his soul, from the mayor to the police down to the hooligans who load and unload their booty in front of our very noses every day."

A long silence ensued.

"Let's go for a walk. Otherwise I get drowsy and I don't want to nap yet. And buy me coffee, because the way things are going with my pension and my measly income these days . . ."

PROFESSOR SERMONETA DECIDED to walk me to the town's caffè. It took him forever to get down the stairs. "When is your ferry leaving?"

"This afternoon," I said.

"So we have time." Then, changing registers: "They even tried to blame your father."

"My father?"

We were walking the narrow lanes together. I had never walked with my tutor anywhere before. He was not a friendly sort, and though my parents told me that his sternness was his way of keeping pupils in tow, I'd always felt that he had singled me out for the sort of abusive treatment one reserves for unruly terriers. I had heard he had a far gentler side to him, but I had no sense of how to bring it out.

He was holding his cane and focusing on each step down the cobbled lane, perhaps his way of avoiding the subject.

I soon began to realize we couldn't have been headed anywhere but toward vicolo Sant'Eusebio. When we reached the locked-up shop, I found myself struggling not to tell him that I used to come here after our tutorial and that here, as far as I knew, life had started for me.

"I heard the cabinetmaker is gone," I said after a moment of silence.

"Did you know him?" he asked.

Did I know him! I wanted to say. I was in love with him. Still am. It's why I'm here. "I knew him," I finally said.

"We all knew him. I can't say I knew him well, but at night, in the caffè, after a few glasses, he'd always begin singing with that voice of his."

"What voice?"

"Lovely voice. Always the same aria, though, from *Don Giovanni*. He didn't know any other. You know the one,

> *Notte e giorno faticar*
> *per chi nulla sa gradir;*
> . . .
> *mangiar male e mal dormir . . .*

"I forget the rest but he'd sing the whole aria."

I knew the aria all too well and supplied the missing words. My father used to sing it too, I said, the twenty-second variation. Sermoneta laughed.

"But then one night he disappeared," continued my tutor.

"He's never coming back, you know. I heard rumors he may be in Canada."

"Why in Canada?"

"I don't know, Paolo, I don't know." He sounded irritated. I could almost swear he was about to call me a blockhead again.

We left Sant'Eusebio and headed farther up toward the caffè within sight of the castle. "Do you still remember the caffè?" he asked.

"How could I forget? I used to come here with my father at night." Sermoneta remembered; he'd seen us there many times. He parted the curtain and peeked inside. It was dark and empty at this time of the day. But the beefy proprietor was there, as always wiping the counter.

"*Salve, Professore*," he said as soon as he saw us step inside.

"*Salve*," replied my tutor. We ordered two coffees.

"*Subito*," said the proprietor.

I paid.

"Recognize this young man?" asked my tutor.

The caffè proprietor squinted his eyes and took a good look at me. "No, should I?"

"The doctor's son."

The corpulent proprietor mused a moment. "I remember the doctor. I also remember those frightful dogs." He mimicked a shudder with his neck. Then turning to me, "How is your father?"

"He is well," I said.

"Ah, your father, what a good man, beloved and missed by everyone here, *un vero nobiluomo*, a true nobleman. And what a shame about the house." Then, with a wry smile settling on his features and with his palm chopping the air three or four times to ape the gesture of a man about to administer a light spanking to a child, "*Tuo padre, però*, your father, however . . . *un po' briccone era*, was a bit of rascal." He let the sentence trail without finishing his thought, which made me think he'd been simply jesting with me.

He leaned over on the marble countertop, indicating that he was about to lower his voice to a whisper, even though the place was empty. But then he changed his mind. *"Acqua passata,* water under the bridge," he said, *"acqua passata."* Pulling himself away from the counter and slowly straightening his back with a bit of a grimace, he said, "This town unfortunately is all *chiacchiere,* all gossip, and I always tell myself, *Arnaldo, look the other way, look the other way and never spread rumors about the lives of others,* even if the rumors are true. I'm saying this man-to-man, because I think you're a grown-up now and understand these things."

But unable to contain himself, the owner turned to my tutor and, almost on the point of snickering, as though the two were sharing an old private joke, he extended both his index fingers and rubbed them together, an ancient gesture suggesting collusion, secrecy, and slop.

"Acqua passata, Arnaldo," repeated my tutor.

AS I WALKED my tutor back to his apartment, already sensing that in all likelihood I would never see him again, I began to realize that none of this was really news to me, that perhaps, without having the facts, without suspecting, I had always known, known without knowing. I probably already knew when, for years, my mother, brother, grandmother, great-aunt, and I were so expeditiously shipped off the island at the end of every summer, while my father stayed behind to lock up and arrange everything for the following year. Everyone on the island knew the house.

The caffè proprietor's gesture said it all. "Early in the morning when they went swimming," he had said, "then every night in the caffè, and during the winter months too, in case you thought winters were out of the question."

"How long?" I'd asked, still trying to pretend I wasn't the slightest bit shaken by what they were telling me. I was assuming a season, a few months.

"Nanni's parents were very much alive at the time. So he must have been, what, eighteen, nineteen? Why do you think Nanni kept crossing over to the mainland at least twice a month during the winter months? To buy paint thinner?"

Now that I thought of it, it would have taken half a day to close the house every fall, not a whole week to ten days as was my father's custom every year. No wonder, then, that without knowing exactly why, my mother, heeding an ageless instinct, eventually grew to dislike Nanni and found him so sinister and unsavory. I thought that she, like me, was exaggerating her hostility the better to disguise that she liked him and that, by calling attention to his shortcomings and overstating his flaws, she was asking us to disagree with her, and by disagreeing, speak of qualities she did not have the courage to name herself. I had always thought that it was she who had leaked what I'd said about the tremor in his hands. Small wonder Nanni knew his way about our house. He had most likely examined the desk long, long before he came to discuss the job with my mother. The way he pranced into the living room as though he owned the place, knew there'd be a hidden box inside the desk, addressed my father as his pal, and had even gotten the dogs to like him, plus the whole banter between them about swimming across the bay—all such dead giveaways. And those nightwalks with my father—he, like me, craving to run into Nanni and hoping that by extending our walks and making up excuses to delay heading back home, we might in the end run into him at the caffè. I was like a lover who is suddenly able to cobble together facts and realizes he's been cheated on for weeks, months, or even years on end.

But I was not jealous. I was happy. And happy not just for

them. I saw that, even at such an early age, I had zeroed in on the right person and read the truth about me and about him as well. I wanted him, and he would have wanted me, not when I was twelve, but later. I even drew pleasure in thinking that my passion was inherited, that it was passed on, and therefore fated. Fate always leaves a mark, and those of us who are truly lucky know the signs and how to read them. He would have taught me everything, and most likely given me everything. Instead, years after, I sought out the wrong people, learned from the wrong teachers, took from those who had less to give and almost nothing I wanted. As I walked after dropping off my tutor in the early afternoon, I imagined the two of them on the very evening after our departure, having a quick meal together in the kitchen. A feast on leftovers. By then my father would have sent away all the help, and he and Nanni would be alone in the house, possibly listening to Beethoven as they sat on the veranda without candles or kerosene lamps, to avoid mosquitoes and prying eyes. Their days, their hours were numbered, and they knew it. San Giustiniano would not stand them much longer. Surely there'd been signs, threats, who knows.

I pictured them sitting face-to-face over dinner with a glass of wine each, my father spreading his elbows on the table as he did with me to watch the young man drink from his glass. After the meal, Nanni says, "I'll clear the dishes," and knowing my father, he gets up and says, "No, let me. You sit."

It was at moments such as these, at the beach in the morning or in the caffè at night, that my father would discover I'd worked on the frames and the small box. "The boy works well." "I am so happy he's taken an interest," says my father. "He does. Every day. But I have to tell you, I think he has a crush on me." The man sitting with his elbows outstretched, watching the young man sip his wine, would not be shocked, nor would he mind hearing this. He might even be a touch amused—like father, like son, he says. "He's been courting me for weeks," says Nanni, "and the strange thing is that he probably has no idea. I don't think he knows anything."

Nanni stands up now and helps my father with the dishes. "One day he's bound to find out," Nanni says.

"With someone like you, Nanni, just like you."

Nanni was right about one thing. I knew nothing at all.

But had I not eventually learned about the ways of physical love through gossip, hearsay, and foul words, God only knows what I would have invented once seized by the urge to touch another human being.

I MISSED THE ferry and had an hour and a half to kill before the next one. I'd go up to the castle, I thought, and later tell my father that I'd made memories the way we had pledged to do years before. But instead I walked up vicolo Sant'Eusebio and stopped there for the last time, not sure what I was doing or why, yet sensing that he would have wanted me to do just that, because he would have done it for me, or for my father, it didn't matter whom. Nothing had changed. I remembered the baker and began heading his way, remembered the bruises on his arms that had made my father and me laugh, and then, as if it were the sound track to this whole place, I remembered Beethoven's thirty-first variation. Where was Nanni now? I bought two pastries. One for me, one . . .

Part of me wanted to keep walking around town at this hour of the afternoon and pretend that eventually I'd find the shop open. I had forgotten nothing; this could easily have been ten years ago. My mother was still alive, I hadn't met Chloe, hadn't met Raúl, and, for that brief spell one winter during senior year in college, hadn't run into a chemistry student, whose name I never bothered to ask and whose voice I can't even recall because we'd hardly ever spoken on the nights we sought each other's bodies in the dark.

But there was no time, and I could already hear the *traghetto* sounding its horn. With any luck, tomorrow I'd be in Rome.

Would I have the courage to speak to my father about Nanni—and not only about his Nanni but also about mine?

What I wanted was to spot my father sitting at a small table at his favorite caffè, arrive late as he always complained I did, and before ordering anything, take a seat and say to him, "I think he's alive."

"Who?"

"The man you and I loved. He lives in Canada."

And then it hit me for the first time in my life. My father must have always known what had happened to Nanni, and that if I'd wanted to know, all I needed was to ask him. A blockhead indeed, I thought, almost laughing at my old tutor's word.

But my father never spoke to me about Nanni. Nor did I broach the subject with him. I never found out what Nanni ended up doing for a living, or what kind of life he led, married, unmarried, partnered or not. But I do know that letters arrived from Canada. I saw an envelope with Canadian stamps lying on Father's dining table once when I dropped in to see him. But when I came back from the kitchen after making a sandwich, the envelope had disappeared. He didn't want me to know they corresponded. But I was happy they did.

Years later, while emptying my parents' home, I found a small sealed package the size of a shoe box addressed to my father. Judging from the postmark, it must have lain there for three years among so many things that had piled up after his death. "*Sciusciù,*" read the note when I unwrapped and opened the package, "I kept this after you left San Giustiniano. I told you I was sending it back. Please accept it and don't argue. I've known love only once in my life, and it was you."

I had heard the name *Sciusciù* used once but had completely failed to pay attention. Nanni had muttered it before leaving our house, probably on the evening when he came to deliver the desk. It was a French word that my father had picked up during his student days in France and used as an endearment with everyone: *chouchou*. They must have used it with each other.

I replied two years later. "Dear Nanni," I wrote. "We received your package about five years ago. But it is only now that I'm writing to you. I don't know why it took so long to write back. My father died six years ago. We never spoke about you. But I knew. Perhaps you never knew this, but I was more like my father with you than you suspected. Or perhaps you knew. Yes, I'm sure you knew. You've been with me all my life."

I didn't expect a reply.

An envelope arrived a few weeks later. "Maybe you'll like this picture. I had it copied and wanted you to have it."

In the picture Nanni and my father are standing in bathing suits with the sea behind them. Nanni's right arm is resting on my father's shoulders, while his other hand is holding my father's left shoulder. My father, his arms crossed, is smiling broadly, and so is Nanni, both trim and athletic. Only then did I realize that though my father was at least twenty years older than Nanni, in the picture they look so much alike that they could be brothers. I had never thought of my father as a handsome man, and yet, in this new light, he was more than just handsome. It had taken me years to see how much alike the two of them were.

SPRING
FEVER

As soon as I see them inside the restaurant I avert my eyes and pretend to be staring at the menu posted by the entrance. If they see me, they'll think I've just breezed in and out after hastily scanning the day's offerings. To avoid being caught fleeing, I stay put a fraction of a second longer, performing a seeming double take at the menu. I put on my glasses, bring my face close to the daily specials in typical French script on the tiny elementary-school slate board by the door, and seem to be totally engrossed, realizing all along that nothing, not one word I'm reading, is registering. Finally, with an imperceptible shake of the head, which she'll recognize as my usual *nah*, I remove my glasses, put them back in my breast pocket, pivot, and walk out, determined to disappear as fast as I can from the block, from the avenue, from the city itself. My little performance must have taken no more than five seconds.

It is only as I am rushing up Madison Avenue and putting as

much distance between Renzo & Lucia's and me that I notice I'm trembling. From shock, I think. No, from jealousy. Or anger. Then I correct myself: From fear. Actually, from shame.

I, the wronged party, am ashamed of being caught by them, while they, the guilty, couldn't care less: no rush of adrenaline, no rattled frown on her face. From where she was seated in the middle of the restaurant, she would have stared me down, meaning, *So now you know.*

I could let myself think that I immediately slipped out of the restaurant to spare her the stress and agitation of being caught. But my heart is racing too fast for me to think I've done it just for her. I hate not only my sheepish, hangdog, tail-between-my-legs getaway; I hate being so visibly shaken. If I run into people I know, they'll take a quick look at me and ask, *What's the matter? You look terrible.* Do I look terrible? As terrible as the day I got a phone call telling me my father had fallen while crossing the street and was lying unconscious in the emergency room and I raced to the hospital forgetting keys, wallet, and the photo ID identifying me as someone bearing his last name? I don't care if I look terrible.

But I do care.

Yet before walking out of the restaurant, I stayed long enough to prevent them from thinking that I'd skipped away immediately after seeing them. Smart thinking, that.

The thought makes me feel good about myself, and feeling good gives my gait a lively sprint. Maud would think I was in a terrific mood and taking the afternoon off and was most likely headed to the very tennis courts where she and I had met less than a year ago.

I seldom play tennis after 8:00 a.m., but taking time off to play on such a glorious Friday early afternoon feels like a wonderful idea, particularly on this faux-spring day that really happens to be in late winter. I call Harlan, my morning partner. He's a schoolteacher and usually heads back to the courts after school. As always, his voice mail picks up. I leave him a message. Meanwhile, I see a crosstown bus on 67th and Madison and decide to head west just as its doors are about to close. It's the long way to the courts, but I like walking up Central Park West early in the afternoon. I can call her on her cell from the West Side in twenty minutes to see how she'll respond. Then, for future reference, I'll register the chill blitheness of her *Busy, busy, busy, call you later.*

On the bus, I try to list a few things. The sound of Maud's voice when she's happy to hear my voice even if she's at a business lunch and *can't really talk right now.* Her distracted vioce when she's surrounded by noise in a crowded restaurant. And yet the way she looked at him while he was speaking to her— listening so keenly, so engrossed, poring over every inflection in his broad, dimpled smile, her head tilted toward his, his almost touching hers, both heads almost resting against the large mirror right behind them, in what every art student would call a definite Canova moment. Of course she won't pick up the phone when I call. Lucky the man whose companion listens to him, hangs on his every word, asks him to tell her more, *and please don't stop talking,* she says, *I love when you talk to me,* her left arm reclining on the back of the banquette, touching his neck, rubbing the curls above his neck—she is staring, gazing, worshiping. *I'll do everything,* her eyes say.

Her right hand rests on the table, fondling the salt shaker, doing nothing, waiting. I know that gesture. She wants him to hold her hand.

They're talking, but they're staring. They're making love, for Christ's sake.

A woman who lets her hand rub the back of a man's neck that way is obviously not having a platonic thing. A woman who hasn't been naked with you doesn't look so confiding, so eager to touch. She can't have enough of him. They're past holding back, past awkward admissions, past the restless unease of people who are irresistibly drawn to each other but haven't made love yet. These are people who've just started sleeping together and can't hold off touching, everything is about touching. They're playing at residual flirtation long after courtship has served its purpose. And yet that hand resting so doleful and guileless on the table, still fondling the salt shaker—can't he tell she's waiting, waiting for him to put his hand on hers?

When had they started sleeping together? Just recently? Last week? Last month? Will it last? Who is he? How does she know him? Were there others? Was there a clear and tangible moment when she decided to cross the bridge and go over to the other side? Or, as the saying goes, did it all just happen? You head out to a business lunch one day, he stares at you, you let your gaze linger on his, and suddenly, after just a half glass of wine, you catch your breath and the words slip out of your mouth, and you can't believe what you've said, and the strange thing is he's no less rapt than you are, until one of you breaks down and finally asks, *Is this really happening?* and the other replies, *I think it is*. I can just hear them: *What happens at Renzo & Lucia's stays at Renzo & Lucia's.*

I envy them. They're sleeping together. And yet I am not jealous. Because I fear jealousy more than the loss of love.

Why wasn't I aware that something like this was going on in her life? In most cases you're not even aware that you've been suspecting, which is why you never bothered culling the scraps of evidence that kept falling your way every day, every hour, and that you now regret failing to intercept, to examine, to log away in the ledger of heartbreak, resentment, and guile. The eternal yoga classes on weekday evenings; the phone she almost never picks up at the office when she knows I'm the one calling; the drinks after work that always get shuffled around so you can't quite tell when they've morphed into an impromptu dinner; the reading group that never gathers in the same place twice; the meetings at work that happen at the last minute; the laptop she shuts a bit too hastily the moment you walk into the room; and always those cryptic yes-no conversations she says are with her boss calling late from Westchester.

In the evening, she smokes a cigarette and stares into space, listens to music and stares into space, stares into space to be with him, not me. She reminds me of infatuated women in 1940s movies who travel by ship and lounge alone on deck and cannot read and all they want is to stroll about at night until the man they love shows up again and offers to light their cigarette.

Was she thinking of him when we sat and watched TV together, or when I massaged her toes because she said her feet hurt, or when we rubbed against each other in the kitchen and I held her from behind and wanted to make love to her? New doubts flit through my mind, but before I can seize them, they fizzle away. Better this way. There are things I may not want to know or think about. Do my friends know? Have they tried to tell me but backed off when they saw I wasn't picking up the hint?

In the elevator to his place, she fixes his tie, as she did once with my lapel seconds before we rang someone's bell, knowing already that, as soon as they shut the door behind them, she'll tear off his tie, unbutton his shirt, undo his belt, yank him out of his clothes. I like the thought that she'll volunteer to help him with his cuff links, because she assumes all men need help putting them on and taking them off. I want him to fear she's thinking of the men she's known when she removes his cuff links with an expert hand.

I AM ON Central Park West and the sun is beaming on this spec-
tacular clear day. With any luck, Harlan and I will be playing tennis as soon as his school lets out. I'll sweat it out and put all
this behind me. Harlan likes to hit, backhand and forehand, and
we'll play like savages, as he likes to say, because we are taking it
out on those poor yellow balls. Backhand and forehand, cross-
court against crosscourt, and, when one of us least expects it,
we'll hit one of those down-the-line beauties to jostle every last
pout out of our system.

On this budding, premature summer day it will be heaven. I
could take a cab to 93rd. But I want to walk in the sun. At the
entrance to the park on 67th Street, I spot a hot dog stand. This
is exactly what I've been aching for: a frankfurter. I ask for sauer-
kraut, lots of it, and onion sauce too. *You've suffered a great shock
and need to be good to yourself,* says an inside voice. This is the
new normal. I need to learn to live with it. Millions have been
hurt before, millions more will continue to be. I should find
someone to speak to, but—and the thought jolts me because
I wasn't careful to nip it—the only one who'd understand is
the very one I wish to lash out against. I'm like those seeking
comfort or, better yet, advice, from the very person who abuses
them.

The hot dog vendor looks at me, meaning *Did I want something to drink?*

Yes, a Diet Coke as well. With a straw, please. The man looks
up at the sky and comments on the weather. "Beach weather,"
he says, "beach weather, like in my country." He obviously wants
me to ask which country that is, but from how he pronounces
his consonants, I've already guessed. How did I know? he asks.
From the accent, I said. How did I know the accent, then? An

ex-girlfriend was Greek. From where she was? From 181st Street. And before that? Chios, I say. Have I been to Chios? No, never, has he? Never, nor would he, he snickers, hoping I'd ask why—which I decide not to. By the time we've exchanged bits of nothings, I've finished my hot dog without actually tasting it, much less savoring it. So I order another. Same like before? Same as before. This, my last year here, he says as he adds mustard to the already-bulging bun. I don't want to hear why he's leaving. But seeing him standing silent and still before me as he is handing me my hot dog, I can't help but ask him why. Because his wife is not well. What's wrong with her? I ask, figuring homesickness, depression, maybe menopause. Cancer, he replies. "She don't want to go back. But I cannot stay in America if she is not here no more." I reach out and touch his shoulder. "Difficult," I say, imitating my version of Mediterranean compassion in pidgin English. "And how." Two ruddy-cheeked adolescents who look as though they've just tussled in gym class and then slipped on their school uniforms approach the vendor, and after greeting him in Greek, they ask for hot dogs. He's probably seen them grow up and taught them the small Greek they know. A third joins them; all three, I notice, are wearing loosened neckties and smoking unfiltered cigarettes. This is my moment to slink away. I bid the man goodbye. He nods back with a sullen, crestfallen look meaning, *They're too young to know about wives, cancer, and homeland*. I don't know why, but as I struggle with my hot dog, briefcase, and Diet Coke, I wish I had stopped, sat on a bench, and told the Greek that I too was losing someone. He would have understood.

But as I keep walking toward the courts, I realize that I don't share his despair. The thought of Maud and her beau zipping their way up to the nth floor in his Midtown high-rise co-op doesn't disturb me. I can see the two of them walking down a long corridor until they finally reach his apartment door, a bit awkward and hesitant, yet grateful that their steps are muffled by the thick carpeting. The cuff links, the necktie, the image of her legs wrapped around his bare waist, don't disturb me either. I'll play tennis, they'll play at lovemaking. Who's the happier of us? Who knows?

At the 72nd Street entrance to the park, a group of bicyclists have assembled and are waiting for some sort of signal to enter the park. A whole lot of people are sitting on the benches at the entrance, some have been skating and are removing their Rollerblades, others putting them on. The usual skateboards. Most of those lounging on the benches don't look like tourists, and they aren't students either. *Does anyone work?* None except for the Greek.

I think of the poor man selling hot dogs all day, already planning what he'll need to pack up, what to give away, what to remember, what to let go of, things, places, people, a lifetime. Perhaps I too should think of sorting out my things. None of it seems to faze me. I was more disturbed by the possibility of being caught watching the lovebirds than by the fear that Maud had found happiness with another man. She looked so expansive, so ebullient and rapt. I haven't seen her like this in so long. Part of me was even happy to watch her beam, one elbow resting ever so nonchalantly on the thin ledge that was supporting the large mirror behind them as she touched his hair, looking like a model for Mauboussin's bracelets. She is beautiful. So why am I not jealous?

Is it because it's still too soon—this is not the shock, not even the beginning of the shock? Or is it because none of this should disturb the universe if you don't let it, if you don't push, if you don't discuss it, not even with yourself? Can one really not think of this? Maud is cheating on me, my Maud in bed with another man, doing things she doesn't, can't, won't, do with me because he knows how to lead her there, Maud astride me as I look up at her when she shuts her eyes and I'm all the way inside her, except that it's not me, it's someone else.

Soon, I know, I'll be rifling through the drawer where she keeps some of her things in my bedroom. I've done it with others, will do it again, though I already know that it'll be out of principle, not because I need to know, or even care. I may end up being jealous because I have to be.

THE GREEK WAS right. This is beach season already, and the weather is clearly working its way into the midseventies. Soon we'll be planning weekends away. The thought buoys my spirits, and stirred by this presage of summer, I remove my jacket and loosen my necktie. It reminds me of school days when they'd relax the dress code as soon as they caught a hint of spring weather in the air, when afternoons felt long and my mind invariably drifted to the beaches of San Giustiniano. Except I still remember how the lure of sea weather always coincided with approaching finals and my dreaded report card. I want to call her and tell her that I can't believe how beautiful the day is. I also want to tell her that I've had a good meeting and am now headed to the tennis courts. But I catch myself. Things have changed, might change the moment she hears my voice and is reminded of the humdrum rhythm of our days and nights. I must learn to keep my mouth shut. No hints, no cunning winky-wink prods as in, *Oh, was that you I saw at lunch today?* Just try to keep your mouth shut. And don't call.

Suddenly, I feel a growing access of tenderness for her. Is this love, or just compassion for someone who is chasing after romance, the way I and everyone else craves the luster of romance in our lives?

The worst is going to be watching her lie to me and, knowing she's lying, helping her sidestep the small traps I might unintentionally lay down, and by steering her away from them credit myself both for being so magnanimous and so very clever. I must never let on that I know.

Nothing would hurt me more than watching her flinch each time she hears the word "lunch." Must never mention Renzo & Lucia's and stay clear of anything remotely bearing on midday, Madison Avenue, or high-rise residential buildings, or cruise ships from Hollywood B movies from the early forties where new lovers stray from first-class dance floors to meet by starlight on the bridge and watch the moon shimmer on the placid ocean. I am thinking of Paul Henreid bringing two cigarettes to his lips and lighting both at the same time, one for him and one for Bette Davis.

The beauty of romance.

Could I live with her after this?

The real question is: Could she?

The truth is: I could.

I can envision her coming by my place tonight after yoga class, dropping her bag in the kitchen, trying to change and get ready for our dinner with the Plums in Brooklyn. She looks at my face and says, *You're a bit sunburned today, aren't you?*

Whenever she asks about my day, there's always a playful allegation that I might have spent it with one of my young interns. Usually I play along. Not today. *I just hit a few balls with Harlan this afternoon.*

She steps out of the kitchen, stops on her way to the bedroom, and then turns and faces me.

I may have some bad news.

I look at her with a glance that wishes to seem at once earnest and not entirely surprised.

About us, you mean. Us, I figure, is safer than *him.*

I think so.

I'm not going to say a word about lunch, but I won't play dumb either.

I know.

Oh?

I take a moment to gauge whether I'm not on the wrong track.

Is it serious? I ask.

She looks at me and purses her lips as if she's never thought about it in exactly these terms.

I don't know. It could be. Or may not. Too soon to tell. I just thought you should know. She is about to turn on the light in the corridor, but she is still not moving. *This is difficult.*

What I've always admired about her is that in our eight months together difficult admissions have always been civil.

I know, I say. *It's not easy for me either. Do you still feel like going to dinner tonight?*

She nods. But just before she goes to change, she turns around, looks at me, takes a deep breath: *Thanks.*

Welcome.

They say the signs are always there, right before you, but like the stars at night, they are impossible to count, much less read. Besides, signs are no better than oracles. They speak the truth provided they're not heeded. While we were sleeping a week or so ago, our feet had touched, then our legs, then our thighs, and before we were even fully awake, we had started making love, way too soon and too fast, which is when she did something un-usual and dug her fingers into my hair and kept rubbing my scalp with such fiendish abandon as we kissed that without holding back or giving it any thought, we both came at the same time. I had no idea how long we'd been making love or how we got started, or whether we'd even said a word before or during. There'd been no foreplay, no afterglow, no trace, no stain, just a vacuum. We didn't even open our eyes. Two alley cats scuffling in the darkest dead of night slinking away no sooner done. I fell back asleep in a stupor and so did she, her back to me, while I, as always, put one leg over hers. She liked it that way, she said, and moaned herself to sleep. Both of us were late for work that morning. The strange thing is that the next day neither of us uttered the most passing remark about our lovemaking. I could have made the whole thing up.

Something, however, did surprise me in the stubborn ferocity with which we ground into each other's bodies. She kept playing with my hair as if she meant to pull it out. I had attributed all this to midsleep, unbridled, savage sex. Then while shaving, it hit me. She was making love to someone else's body, to someone else's rhythm, not to mine.

Or there was this: her very recent love affair with a kind of salad dressing that consisted of a few drops of regular vinegar, not balsamic, and lots of lemon, with just a tablespoon of oil. Except that the lemons had to be grown in the groves of Sicily, and you had to use salt from the salt pans of Trapani in western Sicily. It never occurred to me to ask where had she learned so much about Sicilian products, or who had taught her to mix *cavolo nero* with anchovies and Parmesan and, of course, lemon juice. You didn't learn this in books or at Renzo & Lucia's. You learned it in a high-rise bachelor pad over lunch or dinner. He can't be married.

Then there's the trip to Sicily we've been talking about,

because she wants to visit the whole island, not just the super-crowded beaches and islands everyone travels to. She wants to visit Erice and Agrigento and Ragusa, Noto, and Syracuse, and then the hill town of Enna, where Emperor Frederick II of Hohenstaufen built his pleasure palace. I have no idea how she came to know so much about the puppet theater in Syracuse, or about tiny Ortigia, which she tells me comes from the Greek word for quail, owing to a semigoddess who hurled herself into the water and became a quail, which became an island, which became . . . I never bothered to ask why this sudden yen for Sicily. I would have been perfectly happy spending a few weeks on the islands off the mainland.

All I know is that Maud, who is so tame sometimes, wants excitement in her life. The woman with the slender arm and the beautifully chiseled elbow resting with such grace and whimsy on the ledge of the huge mirror behind her wants fun, wants romance, wants a fresh, new gust in her life. I am sure she resisted at first, and I can just see him trying and trying again before she finally relented.

Look around you, he says in the restaurant.

Yes, and?

Did you look around?

Yes.

Who is the most beautiful, smartest, most intimidating woman in this restaurant right now? What am I saying? Most forbidding.

Maybe that one over there, she says as she points to a woman who's had work done and is wearing lots of jewelry.

Not her.

Then who? she asks. Maud must love this.

It's the woman sitting by the large mirror who knows that the man sitting next to her is struggling to keep his hands on the table.

The things you say.

I just want to hold you.

Had I ever spoken to her this way? With her there were no balconies to scale, no struggle to win her over, no dashing histrionics, no rivals, no door to ram down or to bolt shut Fragonard-style once I'd stepped into her bedroom that first time after we'd played tennis. The door was always open, and everything had come so naturally, so easily, just as it had in midsleep the other night. We crossed the bridge and didn't even see the water underneath.

I LIKE WHAT I am feeling this Friday afternoon. Come to think of it, what I've seen isn't so terrible, isn't so bad, isn't even interesting. Am I going to be jealous—seriously? Sneak into her e-mail, pick up her cell phone while she's in the shower, try to find out what they text about, or sift through a morass of factoids to determine how they meet, when, where? How cliché!

I roll up my sleeves, remove my tie, and enter the park, heading through the bridle path toward the tennis house. With any luck I'll find a partner if Harlan is not there. It will be good to see who's playing, chat with the regulars whom I haven't seen since Thanksgiving weekend, buy a soft drink, hit for an hour or two, and then lie on the grass till it's time to get back home, shower, and go to dinner.

Keep things in perspective. Think how far, far worse off is the Greek hot dog vendor. This is not the end of the world.

As chance would have it, when I arrive, Harlan has already booked a court and is waiting for me in the tennis house. "Go change," he says. I like the brash tone. It reminds me there are other, speedier things to attend to right now besides Maud. I don't want to think of her. As I take off my watch, I think: For now we're okay, we're not hurt, not damaged, just a wee bit bruised, but not flailing. The self's a touch scuffed, of course, but not the heart. The thought comes to me as I'm wrapping tape around the handle of my racket the way one might swaddle an Ace bandage around one's calf, one's wrist, one's ego. We're good.

One last thought before I head to the courts: Must not utter a word to her about what I'd seen at lunch, not the most elusive hint, nothing. I'll do exactly what the Brits did when they broke the Germans' Enigma code during the war. They knew where and when the Germans were planning bombing raids. But they refrained from stepping up defenses for fear of giving away that they had decrypted the enemy's code. A misplaced word, a doubting glance, a hint of irony, and she'll know.

While I'm finishing wrapping tape around my racket, I call her to say I'm going to play tennis. "I figured, when you didn't pick up at the office. I'm so jealous," she says. So she had called me. Why? "To say hi." When? "Less than an hour ago, just after lunch." How was lunch? I ask.

Haven't I just promised not to bring up lunch? She takes the question in stride and doesn't seem to mind it at all. The usual fare at Renzo's. Actually, not very good this time. Oh, another journalist.

Is this because she spotted me at the restaurant and knows I saw her?

Maud says she has a meeting this afternoon and is heading directly to the Plums' from her office. Does she want to meet me before going to the Plums'? I ask. "No, we'll meet there. Just don't be late? I hate when the two of them gang up on me and go on about their dreaded Ned." I laugh. I've taught her to hate their son, now she dislikes him more than I do. "I'll bring something," she says. I say, "Bring nothing. They plan their dinners from beginning to end. We'll send flowers tomorrow." We say goodbye. She loves me. I love her too.

By then, I've completely forgotten about lunch. If she meant to placate me, she succeeded. Which is probably why I called her. Just telling me that the food was not good lifted a huge load and for some inexplicable reason frees my mind of all worries and doubts. Suddenly tennis seems a godsend. I take out a can of balls, open it, and we descend the stairs to court 14, the one totally in the sun. We are going to sweat, we are going to run, play hard, and think of nothing but tennis. All I want is to be one with tennis. As long as we can be one with something, anything, we're okay. As I walk down the stairs and step on the courts, a rush of pleasure courses through my body, I am tingling with a sense of total well-being. I could do this for the rest of my life and not care a whit, about her, about work, about summer, travel, about anything. I am happy.

We had met here on a Friday last summer. She was looking for a partner. I offered. She wasn't a great player, she said. It didn't matter, I said. We played for four hours that day. It was July Fourth weekend and we had both left work early. Neither had plans for the weekend. That evening, we had dinner at a pub and ate at the bar, which both of us said we loved doing. It was like being alone together, one of us said. Early the next morning, without having arranged it, the two of us showed up to book courts. We played for more than five hours. The courts were scorching that day and many stayed empty. We had to change clothes, biked home, came back, and played till sundown. Shower. Drinks. A late movie. Dinner at the bar? Loved dinner at the bar, she said. The air was balmy, my hands, her shoulders, our faces were moist and clammy. Three Dominicans, one with his guitar, were singing on a bench on an island in the middle of Broadway. We sat on the same bench and listened. I kissed her. We made love all night, playing a Brazilian CD again and again, until, in the days to come, it was impossible to make love without the music. We ended up in Italy later that summer, with the music.

I unzip my other racket cover and remove the racket she bought me as a Christmas present.

Manfred, an ace player in his late twenties, comes over to me and asks if he can join us. We find a fourth player for doubles, an elderly gentleman who is a fixture at the tennis courts. He wanted to play on my side, but Manfred had asked first, and Harlan didn't mind having the old man as his partner. I've never played with or against Manfred before, but after almost two years now I've gotten used to seeing him early every weekday morning. I admire his game, his grace, his build. Occasionally, when our eyes meet, we exchange a few words by the soda machine or in the locker area, but I would never have dared ask him to play with me and have always felt he kept his distance for fear I might ask someday. I imagine there's been a cautious chill between us. Yet watching him grow nervous and almost lose his footing asking to join us this afternoon is like seeing a high school champion look gawky when turning to the class nerd for homework help. His voice was shaky; he must have noticed and tried to dissemble by affecting an awkward laugh. It made me feel strong, proud.

When we were done playing, I could almost feel the old chill rise between us. It would estrange us and we'd be back to perfunctory nods. So before things cool down, I ask if he wants a beer and suggest we play again soon. "Tomorrow morning if you want." "Tomorrow it is," I say, perhaps too fast, fearing he might change his mind. Since I had a reservation with Harlan on Saturday, I say I'll give mine up to someone else. "Do that," he says. I feel elated. We leave the park and head to a café for a quick beer. I'm sure he knows I've got a crush on him.

————

WHEN I STEP into the Plums' home this evening, I am confronted by a replay of today's lunch. Maud is seated in the middle of the large horseshoe sofa on their terrace next to him, their legs crossed, with their knees facing each other, creating an intimate, locked space between them. And as at Renzo & Lucia's, her arm is nonchalantly extended on the back of the sofa with her hand almost grazing his hair again, that languid, whimsical Mauboussin smile fluttering on her lips, the same elbow, the same sleeveless arm, the same bracelet. Around them are four large floor candles, casting a shimmering glow over her skin. It's a good thing I'd had only a beer with Manfred and decided not to drink anything else. I need to be in complete control of my tongue, seeing as I nearly risked ruffling things when calling from the tennis house. With another drink I might end up sending the two of them a glowering frown that barely disguises my displeasure.

She is about to introduce him to me but he interrupts, seemingly very eager to meet me. "I am Gabi," he says, setting down his drink to stand up to shake my hand. He looks me square in the face, beaming enthusiasm, a frank, spry, almost feral gaze that won't look away. He is trim, handsome, with a touch of a blush on both cheeks that shouts athletic vigor and good cheer. I am intimidated but not at a loss for words.

Tonight there are the Plums, plus another couple, then Mark, who is probably there for Nadja's benefit, and then Claire, serene, even-tempered Claire who never laughs at anything I say and who must think I'm a total fop. Coming out of the kitchen, Pamela tells Duncan, her husband, that Nadja isn't quite ready for someone like Mark, "She's still on the rebound." "Our born-again spinster should be over it by now, because, let's face it, Sleeping Beauty she isn't," he says. "Shush!" says Pamela. "Just help me finish building this pyramid with these clementines here," she tells Claire and me. Claire sets to work right away, as if she'd been building pyramids with fruits and vegetables all her life, while I laugh, having no idea how to build such a pyramid. I know what she's thinking: *He is so hopeless.* Meanwhile, Pamela has hung up the phone and comes out onto the balcony to tell the guests that Diego and Tamar will be late as usual because of problems with their babysitter. "Besides," she adds, biting her lips as she observes our progress with the pyramid, "I think they're going through a rough patch." "They're always going through a rough patch," interjects her husband.

Duncan and Pamela are an older couple and love hosting younger guests. Meanwhile, I am terrified that their son Ned might be asked to join us for dinner. He always monopolizes the conversation, going on about some obscure artist he's discovered and wishes to promote. But he is there only for cocktails I am told—needs to meet a very important client for an appraisal. "Our rising star at Sotheby's," says Pamela. I look at Maud. She has intercepted my sneering glance and is reciprocating it with a tacit, clandestine smirk of her own. In this we're a team, and the silent back-and-forth between us confirms our solidarity. She's my best friend. We read each other. "So, how was tennis?" Gabi asks. "Yes, pray tell us about your tennis," Maud adds with her usual allegation that tennis is just a nickname for my latest fling with another college intern.

I am once again tempted to send a stony glare her way. She senses I'm in no mood for jokes and she backpedals. "But he had a very good meeting this morning, and this means a lot."

"What kind of meeting?" asks Gabi.

"We're merging with a smaller house that's been failing for years." I say this hastily to avoid engaging in a conversation with him.

"So why did you merge if it was failing?" asks Gabi a bit too abruptly. Despite his obvious charm, he must be a hard-bitten man who doesn't mince words.

I must have frowned at his question. "I am an Israeli who's lived in Italy, not all of me is smooth velour yet," he explains.

"Where in Italy?" I ask, forgetting I should avoid asking questions, especially when I'm not eager to engage. But now that I've asked, I dread the answer.

"Turin."

"Primo Levi's town," I add, relieved it isn't Sicily.

"Yes, Primo Levi and Carlo Levi and Natalia Levi and all the Levites of the world, down to the city's most visible tower— more Jewish than Tel Aviv, which is where I'm from. Not surprisingly, my grandmother was from Turin and her last name was, take a guess, Levi too."

We laugh.

"Gabi is a foreign correspondent."

Gabi has clearly been a soldier as well. He's got it all, I think.

"For which newspapers?"

He rattles off a few names, then says, "Italy, France, Germany, Israel, the States—"

"You name it," I interrupt, to make light of his impressive catalog.

"Gabi's *syn-di-cated*," says Maud, with the faintest touch of humor, both to compliment him for his successful career as a journalist and as a way of defusing the implied sarcasm in my comment by alleging we're ever jovial by nature.

She's still on my team, but she's got his back as well.

This can go on for hours. We're volleying sprightly cross-court shots, but she's the one putting a spin on the ball.

"So explain to me why the smaller outfit is merging with yours?"

"Is this the Israeli or the Italian asking?" I ask, irony still inflecting my voice.

"It's the Israeli wearing mercerized Gallo socks under roughshod army boots."

"Tactful answer," says Maud.

"Tactful or not, I know he'll want to tell me everything about the merger before the evening is out. Can't you see he's already dying to tell me."

We burst out laughing.

"They're merging with us because they have a very solid backlist, which we want and which they'll lose if they fold before the year ends."

"And by 'us' you mean you."

"And others."

"How many?"

"We are legion," I joke.

"You must be very good at what you do."

I decide not to answer. But I don't mind the flattery. I know what he's up to. We've been exchanging mock potshots. He is targeting, I am deflecting. But this is not hostile at all. This is almost like flirting.

Ned, the genius son, slaps down his glass on the meticulously set dining table and says he needs to leave. He's stained the tablecloth.

We look up from our little coterie of three. "And go in peace," I mutter to Maud. Maud forwards my comment to Gabi, who doesn't react and may not share our aversion to Ned. We may be bandying jokes between us, but in case I forgot, he and I are not on the same team.

But then he says something I cannot hear. She tells him he's totally wrong. "Won't be the first time," he replies, and the two start laughing. Either it's about Ned or about one of my assistants. Or about me.

At some point, perhaps to say something, I ask a question that comes naturally and that's been hanging in the air: What brings him to the States?

"I'm writing a piece on biotech companies specializing in gene splitting and cancer research." There is a pause after this mouthful. "This is how I know Maud."

If his remark is meant to soothe me, it works. Now I know the official reason behind their lunch.

I also know why she never thought of bringing up the lunch. It was routine PR stuff.

But I'm not so easily conned.

Dinner is announced. Everyone is so comfortably ensconced on the large sofa overlooking the city that no one stands up. Pamela announces that we are all far too friendly for formal seating at the table, we can sit wherever we please. But still no one moves. So she comes over to me and, extending both arms, pulls me out of my seat and says that to punish me for resisting, she'll sit me at the head of the table. As usual, their large table is meticulously set for a feast, with its thickly starched linen napkins sticking out jauntily from wineglasses like overgrown blooms on steroids. Pamela notices the reddish stain Ned's glass has left on the neatly pressed tablecloth. She examines it and hands the glass to the waiter, and all she mutters is, "One of these days, one of these days, kiddo . . ." On the way to the dinner table, Maud says she'd have strangled him. I take her aside, kiss her, and simply apologize for being late. I ask her when she got here. She was the first guest tonight and came up the elevator with dreaded Ned. "Full of himself, you've no idea. I'll tell you later, but he is more repellent than ever."

She's trying to shake me off by going on about Ned. I know the trick.

When did Gabi get here?

"Oh, much later." So they didn't come together.

Of course, they could easily have planned it this way: *You go first. No, you go first.*

The guests improvise a seating arrangement while Pamela decides to sit at my right. To my left is Nadja, who usually won't speak unless spoken to, then next to her there's Mark, who'll speak to anyone provided it's about himself. The two are meant to get to know each other, otherwise it's going to be polite non-starter talk all evening between Nadja and me. I am relieved that Gabi sits next to Mark. But before I have a moment to relish the arrangement, I notice that Maud has taken the seat between Gabi and Duncan, who sits at the other head of the table. I don't like this at all. Next to Pamela sits Claire, while the seats for the couple in the rough patch are still empty.

No sooner do Maud and Gabi sit than they pick up where they left off. They are engrossed in something. As with lunch, I see but cannot hear.

When everyone is seated, Pamela waits a few moments, then taps her wineglass with a spoon and we all grow quiet. I hate the faux formality of speeches before dinner with people who are, as she just said, far too friendly. She, I have always suspected, may be the polished version of the rough draft her son still is. I begin to dread this dinner. Paula starts by welcoming us. Pardon the terrible mess in the hallway, she says, but we are all regulars here, and for some, this is our second home, but this is Gabi's first time here, and so this dinner is to welcome him to what we hope will be his new home away from home, especially now that he is immersed in such important work.

After toasting with Chassagne-Montrachet, everyone starts eating Pamela's raw scallops, while silence hovers over the table.

"What's his work about?" asks Nadja, breaking the silence. Mark, whom I've known since college and who was always good at class participation, wants to show that he has been listening attentively and dutifully relates what Gabi's work entails. "Most of us know nothing about cancer research, much less about gene splitting, so it's always good when someone brings us up to date," he says. He hasn't changed since his student days—the first to raise his hand, the first to walk up to a teacher after class, the first to hand in his blue book. We talk about the very little we know about cancer research, but Gabi isn't listening. Mark, I can tell, is trying to draw Maud's attention, but she can't hear him. All I can make out, despite Mark's lengthy explanations about some latest developments in gene therapy, is that they're talking about a small town called Enna.

"Where is Enna?" Nadja asks, clearly less interested in Mark than in Gabi.

"Enna sits on top of a hill in the middle of nowhere in Sicily. Like Masada," Gabi adds. "There too a huge massacre took place, but this one was committed by the Romans who had decided to clean out the town of its inhabitants. Masada was more tragic."

"Why?" asked Nadja, who is no longer listening to Mark.

"Oh, because in Masada the victims committed mass suicide to avoid falling into the hands of the Romans, who would have tortured them, killed them, or sold them as slaves. Enna, by the way, knew its heyday under Frederick. He founded the first university in the world, in Italy, and created a culture that housed Normans, Greeks, Arabs, Jews, French. Italian poetry, by the way, was not born in Florence as so many think, but in Sicily. The town of Enna was finally given back its original name by none other than Mussolini."

"What did it used to be called?" asks Nadja.

"The Romans called it Castrum Hennae, meaning Castle Enna, but the name was further corrupted by the Byzantines into Castro Yannis, John's Castle, which the Saracens, once they occupied Sicily, renamed Qas'r Ianni, which in Arabic means Yannas's Castle. In Italian it was known as Castrogiovanni until Mussolini, who loved the grandeur of antiquity, finally dusted off its millennial tiers and allowed it to take back its true name."

Then, seeing that more of us are listening to him than he thought, he smiles, interrupts his description, and adds, "We're all a bit like that, aren't we? Like Sicily, I mean."

"How so?" asks Claire, who is probably speaking to him for the first time tonight. Claire would never have asked me to explain anything.

"We lead many lives, nurse more identities than we care to admit, are given all manner of names, when in fact one, and one only, is good enough."

"And which identity is that?" asks Mark, clearly trying to score a point.

"Might take too long to explain, my friend," replies Gabi, "and, besides, we don't know each other well enough yet."

But the mention of Sicily bothers me. As Gabi continues talking about Frederick II, I can't help but look at Maud. I try to catch her eyes. But she knows why I'm looking at her, which is why she is staring away from the table and then looks down at her plate. She knows I've guessed the cause of her craze for Sicily and that it all has to do with him, doesn't it? Never have clues been so transparent or fallen so effortlessly in my hands. One has to wait weeks, months sometimes, to link the pieces. Here, even thickheaded Ned would have put together the puzzle.

Couldn't they have rehearsed this any better? He was a soldier in the most sophisticated army in the world, and she, despite her quiet, subdued manner, has brains to outfox the emperor of tricksters. Didn't they even have a plan?

Maud asks him to tell her more about Enna, and Gabi right away launches into a long tirade about the life of Frederick II, about Enzo, his son who spent the last twenty-three years of his life in prison in Bologna, and of another son, Manfredi, who died in the battle of Benevento, and as Dante reminds us, *biondo era e bello e di gentile aspetto.* Maud is holding her chin in another rapt Mauboussin pose that I find spellbinding. She is beautiful, she hangs on every word he speaks, she's so in love, and the irony is that she may not even know how hopelessly smitten she is, while the other irony is that I'm not upset, though I should be and could easily see how another man would yell or slam his palm on the dining table in front of all the guests and, later that night, run his fist through the bedroom door when she locks him out because he's become impossible to live with. And perhaps I am hurt but don't know it either and don't want to know it, because on hearing the name Manfredi, which I thought entirely mine to own in this room tonight, my mind drifts to the thrill awaiting me tomorrow morning at seven on the tennis courts. I'll be playing with a champion. I want to tell everyone about my Manfred and how absolutely handsome he is when he takes everything off before showering and the marble of his hairless chest is so taut that one must struggle not to touch to feel whether marble is indeed like flesh. Today was the first time we'd exchanged more than banal locker room banter; usually I say a few words and he answers in fragments, almost as an afterthought, so that neither of us can say we actually talk. But today, something was different. I must have looked absent, fragile, angry; I had no one in my life. Is this why he finally sensed it was easy to speak to me? Because I looked scuttled and undone, human? Or was it the inflection of success on my face following this morning's meeting that made me desirable? I wish I could recall his faint, tremulous German accent when he asked to play doubles. Would someone help me remember his voice and tell me more about him if I too uttered the name Manfred at the dinner table tonight?

I am looking at her as she stares at Gabi, who is going on about the Holy Roman emperor who wrote a book on falconry while sitting in the navel of Sicily, and all I'm doing is thinking of her in her favorite position. With her eyes closed, she loves placing her knees on my shoulders, which are his shoulders now, one knee first, then the other knee, her vagina pleading for him, which is where I know his left hand is right now, getting her all worked up as she struggles to keep her composure without altering that dreamy model's look that says *I am all jewels, I am all ears, I am all yours, all the way.*

How am I going to sleep with her tonight? Or touch her after this? And what if she attacks me in the middle of the night as she did the other night? Will it be with blighted love that I'll respond, or will I go at her with venom and rage in my groin, knowing that even if she's making love, it's not with me. I'll just be picking up where he's let off—man-to-man business, with woman as the middleman.

I'm looking at her. She is like someone new. I love her long, slender arms, and the shoulder that's been completely exposed since this morning, and that necklace giving her a beguiling quality that I haven't seen in a long time.

The doorbell rings and we can already hear Diego's and Tamar's voices. "I know, I know, terribly sorry, but we so wanted to be here," shouts Tamar from the hallway as she approaches the dining room. "But we haven't even started dinner," reassures Pamela as she welcomes the two, and we all hear Tamar's rapid-fire series of shrill, hysterical giggles meant to absolve her for being late. Tamar swings her clunky square Goyard handbag as she walks around the table toward her seat and clicks open and shut her bag each time she forgets whether her cell phone is turned on or off. Diego, tall, with a full, blondish mane and a colorful pocket square in his dark jacket, sheepishly follows his wife and ends up sitting right next to Claire. He isn't happy, his fashionable five o'clock shadow makes him look like a hired thug who's just been scolded by his wife and told to wear a dinner jacket. The couple in the rough patch. Then, thinking of us, I realize we're in a rough patch as well, except no one here even suspects it.

By now I am in total agony. Maud and Gabi are clearly touching, cannot but touch. The Mediterranean macho has gone one further, and after moving his seat closer to Maud's, he lets his left arm rest on the carved crest rail of her chair. Right away she brings her hand to the table, to telegraph there's nothing going on here. But then, as if there's been a change of mind, it goes back into hiding behind the skirt of the tablecloth.

Oh, vile, deceitful woman. I am reminded of *Pagliacci*, which we've seen together this winter. He's the lover, she's the harlot, and I, in case there was a doubt, the clown.

A strange thought crosses my mind. What if I dropped my napkin and, bending down to reach for it, took a peek at what's going on under their end of the table. What would I find? Her white hand gently, awkwardly stroking his totally exposed, swarthy Sabra cock, which curves upward to give more pleasure.

Question is: What will they do with the mess?

The answer couldn't be simpler. She'll use her starched linen napkin with the giant *P* for Plum embroidered in golden filigree, which each one of us plucked from our wineglass as soon as we sat down.

They're laughing again.

Or pretending to laugh.

I bet she's rubbing him even harder as they're laughing.

Which is why they're laughing.

And again I think of young Manfredi of Sicily and of my Manfred who comes out gleaming from the shower room every morning and who knows I'm looking because he is so hung.

Meanwhile, I can't find a thing to say to Nadja on my left. I'd much rather talk to Claire, diagonally across from me. She is always so quiet at these dinners, so cautiously unreachable, radiating a sort of unsullied, Pre-Raphaelite vagueness that I find both chilling and chaste. And as I'm looking at her, I am, as on previous such evenings, trying to imagine what kind of a person a passionate kiss might bring out in her. Would she remain tame, irresolute, or turn savage? I want to unleash the beast in her. I can almost imagine how we'd kiss if I stopped her past the empty corridor, put one palm upon her cheek, and brought my mouth to hers. She is trying not to lift her eyes. But I know she knows I'm looking, knows what I'm thinking. She never looks at me.

At some point, Diego complains of a recent Italian film everyone has been talking about. Not only was the acting terrible but the main plot line couldn't have been more unintelligible. His wife liked the film and thought the acting amazing. So did everyone else in Hollywood, hence the Oscar. "But I wasn't convinced," he says. "You're never convinced," she rebuts. Duncan intervenes. "Why aren't you convinced?" "Why am I not convinced?" asks Diego rhetorically. "Because what a man wants in a woman when he and she are in love is passion, trust, mischief, sorrow, and a shadow of anticipated regret." "What hogwash! *Sois belle! Et sois triste!* Be beautiful and be sad," she replies, quoting Baudelaire. "What you men really want from women is surrender." Diego shakes his head with a resigned, philosophical smile.

"What we want . . . what we want from a woman is a sandwich and some indecency." "What!?" she snaps back. "Nothing," he replies. "Well, you'll get neither from me." Diego smiles one last time and rolls his eyes. "Big surprise!"

Duncan attempts to change the subject and takes it back to another film. But when the subject of films peters out again, it becomes obvious that however we try, the dinner talk is destined to remain rudderless, without fun, spunk, or spontaneity. Even Nadja tries with me. Then she tries with the Israeli, then with Pamela, then with the Israeli again, but the sparks never catch until it's clear to everyone that dinner talk has turned into long-winded drudgery.

Except for the two lovebirds twittering away on their little perch.

There was a moment when I caught Claire's gaze. Then she looked away, or I did. It didn't happen again.

All I can think of meanwhile is the lovebirds, their touching, their incessant giggles at the far end of the dining table, behaving like a pair of naughty teenagers skinny-dipping on a secluded Mediterranean beach in the very early morning while the rest of us continue lumbering through a gray, silent, sunless no-man's-land filled with desiccated driftwood and broken shells. After this, I'll never trust her. Even if I were totally and entirely mistaken, how could I trust her after what I've belched out in my sick head today? Their coaxing, their merry taunts, the penis holding, the cum surreptitiously wiped off her hand, which she'll forget to wash away when she comes to bed tonight—don't they look flushed, the two of them? They're a couple. We're not. And here I am, trying to find something to say to Nadja while nursing the perpetual nattering in my head.

After dinner we are invited for coffee, desserts, and cordials on the sofa lining the balcony. Duncan is still trying to save the

evening and points out to the skyline. "Can you believe this
spring weather at this time of the year?" he exclaims. "*Spring-
time,*" says Diego, about to break into song. "This is New York,"
snaps Tamar; "could turn into winter any moment now." "I just
love the view," says Duncan, still trying to defuse the tension.
"I'm so glad we made the move here five years ago. I hated the
Lower East Side. Just look at this." He points to the bridge.

Everyone's busy taking in the stunning nightfall view while
a waning, livid glow hovers against the buildings of Manhattan.
"This view always reminds me of Saint Petersburg," says Duncan.
"In Saint Petersburg, they don't sleep in June. The city is up all
night, because it's still daylight." "Wish we were in Saint Petersburg tonight," Nadja says. "I heard they open the bridge on the
Neva and people throng the riverbanks." "What's the Neva?" asks
Diego. "A river, for Christ's sake," says his wife. Pamela throws
me a complicit glance, meaning, *The rough patch is very rough
tonight.* "Look it up!" she snaps. "Strange things happen on such
nights," I say. "Strange things happen to other people, not me,"
replies Nadja. "Me either," Tamar says. A quick look from Claire
tells me she's picked up on the *me either* too. It's the only time she
and I exchange a message meant to stay between us. I want to
come up to her and say something funny, stirring, and clever,
but I can't think of what to say. The two of us are now leaning
on the parapet facing the city, her hand next to mine, touching.
I do not move my hand away, figuring she'll shift hers first. But
she doesn't. I'm sure she isn't even aware we're touching. "Surely
there's a life out there better than this," I want to say. She'd look
at me and think I'm a lunatic. So I keep quiet.

Duncan stares out at the skyline, then looking up he points
to the water tank standing at the very top of his terrace.

"I hope none of you minds the water tank," he says. "They've
been working on it for weeks now with no end in sight."

I look up and down on the floor of the balcony and spot a litter of tools and toolboxes stashed away in a corner not too far
from the sofa. "They're rebuilding the water tank. It's very old!"

"People tell us that Hopper painted this very water tank from
his own home across the river," adds Pamela.

Maud tries to say something about Hopper but changes her
mind, especially since Mark steps in.

"Did Hopper live across the river?" he asks, seemingly
incredulous.

"Ned is convinced he did. In fact, he showed us pictures."

"I wasn't so convinced," says Duncan.

"I was," says Pamela, "but I'm Ned's mother."

"Well, it's a very good story," says Mark, turning to Maud, as
though apologizing for cutting her off.

"To think that we're sitting on a balcony that was painted by
Hopper himself," muses Gabi. "What an amazing privilege."

Duncan doesn't care for Hopper. "Tired of the same old houses
in Truro, tired of the same water tanks, tired of all those dejected, vacuous people staring out of unwashed windows." He
leans over the parapet and stares out into the floodlit city. "So,
which is better," he turns around and finally asks those of us
seated on the sofa, "to be here in Brooklyn staring over at Manhattan's skyscrapers or to be in Manhattan looking at Brooklyn's
water tanks?"

It was the sort of statement made half in jest and half to accen-
tuate the spell of lights shimmering on the East River, offering a
sight nowhere else seen in the city except from his terrace.

"Oh, you sound like that tiresome author who's always writing about being in one place and wishing to be in another,"
cracks Claire. "Besides, hadn't we settled the matter last year
when you asked the same exact question?" She's right. We'd had
this conversation exactly a year ago, and, as we watched the sky

turn dark purple, the issue about where one was and where one longed to be seemed dead on arrival. We never resolved it. But I liked the spunky comment. So unusual for Claire to be outspoken. "I wish I could find a place where it's always daylight," says Tamar, referring to Saint Petersburg. "I love life too much."

"With your attitude?" mutters Diego almost to himself.

"Yes, with my attitude," she rebuts. He is silenced.

"Saint Petersburg is just an idea," says Gabi, probably seeking to stem their sparring. "It's built on slush. To most of us, it's like a city that doesn't quite exist, a city made for books. We don't really believe it exists even when we're there. A city where you can't sort out twilight from dawn and where at any moment you could run into Gogol or Stravinsky or Eisenstein, to say nothing of Raskolnikov or Prince Myshkin or Anna herself. A city of elusive, untold wants." And so saying, Gabi stands up facing Manhattan and, holding his wineglass next his mouth to mimic a microphone, begins singing the opening lines of a song about Nevsky Prospekt when the Red Guards light up fires in the cold to drive away wolves and how it's still possible to spot Nijinsky, whom Diaghilev of the Ballets Russes fell hopelessly in love with, hopelessly in love, hopelessly in love.

I would never have been able to put his spontaneous singing voice with the man who'd been talking to Maud at the dinner table. Here another person had sprung forth, with a much younger voice, and a far younger, soulful self. No wonder she likes him. *I* like him. Even Diego likes him. The two begin chatting in Italian. I catch myself wishing to join in.

Left alone as I lean forward with both arms on the parapet, I am thinking of Manfred with me now—he and I, our elbows touching just moments before he shifts and puts an arm around my shoulder. *Oh, Manfred.*

———

"YOU DIDN'T EAT anything," Maud tells me as she approaches and sits next to me on the sofa holding a cup of coffee.

"No. I played with the food, moved it around the plate a bit so it wouldn't look too obvious. I wasn't hungry."

"Why?" she asks.

"Not in the best of moods, I guess." I can tell I'm almost on the point of blurting out what has been upsetting me since lunchtime.

Did I want coffee? A cookie? Half a cookie, maybe?

By now she knows I'm upset, hence the attempted molly-coddling.

Gabi walks over to us with his cell phone in his hand, having read a text. He is about to light a cigarette.

"Oh, I'd love one too," says Maud.

He takes out another cigarette from his slim alligator case and places both cigarettes between his lips. He lights them, then hands her one. "I've seen it done in a movie, and I've always wanted to do it," he says. Never have I been given such ocular proof that they belong together. He offers me a cigarette as well, but I tell him I've quit. "One couldn't hurt," he bandies back, playful as ever. "Yes, it will," Maud jumps in, rushing to my rescue. We're back to being a team. The three of us are sitting next to each other on the horseshoe sofa overlooking the river, Maud between us, with the other guests sitting on either side of us. We're enjoying the fresh evening breeze from the ocean. I've always loved the way Maud raises her head, lifts her chin, and blows away the first puff of smoke. Everything feels cozy and snug here. Gabi cracks a joke about the couple with baby-sitter issues: the husband docile yet fuming with pussywhipped rage, the wife who claims to love life so much. "The mother of all humbug," says Maud. "He is no more docile than she loves life." "We call them the rough patch," I say. "And what do you

make of her bag?" she asks. "It's a suitcase for train compart-
ments." Gabi giggles loudly. Maud hushes him, but it's clear she
is enjoying the rakish dig at the handbag and at the woman who
owns it. "She probably carries wipes, bibs, and pacifiers in case
her babysitter calls." "Or a rolling pin to hit Daddy with each
time he opens his mouth to ask for a sandwich!" We laugh, and
laugh again. "How long do you give them?" asks Gabi, seemingly
cutting to the chase. "A few months," I say. "Maybe, but he loves
her," says Maud, coming to the husband's defense.

"Maybe he loves her, but she clearly doesn't love him," I respond. A moment of silence.

"Actually, I think it's the other way around," says Gabi.
"She is angry he doesn't love her, because she still loves him
but is disappointed with his listless caresses and that sprig of
tenderness."

"How do you know?" Maud asks.

"I know."

He muses, says nothing, takes another puff.

"How do you two know each other?" Gabi asks.

"We met on the tennis courts. It was all quite sudden," I say.

"So you two love each other," Gabi says, turning to me and
then Maud. It's not really a question, but it sounds like one.

"Why do you ask?" Maud asks.

He shrugs his shoulders. "No reason."

Gabi must have had more to drink than I thought. But I'm
growing to like his prickly wit, his jabs, his impish humor. I am
revisited by memories of dorm parties, three of us slouching on
a sunken old sofa in a frat house watching everyone else come
and go, poking fun at each one, most likely because all three of
us are nervous and drunk.

But then a thought stuns me. If a frat party, then we're all just
good friends: she is not my girlfriend yet, she is his girlfriend, I'm

the one just tagging along because I want everyone and everything he loves. They're the couple. We're not.

Another thought scares me even more: At what point tonight does one of us discreetly disappear? How on God's planet does this evening end?

I nurse a vision of the two of us in the cab home, both of us uneasy, tired, listless, and quiet.

Want to talk about it?

She looks at me with her all-knowing gaze that says, *No, not really.*

Why not?

There's nothing to talk about.

I look away, nod, and say nothing.

But she reaches and holds my hand.

Hey—

Yes?

Thanks.

I wait a few seconds.

Welcome.

But I don't feel so kind. I'm angry. And I no longer know why. Part of me feels this whole fever could wash away the moment I spot one tiny, reassuring sign from her, but I also know that once incubated, anger won't go away unless it erupts. I don't dislike this sudden urge to be cruel to her; I don't even want it to slacken, because it gives me strength and clarity, the way anger, rage, spite, and bile make Homer's soldiers bolder and meaner. I like this surge, as if a part of me already wishes to run my fist through a door to prove to her how it feels, because anger fills my lungs and makes me want to puff out my chest and be a man, the way I was a man when I finally told Manfred to move out of the way because I wanted to be the one to put away Harlan's strategic lob with a perfectly aimed overhead slam, which in fact was my proudest moment this afternoon, this day, this month, this year, especially after Manfred put both hands on his hips and, nodding approbation, said, "Wow!" That admiring and spontaneous *Wow*, uttered ever so gallantly in his soft, mellifluous German voice, filled me with such bliss that moments after hearing it I said, "Buy you a beer."

I've gotten to like Gabi, and I want him to like me too. If he's putting his arm around the back of her seat, I don't mind if it reaches me too. And as if he's heard me think this, or maybe because I might have moved closer to him without even knowing it, his arm drops on my shoulder, and his hand is now rubbing my neck with tenuous, absentminded motions that could easily have mistaken me at first for the leather edge of the sofa. It's as though he wishes to assuage all my worries about Maud and at the same time stir something else in me, and I can't tell which it is, and I like not knowing, and I don't want him to stop, and I lean my head forward to let him rub my neck more deeply and let his hand linger there as long it pleases and undo all those knots, while I shut my eyes to relish the soothing massage, which I know he knows may not just be a massage, though maybe that's all it is, a massage. Without looking, I know she's guessed.

After coffee there are schnapps from various countries served in tiny grappa glasses, which the Plums bought last summer in Castellina. "We had them ship twenty-four of them, don't know what we were thinking," Pamela explains. Without meaning to, all three of us keep trying one liqueur after the other. Gabi, I should have known, is a connoisseur and keeps examining the labels on the bottles for the eau-de-vie he likes best but can't find it. "Either way, I'll pay for this tomorrow," says Maud. "So will I," says Gabi. "All of us will," I add. A smile from Maud almost says *Parrot!* Nadja, who moves a chair next to Gabi, asks if she could try some of his, since there are at least four tiny vials spread before him on the tea table. She's never had schnapps, she says, what is it? He explains, she listens, then plies him with more questions, until he grabs a tiny glass containing Pear Williams and suggests she try that. She holds his glass with tentative fingers and takes one distrusting sip. "Not bad, right?" he asks as though speaking to a child. "Actually, quite good. May I finish it?" "Be my guest." Then, standing up, he leans over to me and Maud and says, "We need to split." She's been trying to make conversation with him all evening and is obviously going in for the kill. He snickers, and so does Maud. "If she only knew," he whispers. Maud laughs. I can tell Nadja noticed, though she is eager to join in the laughter. I ask if she'd like to try my grappa. She gently pushes the drink away, saying she doesn't want to pay for it tomorrow either, and laughs, possibly thinking that tomorrow's hangover was the reason why Gabi and Maud had laughed. "We really should be leaving," Maud says, as though apologizing. She casts one languorous farewell gaze to the view from the terrace, as does Gabi, as do I as well. "The view," we repeat in the elevator, "the view."

Outside the Plums' building, the air is still humid and I find myself already missing the terrace with its incipient chill draft and expansive view. Part of me wishes we hadn't left so soon. I enjoyed the sofa, the candlelit balcony, the many drinks, and the company, even the dying conversation at the dinner table where all you needed to do if things stalled was to look out to the skyline and enjoy Pamela's occasional comment or watch the couple in the rough patch spar over this or that. Even Nadja's last-ditch effort to open up to Gabi wasn't so bad either. Perhaps we shouldn't have left. Only then does it hit me that I didn't say goodbye to Claire. There was a moment when, on leaving the table, we ended up standing close to each other observing the skyline. Both of us meant to say something but neither could find the words, so we said nothing, Claire and I. This could have been our moment. All she said after a while was "I think Maud's calling you."

It has started to drizzle. My first thought is that I might have to call Manfred and cancel tennis. But then, if he's like me, he'll show up all the same and we'll have coffee and something to eat under the canopy of the tennis house. I love the vision of breakfast while it rains in the park with the few regulars happy to hang together.

If he's like me, he'll know I'll show up even in the rain. But this is good rain. It comes down not in torrents or in sheets that pour down so powerfully that they'll lash about the avenues like sails flailing in stormy weather. Tonight the rain feels so meek and muted that brushing it away with a hand might make it stop. It lacks conviction, has lost its vigor. *Don't bother with umbrellas*, it seems to say. *I'm about to stop anyway, my heart's not in it tonight.*

We were going to say goodbye on the street corner, but Gabi walks us to an intersection where we're more likely to find a cab He's headed to his hotel in the Financial District, we're headed uptown. The usual squabble about who gets to take the first cab. We insist: "Two against one, Gabi," Maud says. So he cowers, and as he opens the door, he kisses Maud on both cheeks, embraces me Italian style, and extends a phone gesture to signify either a warning that we should not forget to call him or a promise that he'd be calling soon. "As usual, had too much to drink," he says, almost apologetically. Minutes later, another cab screeches to a halt. We hop inside and head uptown. Because of the long cab ride, we decide to put our seat belts on, which puts us almost two feet apart. I'm looking forward to the Brooklyn Bridge, especially in the rain. But the bridge also stirs an uneasy feeling, because it has always scared me and I don't like crossing it on foot. Something is eating me but I still can't grapple with it. I am thinking of the old Greek vendor, of cancer, of Gabi, of

Renzo & Lucia's, and of Manfred and the Central Park tennis house when it rains on Saturday mornings and the world feels snug and happy, but it all comes in one breath, and is stirred by too much alcohol. I'm watching the rain spill ever so lightly on the empty street, and I still don't know what's troubling me. Thinking of Gabi's allusion to many lives and identities, I feel I'm just another Sicily—confused and lonely.

My heart's not in it tonight, Maud. My heart's just not in it.

Neither of us says anything.

She touches the sleeve of my shirt. "I like the cuff links," she says. "I'm so glad I got them."

"I like them too."

"I was getting tired of the gold ones you wear."

"I was too. So, what did you think of him?"

We both know who *him* is.

"I don't know. Lovely fellow. He is clever and very charming, but I don't think we'll be able to give him what he wants. Certainly not this year."

"How long have you known him?"

"Two weeks. He's writing a complicated piece, but so much of what he's after is confidential that I know he won't be happy with the very little we can disclose before testing and FDA approval."

"And?"

"I'm more interested in what he has to say about Sicily than I am about what he wants to know about cancer research."

"Are you seeing him again?"

"I don't think so. I spent three hours with him earlier today. Enough. Pamela asked me to meet him, and I did."

Maud wants to write him off. Because she fears him. And she fears him because she's attracted. Classic syndrome.

"Still, you two were having a good time tonight."

"Oh, he is totally adorable. But he drinks—you should have seen him at lunch." *I did see him at lunch!*

Maud sounds too listless and vague, and she's assumed that mildly fatigued air, which is how she deflects subjects she doesn't want to discuss. Fatigue is always such a good cover for her, the way hysterics are for Tamar. She's ducking, because she knows I'm prodding.

But slumped in her seat, Maud does look tired. The darting, dangerous look that comes when she wears dark lipstick has faded from her face.

"Lovely cuff links, though," she says as she reaches over and holds my hand.

"I wore them all day."

"I'm happy you like them. Wasn't at all sure you'd like them, bought them on a whim," she adds.

And suddenly it occurs to me that if ever there's a good moment, perhaps this is it. We could even gloss over it, but I've been good all this time and now I have to raise the subject, even if it tears open the floodgates. Otherwise, I won't sleep tonight. I am still looking at her, and she looks so unlike the woman I saw at the restaurant this afternoon. Is this the person I bring out when she's alone with me, listless and fatigued? Am I even good for her? Am I enough?

"Do you like him, though?"

"I like him fine."

I take this in, mull it over, say nothing at first.

"For a moment I thought there was something."

"You mean between us?"

"Oh, I don't know, maybe."

"That would be too funny. Never even crossed my mind, and I can assure you it hasn't crossed his either."

"Why would it be too funny?"

"Why? I could think of a hundred reasons."

"Name one."

"You mean you couldn't tell?"

I look at her. And she looks at me. I am feeling totally stumped, but finally I see what I was just starting to guess, or had already guessed except that I am still reluctant to let on that I have. Perhaps there's a side of me that doesn't want all my doubts about the two of them so hastily dispelled, though there's yet another part that doesn't want her to see I've immediately intuited what she's barely had time to imply.

"Oh, that," I say, downplaying her disclosure by feigning indifferent surprise.

"Oh, that!" she almost mimics. "Seriously?"

A moment of silence.

"For a while I thought you two had something going on."

"Puh-lease! So this is why you were Mister Grumpy all evening?"

"Was I Mister Grumpy?"

"Big-time."

She imitates my face when I'm pouting. We both laugh.

"Why do you think he asked if we were in love?" Maud asks.

"Why? Because he had too much to drink? Because he had designs on you?"

"No, dear. On you."

I try to look baffled. But I know she can tell.

"So what else is new?" I ask.

"Nothing, I suppose."

And suddenly I know I am saying something, not just about Gabi, or about men, but about me. But I say this looking out the window at the rain that falls ever so meek and docile over the road that leads to the ramp that leads to the bridge that leads to God knows where I'm going with this, though going with it I am.

And there's the bridge at last, vaulting the harbor under the shadow by the piers, the good, staunch, loyal bridge that understands and forgives and has always known, as I have always known, that what I really long for this evening is neither to be on this side of the river nor on the other bank but on the space and transit in between, the way after speaking of Russia's White Nights it wasn't of nightfall or daybreak that Gabi had sung but of that fleeting hour between dusk and daylight which we all longed for on our balcony on this undecided evening that wasn't winter or summer or even just spring.

Soon we'll be riding up the FDR. We'll cross over at 59th Street and then up Central Park West, and eventually pass the spot where the Greek vendor parks his hot dog cart each day, and then the Langham, the Kenilworth, the Beresford, the Bolivar, and farther up the St. Urban and Eldorado and then the entrance to the Bridle Path and to the tennis courts where Manfred stood gaping next to me this afternoon when I fired my cannonball shot and all I could think of at the time was I want to travel away with you to the island where the lemon grows and squeeze the rind of its fruit on you till I'll smell it on your breath, on your body, under your skin.

"Were you smitten?" she asks.

I don't want to lie. "For a moment."

"*For a moment*," she repeats, gentle irony lilting in her voice, as though realizing that, despite my tone, what I've just said was not spoken in passing.

Again I look outside the car.

"How long has it been?"

I am thinking of Manfred now, not of Gabi, but it doesn't matter.

"A while," I answer. "How long have you known?" I ask.

"A while."

I can hear it in her voice that she's smiling. I don't ask her how, or when, or why in all these months we've never spoken about this. But I feel as though it is she who stepped into the restaurant today and witnessed for the first time what she's probably always known but, like the Brits during the war, knew better than to say anything about.

"And all this time I thought it was Claire," she says.

I shake my head to mean she couldn't be more off the mark.

Silence sits between us. We seem to understand why. Finally, I utter a pallid yet grateful "Thanks."

When I turn to look at her, all she says is "Welcome."

We hardly need to say another word, but I know that right now, in the cab, of the two of us, it is I, not she, who's crossed and gone over to the other side.

"Am I going to lose you?" she asks, and then pauses, as if wondering whether I'm no longer paying attention. "Because I don't want to lose you."

I say nothing. But I don't know if what I'm about to say is the truth.

MANFRED

know nothing about you. I don't know your name, where you live, what you do. But I see you naked every morning. I see your cock, your balls, your ass, everything. I know how you brush your teeth, I know how your shoulder blades flex in and out when you shave, I know that you'll take a quick shower after shaving and that your skin glows when you come out, know exactly how you'll wrap a towel around your waist, and, for that short moment that I crave every morning in the tennis house, how you'll drop your towel on the bench and stand naked after drying yourself. Even when I'm not looking, I love knowing that you're naked right next to me, love thinking that you want me to know you're naked, that you couldn't possibly be unaware that I long for your naked body and that every night I lull myself to sleep, thinking that I'm cradled in your arms and you in mine. I know what soap you use and how long you take to comb your hair when it's still wet, how you splash cream over your elbows, your knees, your legs, and in between each of your dainty toes, always generous but never wasteful with the cream, which you keep in your locker. I love to watch you inspect yourself in the mirror and seemingly approve the shape of your arms, your shoulders, your chest, your neck. Sometimes you'll stand naked by the long urinal next to me, unaware that I'm trying my best not to look. I never look, don't want to look, don't want to be caught looking, don't even want you to know I'm struggling not to look, though I can hear your stream and, for a brief moment, if only I had the courage, am tempted to slip a bare foot in its way to know the warmth from your body.

You, of course, never look. Ditto on the terrace, when you sit and start eating your morning ration of half a protein bar. Nor do you look when you're stretching your legs against the banister before tennis. I'll never come close to you when you're stretching; I'll wait or find another spot to stretch. But you'll come right next to me, put a leg on the bar, stretch one calf, then the other, and not give it a second thought. I avoid getting close to you because I want to get close. You could almost graze my foot as you did once and never even knew it.

Sometimes, after we've each played for an hour in the morning and you've removed your shirt before showering, I love watching the sweat glisten down your spine. My mouth wants to go everywhere on your body. I want to taste you, I want to know you with my mouth.

You know nothing about me. You see me. But you don't see me. Everyone else sees me. And yet no one has the foggiest notion of the gathering storm within me. It's my secret private little hell. I live with it, I sleep with it. I love that no one knows. I wish you knew. Sometimes I fear you do.

To the rest of the world I might be the most cheerful person who ever leaves the tennis courts in the morning. I'll stroll over to the 96th Street subway station, maybe run into a neighbor, joke with the neighbor, hope you're following not far behind, which always gives me a thrill, even when I know you're not following. Part of me wants you to see me happy, wants you to be envious of what could make me so happy. I carry this alleged happiness all the way to my office, and there I'll greet everyone with so expansive a smile that it hovers on the brink of laughter. I can't tell whether it's real or contrived happiness, but it spills into every aspect of my life. Everywhere I go I affect joy, and by some strange miracle, this counterfeit joy brightens me up as well as those whose lives I touch. People look at me and I know what they think: *He's got a life*. I flirt with everyone, but it's really you I'm flirting with.

No one knows why I seem so happy, nor would anyone guess that the sprightly person so pepped up for the day and whose life seems so pulled together might be a disguised alien loping among earthlings. I seem happy even when I'm alone and couldn't be happy. And yet wanting you does make me happy. In the office bathroom I catch myself whistling. At the salad bar the other day, I was impatient and started humming a tune. "You're happy today," said the lady at the cash register, which ended up making her happy as well. Work makes me happy. All I have to do at times is smile and I've jump-started my heart. At long, tiresome meetings, I'm the one who buoys everyone's spirits with the most fatuous comments. Mr. Mirth-Palaver to the rescue!

It took me a while to suspect that the happiness I feel is not affected. The merest glance from you or the most cursory hello can cause a surge of happiness that lasts a whole day. Even if I can't ever touch you, just looking at you makes me happy. Wanting you makes me happy. Thinking that I could steal one fraction of a second to place a cheek on the damp down on your chest after you've just showered gives more meaning and brings more joy than anything else I've wanted or done in a long time. I think of your skin all day, all the time.

Sometimes work gets in the way. Work keeps me busy. Work is my screen. My whole life is a screen. I am a screen. The real me has no face, no voice, isn't always with me. Like thunder after lightning, the real me could be many, many miles away. Sometimes, there is no thunder. Just lightning and then silence. When I see you, there's lightning and then silence.

I want to tell people. But there's no one to tell. The only person I can think of is my father, and he's no longer alive. You would have liked him. And he would have liked you.

I'm shrouded in silence, like a beggar hooded in burlap, skulking in a cellar. I am a cellar. My passion feeds on everything but air, then curdles like bad milk that never goes bad enough. It just sits there. And if it wastes the heart a tick per day, still, anything that touches the heart is good for the heart, is like feeling, becomes feeling. When I do not speak to you I hope that you will, which you never do, because I never do, because we've stopped talking even before we've started speaking.

You speak to no one at the courts. I once overheard an older man ask to play tennis with you. It took guts to ask, since you're an excellent player. I envied him the courage. No sooner had he asked than you smiled and answered, "I'd like that." I envied the answer he got. It took me a month to realize that *I'd like that* was just polite humbug, meaning *never*.

You're always so quiet. When you take a two-minute rest after stretching before playing, you stand and look out toward the trees with a vacuous, almost woeful gaze that lets you drift so far away. You look sad and ashen. *Are you not happy?* I want to ask. *Do you even like tennis?*

And yet you must be happy. You don't need anyone. You are

like a walled citadel, proud of its battlement and of its colored
pennants flapping in the summer wind. Every morning I watch
you walk to your court, I watch you play, and I watch you leave
an hour and a half later. Always the same, never brooding, just
silent. Occasionally, you'll say "Excuse me" when I happen to
stand in your way, and "Thank you" when your ball drifts into
my court and I hurl it back to you. With these few words, I find
comfort in false hopes and hope in false starts. I'll coddle anything instead of nothing. Even thinking that nothing can come
of nothing gives me a leg to stand on, something to consider
when I wake up in the middle of the night and can see nothing,
not the blackout in my life, not the screen, not the cellar, not
even hope and false comforts—just the joy of your imagined
limb touching mine. I prefer the illusion of perpetual fasting to
the certainty of famine. I have, I think, what's called a broken
heart.

Sometimes I want to turn my head to the bedroom wall and
tell the wall things. But what could speaking in the dark do? I
should give up, but I can't. I'm like someone who never got off a
train that traveled past the last stop.

ON FRIDAY EVENINGS, when I leave the office and am struck
by the torrent of traffic lights—the cars, the buses, the clamor
and frenzy of bicycles and delivery boys cutting ever so close as
they speed through one red light after another, and all those
people doing things, going places—just a whiff of the brisk night
air and it'll all come back to me: I'm wasting my life, I am so
alone. A rush of tenderness fills my heart. But I'm not fooled.
Tenderness is sham love, easy love, the muted, civil face of love.

Sometimes on those evenings I'll put off going home. Why
go home? To face what? I prefer to linger on the sidewalks and
make up reasons to walk to the next bus stop, and to the next

one after that. Or I'll step into this or that store and forget work, forget everyone, and let myself sink deeper, because I want to suffer, I want to hurt, I want to feel something, even if I know that thinking of you never lasts long enough, and that swept by the scents and the press of a large store, my mind will invariably drift to other things, other faces, and in the crowd I'll lose you and won't remember your face.

On one such evening at Barneys, I ran into Claire. "I'm thinking of buying a tie and can't decide which of these two." She was buying a tie as well. "Who's the lucky man?" I asked. She gave me a semi-amused, reproachful smile, perhaps to mean *Must you always joke?* "Just my father," she said. She had already picked a tie and was walking around with it to make sure there was nothing else she wished to buy. "How about you?" "Can't decide," I said, holding one tie in each hand and catching myself imitating the seesawing motions of a scale. "Wouldn't it be just like you to waver?" she asked, still amused but also chiding. I did not answer. Instead, I asked what she was doing after buying the tie. "Nothing." Would she have a glass of wine with me on 63rd Street? She hesitated. "It's Friday night, Claire." "I promised . . . ," she started but then relented. "Fine. One glass." We buy our ties. "Come. I'll tell you all about my obsessive romance with neckties and how I court them, love them, and am forever loyal to each one." But all I wanted was to talk about you. She laughed. She humors me. But I know she doesn't approve. I never told her that I had wanted to buy you a tie as well. Then I chickened out and didn't buy you one. But an hour later, I am alone again. I know how the evening will turn out. If only I could dream of you. Sometimes I do. But not often enough. Dreams are like practice runs and mini-rehearsals; they tell us what we'll do, when to ask, how we'll touch when the time comes, if the time comes. In the morning, when I stand naked in front of the mirror, I like to think that you're there behind me. Then you'll come closer and stand flat against me, naked as well, your chin resting on my shoulder, close to my collarbone, your cheek glued to mine, your arms around me. I smile at you and you smile back. We're good together. We've had a good night. I want to hear you say you liked what we did. *Did you really?* I ask again, as if I need you to repeat it, because I won't quite believe it myself until I've heard you say it. You bite your lip and you nod four or five times.

I know this nod. I've seen it many times on the tennis courts. It's your quiet way of driving a point home, of following a tennis ball and watching it land exactly where you aimed it. You never pump your arm when you score, you never exclaim anything, you don't even smile when you fire a perfect backhand straight down the line. All you do is nod several times. Sometimes you bite your nether lip. That says it all. It's what you do when you catch your body in a mirror in the locker room and check yourself out, especially your shoulders, which you know are perfect. Sometimes you'll even turn sideways to eye your shoulder blades, which you flex once or twice, and then nod. You approve. It's what happens when mind, will, body, earth, and time are in total alignment. It's probably what you did—the nod thing—as a child when hurling a flat stone and watching it skitter on a large body of water, three, four, five, six, seven times. Or when you'd spot an A+ when your teacher handed back the weekly science quiz on Mondays. The nod thing again. It confirmed that something you worked on and saw through finally gave you pleasure. Sometimes, though rarely, when you hit a ball hard, you'll grunt. I love to hear your muffled grunt. It makes me think that this is how you groan when you come. I like thinking of you coming. It brings you down to earth, makes you human, gives a sound to exertions that might otherwise slip unnoticed. I want to see your face when you come.

I look at myself in the mirror as we're shaving almost shoulder to shoulder in the tennis house and imagine you're sending me the nod. I wonder what it must be like to be you, to look in the mirror whenever I catch my reflection and simply nod two to three times. To have your skin, your lips, the palms of your hands, your cock, your balls.

Everything about you is perfect, willed perfect, deliberate. Everything in its time, from the first half of your protein bar before stretching your legs to the second half of your protein bar when you leave the locker room on your way out to the subway station. Timeliness in all things. Which is why I've never asked you to even hit a few balls with me. My skittish, uneven playing would irritate you no end.

You arrive by 6:45 and you leave at about 8:20. By 8:30 you're at the 96th Street station, carrying today's paper in your right hand. You ride the downtown train to 34th Street and then you change for the uptown R or N to Queens. I know, because I followed you once. Twice, actually. Every weekend I am sure that you have your hair trimmed, because it's always shorter at the start of the week. On your way to or from the barber, I bet you pick up the shirts you delivered last Saturday and drop off this week's laundry. I know that you have your shirts laundered because in the morning you always tear out the tag stapled around the lowest buttonhole. I'm quite certain that you iron your pants before going to bed every night or early in the morning before tennis. I can just see you occasionally putting down the iron to eat from a bowl of high-protein cereal. You never rush through anything; everything in its time, down to the way you store your clothes in the locker. You'll fold your scarf, then hang your jacket and trousers on the hanger you keep in your locker, and finally fold your paper and stand it so it won't crinkle in the locker or stain your clothes. Everything is minutely taken care of and premeditated. When I think of what kind of work you do, I am almost sure you're either an actuary, an accountant, or a fussy patent office clerk who prefers not meet clients.

People like you live alone, like living alone. God, you must be dull.

You probably were no different as a little boy—the kind of classmate everyone admires and envies but secretly hates. I can just see you leaving school, dutifully saying goodbye to your homeroom teacher, and heading home early every afternoon. You look happy. You don't mind walking alone. You're neither slack nor rushed as you think of what's awaiting in the kitchen. Unlike others your age, you're still wearing shorts and you don't care what anyone says. Along the way home, you're already planning how to tackle your homework, knowing that if you finish on time you might get to watch your favorite show and later, after supper, go back to the book you've been reading. I imagine you have two siblings; you're the youngest. The one you're closest to is already in college away from home. You miss him sometimes, especially since you like rowing out with him on Sunday afternoons to fish, the two of you watching the herons standing on the warm sedge, while he talks and tells you about things you know nothing about and you listen. Your parents won't let you use the boat when he's not there; you listen to them too, you always listen.

There are no ruffles in your life, no fretting before exams, no threats of having your allowance withheld, you always know what to do, what to expect, what to avoid—poison ivy, ticks, brambles, and the bad boys who linger around but won't cause trouble if you duck them in time. You're seldom caught by surprise, and you always budget your time. You don't call it budgeting your time yet, but I heard you use the expression once when a tennis player asked you what you did for work, and when you told him and he asked how you managed to divide your time between teaching high school during the day and special education in the evening, you smiled and said, "I guess I budget my time." You were probably never late for school, never late handing in your homework, not late reaching puberty. Punctual in all things. And, yes, unremittingly dull.

AFTER MORE THAN two years, I still know nothing about you. I can't even tell how old you are. Sometimes I'll swear you couldn't be older than twenty-five. But the elusive hints of incipient male-pattern baldness throw me off and give the lie both to your boyish face and to the taut, marble-white chest on which the outlines of blood vessels are as visible as on the face of a child. I'd have settled for thirty-plus, but your voice is too high, which is why I'll fall back to late twenties. The other day while riffling through a box of old photographs, I landed on a picture taken of me at the beach when I was twelve. I hadn't seen this picture in years, and yet it radiates a startling new meaning to me now, because all I want is to show it to you, to draw you into my life, and let you see that the man I am today and the boy I was once are the same person. With you I want to go back to the beginning to restart the story of my life. I remember exactly when this picture was taken. It was late one morning. Two brothers who were going for a swim stopped by to greet my father and stood watching him as he snapped my picture while I felt awkward in front of them and was trying to stand straight and not squint though the sun was in my eyes. I had a crush on one of them and was too young to realize it. Had you told me back then what I want from you now, I'd have laughed in your face; had you held me as I so want you to now, I'd have struggled and freed myself and kneed you in the groin, called you all manner of foul names that I'd dread you'd easily use on me now. Today, all

I want is the courage to ask you to hold me as you might have done when I was in that picture at the beach and, after wrestling me to the ground and holding me there with my mouth biting the sand, tell me not to struggle against you, against your mouth, against my life.

EVER SINCE I first noticed you, I made a point of speaking to everyone else at the courts so that you might get to know me, if only by overhearing my conversations. I wanted to let you know that I love laughter and good cheer, and that despite being friendly with just about everyone, I am no fool.

I love starting conversations with people whom, in other circumstances, I wouldn't even notice. I've made friends with the help, one of them the pert Wendy at the concession stand whose real Chinese name is not Wendy and with whom I flirt every morning when I complain about her coffee. And then there's the handyman who's told me the story of his life and how he had to flee Russia and now lives on Staten Island with his Dominican wife and needs to leave home to take the ferry by four thirty every morning to show up at the tennis courts on time. I know about his daughter who works nights as a nursing assistant at Mount Sinai and about his sister-in-law who lives with him ever since her accident. I've also spoken to another handyman in my broken Spanish. Now he seeks me out, wants to talk, may even have mistaken my overzealous camaraderie for friendship.

In the tennis house I am forever again Mr. Mirth-Palaver, the one everyone greets and around whose shoulder everyone, from the players to the handymen to the tennis coaches, likes to put an arm when they pass by. Some even shout my name. I want you to know my name. I want you to know I'm five lockers down from yours. But as soon as I see you, I freeze. Should I look, or pretend not to? Should I speak, or say nothing? Better say nothing. For there are indeed days when the whole thing fritters away like a bad dream and I begin to scorn you. I like scorning you. Sometimes I'll coddle those moments when desire seems to have totally ebbed and indifference has chilled the little that's left. Then I thank my stars for helping me hold my tongue. I look at your ass, your cock, your face, and feel nothing. The circuit is always the same: from attraction to tenderness to obsessive longing, and then to surrender, desuetude, apathy, fatigue, and finally scorn. But then, just hearing your flip-flops on the wet pavement of the shower area reminds me that indifference was just a reprieve, not a verdict. By the end of your game, your white shirt is all damp and sticks to your chest, and I can make out your rib cage and your abs, not an ounce of fat, the six-pack no secret though never declared. Scorn disappears. I want to bury my head in your chest the moment you remove your shirt, I want to wrap the shirt around my face. So I watch. After taking off your clothes, you'll put them in the usual white Apple plastic shopping bag and pull the drawstring tightly before dropping it into your swanky leather messenger bag. Sometimes I've watched you toss your damp shirt and shorts into your bag as if you've suddenly lost your patience with them and refused to be neat. I love the scruffy you. It makes me long to know the unkempt, unbudgeted you, the you who needs others and makes room for them at night and likes dessert when having a story told before bedtime.

IT'S BEEN HAPPENING again this year. Before shaving and showering, you'll still come to where the sinks are, close to where I'll be standing and shaving, and for a split second—and this is my moment—you'll stand behind me totally naked. If my timing is right, I'll keep shaving and observe you in the mirror. But just sensing you are scarcely inches behind me is enough to send my

heart racing and bring me to the brink of doing something fool-
ish, like leaning back to feel your chest, or turning around to let
you see that I'm getting hard. I like when my heart races, when I
start to forget things, when I cease to care and all I want is for
you to reach over to me, and without warning rest your towel,
rest the light stubble of your unshaved chin against my back
and lock me in your arms, your cock tucked between my cheeks,
staring at ourselves in the mirror as though after a good night
together. This is when I must think other thoughts, this is when
I push my cock against the rim of the sink to keep it in check.

Sometimes, as you did last year, you disappear for two, three
weeks and once again I fear I've lost you. Either you've moved or
found better tennis courts elsewhere. I know we've been through
this before. But this time I dread the signs. I picture you playing
tennis in Queens near your school. And then it hits me: I've lost
you. You now rank among the things I'll always regret: opportu-
nities lost, children never had, things I might have accomplished
or done far better, lovers who have come and gone. In a few years,
I'll remember this shabby tennis house and its puddles and think
back on the splash of your yellow flip-flops. I'll remember the
courts in late winter, when only the regulars and the diehards,
including old Mrs. Lieberman, play, or April weekday mornings
or May afternoons when lilacs bloom all over Central Park, or
when the silence that hovers over these courts and over the park
by eight in the morning is as spellbinding as the silence on empty
beaches at the break of day. I'll look back to that beautiful backhand of yours, how you knelt down in something like silent
worship for the death blow you were about to strike and then,
having slammed the ball, stood there, staring at your befuddled
adversary, biting your lower lip as a humble disclaimer in the face
of heaven's silent praise. I'll regret that nod, because it is the nod
I picture on your face whenever I imagine my cock entering your

body, slowly, very slowly at first, and then, when I'm all the way in and want to tell you that this is the best life can offer, you'll nod again and bite your lip, which I now want to bite more than anything in the world as you finally reach up to me and kiss me with your tongue deep in my mouth. What I'll regret is never seeing your face when you come, never holding your knees, or caressing your face, many, many times, or even knowing that tinge of disappointment after sex that immediately begs to be expiated with more sex.

ONE MORNING I arrived earlier than usual. By now I'd made a habit of entering the park at 93rd, not 90th. We entered the park at the same time. I hadn't seen you in weeks. Clearly something could have been said on such an occasion. You did not look at me, and after giving you a chance to say something, I decided not to stop looking at you. This was very unusual. I kept glancing at you a few times, perhaps in an attempt to greet you if you so much as looked my way, but you were staring straight in front of you, budgeting your steps, budgeting your thoughts, your day. Better not disturb him, better not intrude, yours were clearly *get lost* signals.

An hour later, in the locker room, when I saw a huge bandage around your right thigh, I figured I had to seize my chance. "What happened to you?" I asked, with a tone that wished to imply a friendly *what idiotic scrape did you get yourself into?* "Oh, I was just trying to open a bottle of wine that broke a few weeks ago." "Stitches?" "Many." You smiled. Then seeing I wasn't looking away from you, "You're the third person who's noticed."

"Hard not to. Can you play tennis with this?"

"Tennis is easy. It's showering that's difficult."

We laughed.

"I've got it down to a system." And so saying, you produced a box of Saran wrap from your swanky leather bag, plus a collection of sturdy rubber bands. It made the two of us laugh again.

"It's really a lot better. But thanks for asking."

Thanks for asking. There it was. Perfunctory courtesy bordering on dry, dismissive pap. The emperor of clichés. It did not surprise me.

A few days later just as I was opening my bag I cursed out loud. "Can you believe it?" I said, turning to you. "I forgot my sneakers."

"Don't you keep them in your locker?" you asked.

"Normally I do, but I took them to play tennis on Riverside Drive last Sunday."

I looked at my watch, as if I could get back home and make it to the courts in time. You read my thoughts.

"Well, even if you rushed back home you'd probably lose the court. So my advice is sit in the benches, have a protein bar, and enjoy a fresh cup of coffee."

"You mean that slick of gooey tar with or without the curdled milk?"

"Oh, it's not so terrible," you said.

And suddenly I realized that my scorn for the coffee they brew here was all along a simple affectation, an exaggeration meant to draw your attention, like everything I say here. But you weren't biting. You are not given to hyperbole, irony, or wry humor. You say it like it is.

So I took your advice, bought a protein bar and ordered a cup of coffee and took it to the balcony to watch you play. I loved how before hitting the ball, you drew your right arm all the way back and how you stretched out your left hand to aim the ball where you wished to send it. There is grace, and skill, and follow-through in everything you do. No affectation, no exaggeration, just the thing itself. I envied you.

As I watched you play, I noticed you had changed your bandage to a smaller one. I wanted to comment on that and meant to wait for you, seeing as we had started talking.

But why fool myself? We hadn't started talking at all. You were no more thinking of my shoes than I of my protein bar.

Eventually, I ate the protein bar, took another sip of the coffee, poured the rest of it into one of the gutters, watched you play some more, and then, after shaving and showering, left.

I did not go straight to the office that morning. I bought another cup of coffee, walked up the stairs to the High Line, found a quiet, empty spot, and just sat there, staring at the water, at the near-deserted walkway, at the plants and the trees and the bushes, all so vibrantly green that day. I was savoring my misery, trying to remember your voice, or just the words you'd said in case I was unable to summon your voice. But nothing came to me. I wanted to think of you. But nothing stirred there either, except a feeling at once sad yet not unpleasant. I'm in love, aren't I? Yes, I think so. On a paper napkin I'd pocketed after buying coffee at the tennis house, I began to write: *I know nothing about you. I don't know your name, who you are, where you live, what you do. But I see you naked every morning. I see your cock, your ass, your balls, everything.* I had no idea why I'd written these words. But it was the first time I had taken something in my chest about you and put it in words out into the real world. I didn't want to stop, because it was like talking to you now, yet better than talking to you, because I could let down my guard and felt soothed by the words, knowing there was no reason to feel soothed by anything, much less by my own words. I folded the napkin and slipped it in my wallet. I knew that I'd never throw it away.

But as I was about to stand up to walk to my office, I felt something almost like pain in my chest. I liked the pain. And once again I wished my father were alive. He's the one person who'd understand the inflections of what I felt, the sting and the salve braided together like twin serpents going at each other. This is love, he would have said, diffidence is love, fear itself is love, even the scorn you feel is love. Each of us comes by it the wrong way. Some spot it right away, others need years, and for some it comes in retrospect only.

And while staring at the Erie Lackawanna station across the Hudson, I remembered him standing at the dock waving farewell as our ferry was chugging away from the island. Here was a sad man, I thought. Little did he know then that this would be his last summer of love. But knowing him as I did now, he must have feared and indeed foreseen it might never be given to him to find love again, which is why he treasured it until the end.

THIRD WEEK AFTER we spoke that time.

We say hello. For the next two or three weeks, I'll say hello first. Then you'll say hello. But on our way to the courts, never a glance. You budgeted one, not two greetings a day, and our slim quota brings us no closer than when we were strangers. After a few words the chill immediately rises like frost creeping on a windowpane. In no time, I am back to surreptitious glances that instantly shift the moment they land on you, or that shift before even spotting you, so no one could even call them glimpses.

Sometimes, when you're given the chance to avoid my glance, there's no greeting at all. Clearly, we've slipped back to where we were before. At the watercooler, as I'm bending down and drinking, I don't see you standing right next to me, waiting to drink as well. Neither of us has spotted the other until it is too late. "Oh, hello!" I say. "Oh, hi," you say.

When it's time to leave, you roll your orange towel into a ball and slam-dunk it cavalierly into your bag before zipping up the bag and slinging it across your shoulder. You never say goodbye

to anyone, not even to the attendant who is always on the prem-
ises or to Mike, who strung your racket once. Not to me either.
You simply slink away, like those who are either too arrogant
and self-centered, or unspeakably shy and don't know how to be
the first to say goodbye.

A month later, though, you are the first to greet me. Very
unusual. Still, before I let it go to my head, I realize that your few
words were nothing more than a string of commonplaces. The
twisted smile that wasn't so welcoming, the terse wording, the
gaze that turns opaque and nearly flees after saying *Oh, hi,* as
though your whole body felt obligated to greet me when it would
much rather have drifted away. It's the kind of greeting I give
Mrs. Lieberman whenever I'm unable to duck her in time.

Still, three weeks into our first conversation, we've moved
from one daily greeting to sometimes two. Within a month,
you've managed to add: *Have a great weekend,* followed by *How was
your weekend?* or *How are you doing today?* I reply using the same
bromides, hoping to modulate them differently each time to show
that I really mean what I say when I reply with the same tired *fine,*
or *just fine,* or *really fine,* occasionally throwing in a *no use complain-
ing* to add variety to what have become pabulum and hackneyed
exchanges. All along I'm thinking: I've got a crush on someone
who is evidently no less platitudinous than I am. It's all my fault.
I've set it up this way and should have seen this coming. You
budget your greetings, your smiles, your nods, but you never
throw in that minor extra, seemingly inadvertent something to
make me think that you mean more than what you say. Your
words, like mine, are without content, without meaning, limp-
ing signifiers. The old silence was preferable.

We toss occasional remarks at each other the way a tennis
instructor keeps tossing balls at old Mrs. Lieberman, who is trying to practice her forehand after her operation but misses eight

out of ten times. And yet I live for those two to three minutes of clumsy, insipid chitchat: the weekend, the latest movie, plans for the summer that never pan out, your thigh, my tennis elbow, and again your thigh, my brother, your brother. I live for this. And if this is all there is, well, this is all there is.

BUT NO ONE can prepare for the worst. The worst doesn't only dash hopes; it tears through everything in ways that are almost meant to hurt, to punish, to shame. Despite my most sobering forecasts, life can still play the cruelest card and scuttle everything—and just when I thought we were sailing past the shoals. This happened on April 26. I can't forget the date. It was the anniversary of the death of my father.

We were discussing the tennis house and how it needed a face-lift. "A face-lift!" you said. "You mean a complete and total do-over." I had never heard you say anything critical, much less something that seemed open-ended and did not instantly snuff out conversation. Ironically, I found myself coming to the defense of our poor old tennis house. You listened and then said, "Yes, but when was the last time they had paper towels in the dispenser or even a paper dispenser, for that matter?" And after a brief pause, "To say nothing of toilet paper."

We both laughed about the toilet paper. What I liked was the puckish and playful tone in your voice. I'd mistaken you for a straight arrow. Suddenly you were making me laugh.

Caught by surprise, all I could say was, "I didn't think you noticed things."

"Oh, I notice plenty."

This frightened me. Were you talking about me?

"But I've never heard you complain before," I said.

"You don't know me yet."

I loved this. The possible double entendre in your words, the air of impish mischief, the hovering promise of getting to know each other, the banter that could so easily die in its tracks or, with a nudge or two, take us to exactly where I hoped you were leading us. I was scared, scared of what you'd say to set me straight, scared that I wasn't misreading you at all.

Until now, talk has never gone anywhere. All I do is steal wisps of information in the hope of cobbling together your portrait, the way sketch artists do at police stations. I know you went to Oberlin, I know you come home late sometimes and all you want to do, after tutoring learning disabled students in the evening, is listen to Haydn sonatas, because they make you happy and help you unwind, which you've once said is why you need to play tennis every morning, otherwise you tense up during the day and get impatient with your students.

Our conversation about sad conditions at the tennis house was going well. We'd never spoken so much. We even spoke about your college years, and how difficult Christmas breaks were for you when you had to go back home with so many papers hanging over your head followed by the promise to bring back German fruitcakes for all your friends in the U.S. Stollen, I said. I hadn't said that word in so long. You laughed. Which made me laugh, which made you laugh. I could have put all my cards on the table and said it right then and there: *Let's grab a drink one of these days*—said casually, of course.

But just as I was warming up to say something like this, the bombshell. You were talking about schools and careers when for some reason you said, "My partner is a professor in classics." I needed to struggle not to tell you that my undergraduate major had been Greek and Latin literature and that I had translated *Animal Farm* into classical Greek. But this would have sounded so fatuous, as though I were trying to measure up to your partner. Still, I was thinking of finding something to say about my own life as a lapsed classicist when what you had just said finally hit me. You weren't talking about your tennis partner. You were talking about your partner. "He is writing a book about Thucydides," you said. My favorite author, I wanted to add, but didn't. Had you read Thucydides? I found myself asking, even though my mind was miles away at that point. "I had to," you replied. "Twice!"

Clearly, they have a collaborative relationship, I thought, loving the very word I'd spun out in a moment of anger, envy, and derision. *Collaborative.* I could just hear your pieties: *His problems are my problems, my troubles his troubles. We share, we care.* I wanted to laugh at the two of you. But all I kept thinking as I left the tennis courts that morning was, So, you knew, you knew what I was doing when I kept trying to chat you up all these weeks and months. All you needed was to wait for the least intrusive way to play the partner card. *My partner this, my partner that, oh, that's what my partner always says.* For someone who budgets his words, you knew where you were headed the moment you brought up Germany and stollen and Haydn. You must be a good teacher. Nothing you say is without purpose.

What didn't go down well was the sheer simplicity, the tawdry, ordinary, threadbare, flat-footed, mundane simplicity with which you hit me with the "boyfriend" line—the kind of disingenuous aside a girl in her late teens might drop when she says, *This is exactly how my boyfriend feels.*

I felt numb all day.

Partner. With that one word you not only tore down my flimsiest and untold fantasies; you also shattered the romance I'd been coddling for two years. All I could do now was hold fast to the wreckage of what were mere illusions.

That day changed everything. I was devastated, quietly, as though barbarians had swept through my life and forgotten to kill me after slaughtering everyone and eradicating everything, including memory. I couldn't remember what I had wanted from you or how I could even have thought of making love to you, night after night, the very thought of our mouth-to-mouth love robbing me of hours of sleep. I struggled to remember the raw fantasies, but their stirring sound track had gone dumb. All I was left with after hearing the *p* word was a collapsed house of cards, which it had taken me forever to build. What was inside that house, or why I had built it, or what storms it was meant to withstand, or which pleasures it hoped to billet—all gone. A mere nothing, and it was finished.

And here our story ends.

I CAN RELAX NOW. I can speak to you of my life, open up, let you peek into my world as it really is, feel less harried by the things I try to hide from you, stop boasting and saying I had a great weekend when it was altogether insipid.

I try to picture times ahead. One day you'll finally invite me over to dinner with your partner, and we'll talk. Of the classics, of Thucydides, and of young Alcibiades who made a pass at Socrates but was turned down because the philosopher knew the young hunk was way too handsome for him. And we'll talk of Nicias, who was executed because he was a worthier general than Alcibiades and went to his death knowing that the Athenian warriors he ferried across the sea with the promise of glory would die the ignominious death of slaves in the quarries of Syracuse off the island of Ortigia.

And if the two of you come over to my place, I'll pour your wine and your partner's, and it will be a dry white, and I'll cut open everyone's branzino as I'd seen a waiter do in Europe, using a flat spoon, and think to myself, *Better this than nothing. At least he's under my roof.*

And it will be so odd watching you and Maud eye each other with the uneasy premonition of people who can't quite put their finger on what troubles them only to ignore it when they begin to see it. The two of you will end up talking about one thing or another and eventually find a slim something to share in common. And we'd be having such a good time the four of us together and it would seem so natural for people who meet on the tennis courts to join for dinner that we'd forget to ask why it had to be now and not two years ago.

But this fantasy peters out too. It's too homespun, too tame, and my mind can't stand it for long. I prefer to think of sex. But I don't want to think of sex, don't want to see you naked any longer, won't even look when you're naked, don't want to like when I do look only then to catch myself thinking, *This is where his partner's mouth goes when they're alone at night.* And, yes, I do still like. I haven't seen you naked in months, even though you're naked right before me every morning. I don't look, or I look but not to see.

The other day I saw you had a bluish scar on your thigh. I had never noticed it before. I'd seen the bandage, seen the thinner one too, then stopped noticing you'd removed the bandage altogether. The scar made me feel sorry for you, I wanted to touch it, to speak about it, to ask if it still hurt. But I held back. I looked at your face and it was the face of someone with a scar on his inner right thigh. It made you so human. And I loved you human. I wanted to hold you.

You smile when you speak to me. I suppose I smile too. Then just a day later you were bending down to pick up something and I spied, if for the most fleeting second, your anus. It too brought out a feeling verging on compassion, partly because I felt I had trespassed by just looking and partly because it made me know for the first time that you were kind, vulnerable, soft.

I should never have looked. When I thought about it, it made me feel I'd infringed on something wholesome and private and ever so chaste about you, like an instance of the holy that suddenly flares before our eyes and then leaves us speechless, humbled, and shaken.

But then just as I was attempting to wean myself, suddenly you took me completely by surprise. I was playing tennis on court 14, you were, as always, on court 15, and your ball spun out and hit my side of the net. You shouted *Thank you!* as we all do to ask for the ball when it lands on somebody else's court. It's a peremptory *Thank you!* but no one takes it amiss. I hadn't heard you the first time and didn't respond. So you called out again, except that this time you shouted *Thank you, Pauly.*

Pauly! Which is when I realized that I had indeed heard you the first time but hadn't been aware of it.

It wasn't just *Pauly* that you said but *Paulyyyy,* so chummy, so close, so intimate in the way you lengthened the last vowel of what used to be my nickname, that it suddenly tore me out of the tennis courts in Central Park and took me right back to my childhood where everyone at home and later in high school used to call me *Paulyyyy* exactly as you did, because it was an affectionate diminutive underscored with such good cheer and warmth. The boy in the picture I wanted to show you is called Pauly. And you'd hollered my name without even pretending you were unaware of it. The only place where Pauly appears is in a scanned image of my college yearbook on the web. Had you looked me up online?

Hearing my name spoken that way made me more happy than I might have expected. Everything I'd felt and all the fellowship I've been seeking from you had all along been there right before me, except that I wasn't seeing it, perhaps because pride and fear and raw desire stood in the way. But from your mouth

my name had suddenly acquired a new timbre, a new sound, its
real sound. I could have dropped my racket and leaned into the
court's chain-link fence, the way people do when they're ex-
hausted and take a moment to catch their breath, and I wanted
to cry. I interrupted my playing to send you your ball. And then
you smiled and said it again: "Thank you so much, Paul"—as if
my nickname had been a slip you wished to disown.

Still, I felt like a boy who worships a much older schoolmate,
and who, during recess one day, is asked to buy cigarettes for
him at the local bodega. It's no longer a busboy's errand but a
privilege. And I did feel privileged. Your use of my name put me
on a different plane. It was as if you had thrust your hand in my
locker when it was open and seized the apple I keep there for a
snack and said, *I'm taking the apple, you can have my protein bar.*

One thing occurred to me when I had finished playing tennis
that morning. I had never once asked your name or attempted to
know it. My way perhaps of staving you off, of keeping you unreal, of not showing I cared.

Later, after showering and getting dressed, I looked at you
and, from seemingly nowhere, said that I didn't know your
name. I did this perhaps to show you I was fully aware that
you had used my name for the first time that morning and that
the gesture did not go unnoticed. You immediately told me your
name. I would never have guessed. I don't know why, but I kept
thinking it was going to be Friedrich, or Heinz, or Heinrich, or
Otto. And because this is what people do when they exchange
names, I reached out and shook your hand. I liked what I felt
when I touched your hand. I knew that I'd feel some sort of signal race from you to me. Or perhaps I wanted to think I felt it.
But feel something I did. I was not going to keep your hand in
mine, but I wanted to, and I know, by the way you were polite
enough not to withdraw yours too soon, that perhaps you had

felt something as well. Suddenly, and I loved this, I had become the older schoolmate who sends the younger one to buy cigarettes. I loved your intimidated smile. And I loved this about us: we were swapping roles. *He's shy*, I thought.

"Let's grab a drink one of these days."

"Why not, I'd like that."

I had wanted to kiss your hand, to lace my five fingers in all five of yours and know the softness of your palm. Nothing like that happened, of course. But I did look you straight in the eyes hoping you'd know.

I went to work in a halo of bliss. What I failed to notice was that you were walking right behind me by no more than ten paces. I saw this not when I went down the stairs to the subway, or even when I reached the platform, but on the train itself. You had gotten in through another door and had found a seat in the same car. I was standing reading the paper. If you saw me, you were back to your usual silent and averted gaze. We don't speak outside the tennis courts. I didn't want to push things or be obtrusive, so I pretended to be lost in thought while reading the paper. I apologized to someone sitting down when I felt my paper graze her face, but I said it loudly enough for you to hear. I'd been doing this for two years in the locker room: talk to anyone, but talk to no one but you. Perhaps I expected you'd make a motion to talk. But then you didn't need my voice to know I was on the train. You already knew, the way I knew.

And there you were seated, casting that same lifeless, faraway gaze I'd seen on the courts once before as you stared blankly at the nameless humanity in the car. Your legs were slightly parted and you had the back of each hand resting on each thigh with the palms up, in a gesture so helpless, so passive, conveying such resigned acquiescence in your slumped posture that it hurt me to watch an athlete sit that way. I wanted to say something, anything, to break through all our hurdles and ask what was the matter and why were you staring with so forlorn and vacant a gaze at those around you. But who could have dared such a thing? So I pretended to go on reading.

Here I was reexperiencing these old stirrings of tenderness for you when it occurred to me that despite all my vigilance, I was so rapt by the article in the paper that I'd failed to notice we had reached your stop and that you had already left the car, probably brushing right past me without saying a word.

What snuffed the joy I felt that morning once I reached my office building was what you'd said when I asked about drinks. "I'd like that." Yours, I remembered, was not a yes. It was polite humbug.

THAT NIGHT, ON my computer, I did some sleuthing. Not knowing your last name, I typed in "Manfred," the name of your private school in Queens located near the subway stop to which I'd once followed you, the word "tennis." Nothing came up. So I tried a host of words, removed others, added others, even went so far as to follow an old hunch and checked American army bases in Germany. Nothing again. Finally I typed in "Oberlin" and "Manfred" and computed graduation years. And suddenly, to my complete surprise, there was your picture with your full name.

From this I couldn't resist asking more questions. Where did you live in New York? What had people said about you? Did you have a Facebook? Who were your friends? I read everything.

Not only did an address pop up with a telephone number, but on social media up came the name of someone who might be your partner. When I entered his name, the name "Thucydides" came up. Then "Professor, Classics." You hadn't lied. He'd already published a monograph on Thucydides.

I envied the two of you. I could just picture your meeting during freshman orientation week, then I saw you coming back together from the library late at night, every night. Perhaps you'd meet in the library after dinner. Then one winter night on the way back from the library to your dorm he stopped, sat down on one of the benches even though it was freezing, and said, "I just need to know, Manfred. Do you have feelings for me?"

WHAT CHANGED BETWEEN us was the dissolution of what seemed a war of nerves. Now it was you who'd start conversations. My plodding *Fine* to your *How was your weekend?* turned into a litany of things you had done or gone to see. I found out about your father and his bone marrow transplant, and about the sorry state of the central air-conditioning in your apartment on 95th Street, and about your elder brother who had gone back to Germany, and the black-and-white films you and your partner liked to watch on Turner Classic Movies. You didn't speak about sports, didn't even ask if I had watched the French Open. Rather than overlook the decaying state of the tennis house as you'd done before, you began to make fun of the grimy sink where we shaved, the puddles we had to wade through to put on our clothes, the homeless men who would sneak into the tennis house early in the morning to shower or wash their clothes in the very sinks where we'd just shaved and brushed our teeth. "If only my colleagues at school knew we hobnobbed with the homeless every morning."

In fact, one day a homeless man walked in and dumped his dirty clothes in one of the sinks. "What did I tell you," you said. "Hi, Paul," said the homeless man. "Hi, Benny," I said.

As we walked back to our lockers, I told you that Benny's was a very sad story. He had worked as a bartender, but after drugs and one misfortune following another, he ended up homeless.

Lost his license, his home, his wife, his children, and yet had read all the Russian classics and could recite all the ingredients of every cocktail ever concocted this side of the Atlantic. "He's trying to work his way back," I said, adding a touch more earnestness in what I was saying, perhaps to show that under the veneer of mischief and sarcasm, I was really a good soul. You said nothing. But I liked talking to you as we were getting dressed, because you'd have to face me and thus offer a frontal view of your body, your chin, your pecs, your abs, your eyes. I didn't want to look any lower, so I kept staring at your chest, but staring at your chest made me want to touch it, so I stared at your face, which I wanted to kiss, until I'd looked below your waist before your eyes could follow mine—all this as we're talking about the lapsed bartender who was trying to make a comeback.

"Paul?" said Benny, who had come out into the locker area after wringing his clothes in one of the deeper sinks.

"What is it?"

He seemed uncomfortable speaking in front of you and signaled for me to approach him, finally whispering, "Can you help me out?"

I walked back to my locker, secretly took out my wallet, and sidling back to the bathroom, handed him a few bills. I didn't want you to see. But I did want you to see that I had made an effort to hide that I'd given the poor man money.

"You gave him money," you said when I was back at my locker.

"No, I didn't."

"Yes, you did."

"He's a good man," I finally said.

To which you replied, "Another 'Metropolitan Diary' moment."

We smiled at each other.

"Well, we're even, then."

"What do you mean?" I asked.

"I gave him something too."

It turns out you'd given him far more than I had.

I smiled at you and shook my head with mock reproof.

"What?" you asked, not letting the matter go.

I wanted to say that we thought along the same lines, liked the same things, were more alike than either of us knew. Instead, I ended up saying something entirely different. "That was a lovely gesture and far more discreet than mine."

It ranked among the most saccharine banalities ever to come out of my mouth.

You said nothing.

"What?" I asked, echoing your words.

"Nothing." Then after a pause, "I think I'm beginning to understand you."

"Oh? Tell me more, because I'm not sure I do."

"You're not easy," you said.

"And you are?"

"I suppose not."

We stood there speechless, trying to avoid staring at each other, and though we were both fully dressed and ready to leave the tennis house, it seemed to me that neither of us wanted to leave with the other.

I said I needed to pee. I was giving you the exit line you needed to leave the locker room without me. I felt I was doing the right thing.

THE NEXT DAY, Saturday morning, as I'm heading to the farmers' market, my fantasies take over. It's a lovely, clear, summery beach day, and I'm thinking of what you might have done last night and whether you're gone for the weekend. The weather was still a bit cool, but I had an image of the summerhouse I'm sure you share with your friends and I pictured all of you having drunk too much last night. Yet everyone knows you're an early riser, and last night your friends asked you to get some milk in the morning, maybe bagels and things, and don't forget a few treats, someone ordered. Dreamily, you step out of the house to face this gorgeous morning. You're the only one up in the house and the only one on the lane. This is good. The weather is good. The lanes are quiet, and the silence doesn't let up. I can hear your flip-flops on the dusty slabs. You're happy. Last night, great dinner, good friends, nice talk, good wines, great sex. You haven't showered and you don't plan to until after your first swim in the ocean. All you did before heading out was put on the shorts you wore last night and a T-shirt, no underwear. This is heaven. You're going to surprise everyone by buying something like a cake— why not, you think, especially made locally with strange berries and grains found nowhere but here. I envy you the errand. Suddenly, I am there with you and would love to walk with you, because we've never walked together, and going to get bagels and things plus a treat on a Saturday morning at the beach seems so easy, so uncomplicated, such a source of clear, simple, undiluted joy.

Yet another part of me wishes that you'd asked me instead to pick up milk and breakfast for everyone. I know that once I walk out of the house you'll find a way to talk about me to those who are already up having coffee. They must have heard our moaning last night from the other end of the house, and someone is sure to say something, possibly comical, *The two of you making the beast with two backs, did you two ever consider catching your breath?* Everyone laughs, partly because I'm new among your friends. And you laugh with them, but then, on impulse, you pick yourself up and dash out of the house, and before I'm twenty paces on the lane, you're running after me, *I wanted to come with you.* I look back and smile.

But there's another Saturday scenario: you say you'll head out to get breakfast and ask me to stay in. *Have coffee with Esmeralda. I'll take care of things,* you say. No sooner have you walked out and closed the screen door behind you than we start talking. I'm new to this scene, so Esmeralda hands me freshly brewed coffee.

Be good to him, she says, *don't hurt him.*

But I am good to him.

Do you love him?

Do I love him? I'm crazy about him.

That doesn't seem to satisfy her.

Two other risers totter into the kitchen and help themselves to coffee.

But do you care for him? asks one of the two.

I can repeat this scene in my mind all day.

Everything tells me you care for me. And yet never a sign from you.

That same Saturday night I finally dream of you. I am walking with Maud around the Lincoln Square area. We are just leaving the movie theater when we run into you and your partner on the same sidewalk. It's late in the summer and you've been gone from the courts for more than a week, so seeing you standing in front of me startles me so much that, without even thinking or rehearsing our usual lukewarm hello, rather than shake your hand, I let my palm reach out to you and touch your cheek. I would never have dared this, but part of me can already tell this is probably a dream and knows it's not unseemly to do this in dreams, especially when one's not seen the other for more than a week. Perhaps it's your tanned neck exposed down to your shiny breastbone that stirs the impulse.

But then, in my dream, you do something more startling yet. Not only are you not taken aback by my bold caress in front of your partner, but you actually yield to my palm, because you like this, and by leaning into my hand, you're trying to make my hand stay there. We shake hands right after, perhaps to cover up what has just happened, and then make introductions left and right. Maud and your partner begin discussing how much they liked the film. "He certainly didn't," you say, pointing at me. "You don't say!" says Maud, making a joke at my expense. We ask which way you two are walking. It happens to be ours as well. At some point, she and he drift ahead while the two of us lag behind, almost intentionally putting distance between them and us. We've never walked together, yet here we are, more together than we'd ever been in two years. You grab my hand and don't let go. Surely this is a dream, I think. "Haven't seen you in ages," you say. "Let's walk together."

"But what about them?" I ask, mistaking your meaning, only then to realize that I haven't mistaken it at all.

"They'll live," you say.

And just as you utter these words, I know with unshakable certainty that those few minutes when we walk hand in hand together are, even in a dream, more real and better than anything I'd ever know in life, and that I would be lying if I called what I've been doing all these years living.

The happiness that came with the dream stayed with me all day.

I resolved one thing. The next time I saw you I'd do exactly what I'd done in my dream. I'd touch your cheek, either on the courts, or in the tennis house, or in the locker room, but something like this had to happen.

Or else.

Or else what? Shoot myself? Seriously?

When I saw you after my dream, it was impossible to go through with anything I'd resolved. You were chilly again, as though you'd intercepted my dream and were so horrified that you thought it best to put distance between us. I wonder if in the universe of sleep, dreams don't fly out and rat on one another's dreamers and hold cloak-and-dagger meetings in the side alleys of our nights where they slip coded messages, which is perhaps exactly what we want them to do for us when we lack the courage to speak for ourselves. Dreams inflect our face, our smile, and on our voice lingers the timbre of desire we weren't willing to hide while dreaming. I wished you'd taken a second look at me and said, *You dreamt of me last night, didn't you?*

When I saw you again the next morning, the element of surprise, which would have justified a seemingly spontaneous show of affection, was undercut by your immediate complaint about the poor maintenance of the courts. Then on Thursday you didn't show up at all. I'd have to wait forever, till Monday.

And yet the joy of having run into you in a dream was still not wearing off, nor could I hide that joy; it touched every hour of my days, so that what I grew to fear was not that you wouldn't turn out to be the person I met in a dream, but that the joy that came from the dream the moment you held my hand and said *Let's walk together* would, without warning, without my knowing it even, gradually and unavoidably evaporate. How to coddle it, how not to let it go . . .

Early Friday afternoon, I decided to head to the courts. It was an unusually warm day for early spring, and I wanted to put everything that had happened to me that day behind me and enjoy the weather. I had spare clothes in my locker and had no need to go home to change. Then, as I was entering the tennis house, there you were, Manfred. It was three o'clock in the afternoon, I almost never go to the courts at that time, and, as it

turned out, neither do you. You had left school early and hadn't
reserved a court. You asked me and Harlan if we could play doubles with you if you found a fourth partner. A fourth would be
easy to find, I said. As luck would have it, you spotted the elderly
gentleman who had once asked you to play but had never dared
ask again. He readily accepted and rushed to his locker to pick
up his racket. It was clear that you hate asking people for anything. You seemed so diffident and unsettled in asking me to
play with you that to put you at ease, and perhaps because Harlan was present when you asked, all I could do was raise my
palm and let it stay on your cheek and say it was perfectly okay,
really okay. You didn't shy away from the gesture, nor did you
lean into it. But you smiled and I smiled. We didn't say a word.

"This makes me very happy," I ended up saying. "We've
never played before."

"I know," you said, "me too."

Neither of us was quite sure what the other meant, but, as in
dreams, our words could be taken in so many ways, which was
fine too, because we liked thinking they had more than one
meaning, one obvious, one not so obvious, one hinted at but so
muddled that neither of us knew which to grasp, because each
was so laced into the others that all three ultimately meant one
and the same thing.

"Maybe we can grab that drink afterward," I said. Perhaps I
was pushing things.

"Oh, yes, *that* drink," you said, as though to show you hadn't
forgotten there'd been a vague allusion to a drink once and that
it hadn't escaped you at all. For a second I thought you were
making light either of the idea of a drink or of its coded meaning. Your empathic irony surprised me. Were you going to be
difficult before turning me down?

"But I'm buying," you said.

After tennis, we go to a bar on Columbus Avenue. It's four fifteen in the afternoon, the sun couldn't be brighter, we're sitting in our damp tennis clothes at a bar-café on the sidewalk. Our bare knees are touching, and neither you nor I is pulling back. We could make small talk. But I'm older, I cut to the chase.

"Tell me about your partner," I say. Something in the way you react to my words shows you want to pretend they come from out of the blue, but then you change your mind. Not the time for evasive maneuvers; our cards are on the table.

"There's nothing to tell."

"Nothing?"

"We've been together since college."

"But?"

"No buts. I know this may not be what you want to hear."

"So you've known. About me, I mean."

"I am not sure. But I think so."

How delicately you phrased this.

"And?"

"And nothing. I think about you." And then you added, "A lot, actually."

Yours, I realize, is the first real card on the table. I admire this. Mine had been just a joker.

I lower my right hand under the armrest of my chair and grasp your left hand, which is also dangling below your armrest. You didn't expect this, and I can sense that part of you wishes I hadn't done it. But I don't want to let go, not now.

"I'm living with someone too," I said. "But everything you've said, I could say too."

"So say it." This is how you fought back, something catty, touchy in your voice. I like it. Your hand relaxes and is actually holding mine. I am so, so glad I never let go.

"We've been together for almost a year," I say, "but it's you I think of—even when we're making love." Nothing will shut me up now. "Especially when we're making love."

"And?"

I grow silent.

"I want to know."

"And nothing. Do you really want the graphic details?"

"No," you say. "Actually, yes, I do."

I loved how you said this.

"I'm always thinking of you. Even when I'm not looking at you, I'm with you all the time. I know everything about you. I know where you live, where your parents lived in Germany, I even know what high school you attended in Virginia, I know your mother's maiden name. Want me to go on?"

"I could say the exact same thing about you."

"How so?"

"I know your tennis schedule, I know what train you take after tennis, I know where you live, I can go on and on. I know all about Maud too, she's also on Facebook."

I'll never forget the moment when it finally dawned on me that we are mirror images of each other. And yet . . . so many months, so much time wasted.

"What else do you know about me?" you asked.

"I know what clothes you wear, I know the color of every single tie you own, I know that you put on your socks after, not before, putting on your trousers, I even know that you occasionally use collar stays, that you button your shirt from the bottom up, and I know that I want to know you for the rest of my life. I want to see you naked every night. I want to watch you brush your teeth, watch you shave, I want to be the one to shave you when you don't want to shave, I want to be in the shower with you, I want to rub lotion on your knees, your arms, your inner thighs, your feet, your dainty little toes. I want to watch you read,

I want to read to you, I want to go to the movies with you, I want to cook with you and cuddle up and watch TV with you, and if you don't like chamber music, I'll drop my subscription and watch action films with you, if that's what you're into. I want to lie naked with you now. All I want is to be with you, to be like you—"

You did not let me finish. "I want to call you tonight."

Your words hit me in the gut. You could have said, *We're fucking tonight,* and it wouldn't have stunned me more.

"I'll put my phone on silent," I said.

"So will I."

As you withdrew your hand from mine, you let it rest on my knee.

"On second thought, I don't think I'll call you tonight," you said.

"Why?"

"Messy. I don't want anyone hurt."

A moment of silence threatens to erase everything that has just happened between us and seems to throw us back to where we'd been last week, last month, last year. I had to say something.

"I don't want this afternoon to turn into nothing," I said. "I don't want to lose you."

And as though this would prevent you from changing your mind, I took out my cell phone and showed you the picture of me as a twelve-year-old.

"This is who is speaking to you now. Earnest, horny, so scared."

You looked at the picture and nodded, and I know you understood that I was desperately trying to build the flimsiest pontoon bridge between us.

"Will you think of me tonight?" you asked.

I snickered to show there was no way that I wouldn't.

"Will you?" I asked.

"I don't know yet."

This threw me off.

"Just teasing, Pauly, just teasing. Tennis tomorrow?" you asked.

"It might rain," I replied.

"But you know I'll be here. You know I'll wait. And you know why."

"Why?"

"You already know why."

I couldn't resist. My hand touched your face, and better than in my dream, this time you didn't just smile, nor did you just lean into my palm. You cupped your hand over mine and let our hands rest there together.

"I have so much to say."

"Me too."

Once home, I go online to look for your picture again. I stare at your face. You are smiling, faintly, possibly at me. I want to close the page but I can't stop staring. All I want is to look at you, touch your face, I want this face to be in my house, my office, my life. I want it so much that I am suddenly gripped by the worst fear: tomorrow morning you won't show up. I'll be there, waiting, and you won't come. I'll wait for you, and keep waiting, even if you're two, three, four hours late, I'll wait in the afternoon and by evening still say I shouldn't stop waiting. I don't know why I'll wait or what I mistrust and fear so much.

All through dinner at Pamela's, I keep thinking of your voice and of how I'm never able to summon it in my mind. Everyone at the dinner table is talking, we drink too much, and as I keep rubbing the wristband of my watch under the table, I like to think that it's your wrist I'm holding, not mine, and if not your wrist under the table, then it's your hand gently cuffing my wrist, and the more I touch my wrist, the more I want to think it's your hand squeezing my cock. It makes me happy. And it makes me miserable. By the fourth glass of wine, I become aware of myself struggling not to tell everyone at the dinner table, *I'm luckier than all of you sitting here tonight, I'm in love, desperately in love, and this is total agony, and none of you is helping, because from the look on your faces, none of you knows a thing about love, and frankly, neither did I until now.* I keep quiet, but if you walked in on our meal like a resurrected Jesus and said, *Come, walk with me, Pauly,* I would stand up, drop my napkin on my chair, leave my wineglass still full, and make the most perfunctory apology to Maud and the other guests before being spirited away by you. If I have to pay with my life to hear you say, *Come, walk with me, Pauly,* I would do it.

But you do not appear. And however I squeeze your wrist, I cannot make you stay. My smile fades, I stop talking, and am Mr. Mirth-Palaver no more. And I am the most miserable man alive, and more so because no one at this dinner table has the slightest notion of what's tearing me up. And yet, what if each of us at this very table were a monsoon-ravaged island trying to look its best, with all of our coconut trees bending to the winds till hopelessness breaks their backs and you can hear each one crash and all their mealy, hardheaded coconuts pelt the ground, and still we'll keep our spirited good cheer and add a lilting sprint to our gait on the way to the office every morning, because we're each waiting for someone's voice to tear us out of our bleak and blistered lives and say, *Follow me, Brother. Follow me, Sister.*

I turn to my right and look at Pamela, and to my left at Nadja. Maud is speaking to the man at her right. Are they all looking for someone to take them away and save them from themselves?

And there is Duncan getting old, and there is Diego, and as always Claire, who never laughs at anything I say, who always looks as though she's struggling not to tell me what a dolt she really thinks I am—is Claire also waiting for someone to come into her life and say, *Follow me, Claire, just follow me?*

And suddenly I realize that you did ask me to follow you today and that you held my hand when I touched your cheek, and that what scares me more than going to the tennis courts tomorrow morning and not finding you is finding you waiting for no one but me, just me, Manfred. You'll be sitting under the canopy, holding your two rackets between your knees, and, seeing me, you'll say, *The courts are wet today, they said it might even snow tonight,* which is what I'd have said had I spoken first, and it would be my way, and possibly yours as well, of saying *We have the whole day to ourselves and the night too, come, live with me.*

STAR
LOVE

hadn't seen Chloe in ages. We met at a party on the Lower East Side and were the odd, unpaired two in a roomful of people who had all stayed in touch since college and whose toddlers were now starting to attend the same preschools. It was only a matter of time before we found each other. We joked a bit about ourselves—*Still unattached? Still unattached*—then we joked about some of the guests who hadn't changed—or, as she said, improved—since senior year, joked with an older couple who, seeing us chatting outside the master bedroom, asked whether the twins sleeping inside were ours, and finally found it strange that neither of us was eager to stay much longer at a party we'd both gone to for want of anything better that Friday night. All of it brisk and chipper talk that made you want to stick around and put an arm around her, which is why I waited for her and wouldn't leave until she did, but then stayed on till we closed down the party around two in the morning, which is also how I ended up walking her home six or seven blocks away. She said she couldn't believe she'd stayed so long. When I asked why she had, she looked at me with a *duh!* smile, meaning, *For the same reason you did.* I didn't argue or put up a front or try to come up with some far-fetched reason to pretend I didn't understand. She didn't press the point. All she asked when we reached her building and stood outside in the cold was how long would it take me to ask to come upstairs, because, in case I was wondering, the answer was yes.

Blunt, curt, and snappy, like the swat of a frisky cat.

She had barely opened the front door to her building when I put both palms to her face and kissed her. I had forgotten that this was the feel of her mouth, of her tongue, of her teeth. I remembered noticing her taut, dark lips and their surly upward curve, which always suggested ill temper in our college days but were now signs of a far tamer, less daunting woman. We kissed and undressed by a settee under the bay windows facing her empty, snow-decked street. She poured wine in two iridescent glasses that had belonged to her parents before they moved to Florida. A large black fan, sitting on the windowsill, kept staring at us like a baffled raven that had never seen two people tear off each other's clothes. "Look at me," she pleaded in bed. "Look me in my eyes and don't let go." At first, I didn't know what *Stay with me, just stay with me* meant, but she gasped these words with the bruised sensuality of a turtledove that wanted nothing more than to have its crown soothed, and soothed again with gentle, reassuring motions. "Yes, just keep looking at me like this, just like this, and look at me when you come, because I want to see it in your eyes," she said as her eyes bore into me with a gaze that told me sex without staring was as paltry as love without sorrow or pleasure without shame. I wanted to see it in her eyes as well, I said. I'd never been like this with anyone before.

Later that night I couldn't stop myself from asking how

she knew I'd been waiting to leave the party with her. "Simple," she replied, "because I kept hoping you would. You and I always thought on parallel tracks. Besides . . ."

"Besides?"

"Besides, it was written all over you," she added seconds later.

This is what I remembered liking about her: volleys of dark mischief, and always a suggestion of danger that was never quite unwelcome, plus the taunting put-downs that were instantly taken back and buffed with a hasty apology that won you over with what you'd been craving to hear, because she always spoke your thoughts as if she'd been reading them from inside your head. I liked her barbs that poked and didn't mince words and aimed straight for the bashful little truth she'd seen you hide and knew exactly where to find it when you claimed you couldn't remember, because this is where she'd have hidden it herself. In the end I had to tell her: "You know I was crazy about you senior year."

"Not true," she said.

"Why not?"

"I was."

"Now you tell me?"

"Now I tell you."

There it was again: the impish taunt laced with the hurt avowal from the girl who in college had always kept me on tenterhooks. Even her smile had troubled me in those years. It seemed a veiled come-on shadowed over by a snarky *Don't even think of it.*

That night the dream long given up years before was, like a borrowed book, finally being returned after sundry roundabouts and forwarding mishaps. Without knowing it, perhaps, we'd been waiting to turn back the clock.

We had a makeshift breakfast on an old dining table that had come from her parents' apartment in Peter Cooper Village, made love again, then without showering walked around the West Village and the Lower East Side until early Saturday evening. We spent two nights together, had coffee and pastries on MacDougal Street and dinner twice at a small place across from her home on Rivington called Bologna, where the waiter took a liking to us and gave us a second Chianti on the house. I reached out and held both her hands from across the table and said that this was worth the wait. Yes, it was, she said.

Then, without explanation, she failed to return my calls and disappeared.

"I moved on," she said when we met four years later at a party in the same apartment on the Lower East Side where we'd once again both drifted for want of anything better to do that night. Things turn sour, she said, they so often did with her, plus she hated the fallout, the postmortems, the rancid days when one or the other gets too close but the other doesn't.

How could she call them rancid when they had barely blossomed? It—*we*, she corrected—belonged to that one Friday night. Saturday was touch-and-go. Sunday was a mistake.

So, four years later she remembered to the day exactly what we'd done.

"But Friday night?" I asked, clearly wanting to hear more about that one night, because I knew she'd have something good to say that I wanted to hear repeated now.

She didn't need to search for an answer. "Friday night was meant to happen since freshman orientation week, if you care to know."

I did care to know, I said. I had no idea.

"You don't say!"

But the wave of irony in her voice, along with the implied

barb, flooded over me and told me that, for years now, she'd been holding a muted grudge or something bordering on the kind of bitter pardon that never finds peace and hardens into a bile stone.

"I wish I'd known," I said.

"You do now."

This was still bubbly party banter, and I could see she was already trying to untwist the knife she might have accidentally plunged in. I attempted a quick comeback in flip, lilting, chitchat mode, but there was nothing I could say to undo or at least recast the past. "Besides," she finally added, as though this justification might clear the air once and for all, "you yourself were already starting to backpedal that weekend. Perhaps we were both paying up long-overdue library fines."

"It wasn't a fine to me," I said.

"Well, not to me either. But I wasn't going to sit and wait for things to blow up in my face."

I gave her a startled look.

"You weren't exactly Mr. Available Forthcoming. You were growing moody and sullen. I can always tell when a man starts whiffling and waffling by Saturday afternoon and turns downright mopey and cries for space as if he'd timed out and violated undeclared furloughs. I'm sure part of you wasn't so sorry to see the thing go."

But then, in a move that still managed to catch me off guard, after turning the tables on me, she turned them on herself: "Maybe I wasn't doing it for you. Or wasn't what you expected, or wasn't enough. Or maybe you wanted someone else, something more. We weren't gelling. I've been there enough times to spot the obstacles ahead. As I said, we were terrific for a Friday night, no questions asked."

"Well, maybe Friday itself was a mistake," I said, eager to

drive my own nail into the coffin, since this is where she was headed.

"No, not a mistake at all," she corrected. "It just wasn't going anywhere. All we were doing was catching up."

"Perhaps there was nothing to catch up to."

"Maybe. Which explains why we always chickened out."

I looked at her and said nothing.

"We did," she repeated.

"*We* did?"

"Okay, I did," she corrected.

Like an old couple remembering their first dates to fan the embers of a dying fire, we were trying but failing to bring back the levity and the joy of finding each other again after so long.

I told her I remembered one night in particular.

"Which night was that?"

But I knew she remembered.

A day before Christmas break, senior year, as we were walking back from the library with loads of books each, she stopped, sat down on a freezing bench, and asked me to sit next to her. I had no idea what was on her mind but felt it had been waiting to happen a long time and finally it had come. I was nervous but I sat down. I remember her very words: "I want you to kiss me." She did not give me time to react or even to get ready but kissed me right on the mouth, her tongue already searching mine. And then she said it: "I want your spit." I kissed her as passionately as she kissed me, more passionately in the end, because I let myself go and didn't have time to think and was happy not to think. *She wants my spit*, I kept thinking.

I walked her to her dorm room, she opened the door, said her roommates were sleeping, and before I knew it we were once again kissing violently in the hallway. She had slept with everyone I knew yet had spent more time with me than with all of them put together. She did not let go of my hand and led me into her suite. I kissed her on the sofa and I was already putting my hand under her sweater and could smell the skin of her collarbone when, without warning, something changed. Maybe it was a light in the bathroom, or muffled laughter in her suite, or maybe I'd done something wrong, or had failed who knows what test, but I could tell she was tensing up. Then she said it: "Perhaps it might be better if you thought of leaving before they wake up"—as if what we were about to do might trouble either us or the others, asleep or not. But I said nothing. I walked out of her building and crossed the empty quadrangle all the way back to the library under the glittering Christmas lights on campus, trying but failing to understand what could possibly have made her change her mind so abruptly.

The next day we went our separate ways for Christmas break. A month later, when we came back, we were strangers. We avoided each other everywhere. It lasted another month. "You were so mopey in those days," she said.

Her taunt didn't bother me now. I liked being taunted. After years in the real world, I had shed some of my indecision, my fears, hurdles had come down, the risks not a worry—*if I get burned, I get burned.*

I didn't tell her that it had taken more than half a year to get over our two-night stint of four years earlier.

We exchanged e-mail addresses, both of us thoroughly aware that neither really meant to drop a line. But we weren't leaving the party yet. I ended up taking her home. Same six or seven blocks from the party, same cold entrance to her walk-up on a snowbanked Rivington, same hesitation at her stoop in the wee hours of the morning. What surprised me more than going through the motions of the last time was the unruffled ease with which one thing had led to another, as if my hesitation and hers were staged for the benefit of an observer who'd been dogging our footsteps to remind us that according to the old saying no sane person should presume to step into the same river twice.

Her place was the same. Same overheated studio, same scent of a hidden litter box, same clang of the front door that finally slams shut, same old wobbly black fan perched by her windowsill like a stuffed raven I'd once named Nevermore. When she saw me dawdling by her kitchen with my scarf and beanie still on, she said, "Stay tonight."

She made love the exact same way, told me how she kept hoping I'd stay late at the party but didn't want to show it in case I wasn't going to meet her halfway—which is what she'd more or less said on our first night together—and though I knew this would be over and done with by Saturday afternoon, I let myself go as I'd done the last time. "Look at me. Look at me, and talk to me, just talk, I beg you," she said, and everything I was and everything I had in me to give was already hers to take and stow away if she wished or to toss down the chute if she preferred. "I love how we make love together—you of every man I've known. I love what you love," she then said. And she loved the smell of me, and she wanted me like this every day and every night and every morning of her life, she said. I loved that she spoke to me this way when we made love; it made me speak like this as well. I stood, picked her up, sat her on the kitchen table—we were going to baptize the table, I said. You of every man I've known, she repeated.

After sex, I said, "This was fate."

"This was nice," she replied, putting things in perspective, meaning, *Let's not overdo it.*

Then realizing she might have snubbed me without meaning to, she added, "You haven't changed."

"You haven't either."

"Are you so sure?"

"Quite sure."

"I've been through a lot since the last time," she said as we snuggled naked on the same old love seat afterward. I liked how she called it *the last time*. "It doesn't show," I said. "Trust me, I have." Did this mean she was less likely to bolt, was more vulnerable, tamer, eager to stay close—had she been badly hurt?

Too many questions. She had a boyfriend, she said.

"Serious?"

"Enough."

I didn't bother to ask where that left us. There was no *us*. When I made a show of getting dressed the next morning, she said I didn't have to leave yet. The "yet," a Freudian slip almost, told me it was only a matter of time before she'd remind me it was indeed time.

Naked over breakfast, we talked. Yes, she still did yoga every morning. Yes, I still played tennis before work. No, I hadn't found anyone. Well, I haven't either, she said, now downplaying the boyfriend. Staring around the room, I told her I recognized her kitchen table. "You remembered," she said, surprised that this thing called time had happened to us after all. She came over to my corner of the table where I was eating an English muffin and, seeing me getting hard, lowered herself on my lap, facing me, her bare thighs now straddling mine. I loved how she did this. "I've always thought of us just like this, you, me, and an English muffin," she said. "Why?" I asked, not thinking that this was my turn to echo what she'd just said. "You make me like who I am and what I want." "Haven't others?" "Not like you." "Doesn't he?" "*Him?*" So she liked us? I finally asked. "Always have—skimpy, transient, scuttled us," she added. And there they were, her dark, bruise-colored lips, and there were her eyes that bore into me and made me want to rip myself open with a kitchen knife and put my heart on her parents' kitchen table for her to see how that little organ wobbled and jiggled when she spoke such intimate words to me. We were still naked, and speaking so honestly to each other aroused me, but neither of us was fooled by the passionate kissing or by what the rest of our bodies were doing. This was candid goodbye talk, and even as she grabbed my cock and lifted herself ever so slightly and slipped it inside her, I knew the meter was running. "Don't shut your eyes, please, don't shut your eyes. And hurt me if you want, I don't care, I don't care," she implored.

Later, after I got dressed, "Not going to be mopey, are you?" she asked as we began hugging at her door.

Wasn't going to be mopey, I replied.

I recognized the stairway. I remember thinking how everything between us was back to the same again, because spending the night together had neither changed nor settled a thing, and that, despite the years and lovers I'd known since college, I was no less vulnerable or any more toughened than I had been on that faraway winter night in February during senior year when we made up and ended up collapsing and sleeping on the same couch while staying up two straight nights translating Orwell into Greek on our joint senior thesis. Time, as far as we were concerned, had altered nothing.

When I reached her main door and stepped onto the sidewalk, the only thing that had changed was not heading straight to the bodega across the street to buy cigarettes. I had quit smoking again. She'd once complained that everything about me reeked of cigarettes. I wanted her to know that I had turned a new leaf and moved on. But I had forgotten to tell her; now there was no point.

We didn't see each other after that weekend. But our e-mails were incessant. I was trying to show I'd long learned to keep my distance—if that's what she wanted—that I would never intrude and would remain the sidelined friend who didn't need to pretend he was just a friend. It could morph into something more if she wanted, or it could as easily be taken down like unsold clothing from a store window heaped in a pile eventually shipped to discount outlets and hurricane survivors. Friendship on consignment, I called it. On spec, she retorted.

But on e-mail we were lovers, as though a fever coursed through our veins. As soon as I saw her name on my screen, I'd be unable to think of anything or anyone else. There was no use pretending I could wait. I would drop whatever I was doing, shut my door if I was at the office, muffle the rest of life around me, and think of her, just her, almost speaking her name, which sometimes I caught myself doing when one or two words would gush out of my mouth before I could stop them, words I would repeat verbatim to her on e-mail, hoping they'd fly to her screen and stir her like powerful newfangled meds that have an instant effect on one tiny chamber of the heart without affecting the other three. Ours were gasps, not e-mails. Words that thrilled me even more when I transcribed them from my body to my keyboard and that tore out of me like darts dipped in blood, semen, and wine. I wanted my words to erupt on her, the way hers did on me, like buried bombs detonated remotely when we were least guarded.

At home in the evening, I would reread her e-mails of the day, poring over her words until I was aroused, because part of what stirred me more than her words themselves was knowing that I'd have to disclose my arousal as it was happening in my gut and my groin. My mind would look for that string of words like a dog that sniffs for a bone and, when it finds it, or thinks it has found it, quivers with bliss, even when the bone has been inadvertently tossed. Simply thinking of her late on that Friday night after the party when she said she'd never forgotten what we liked in bed—*you of every man I've known*—would make me want to scream that nothing in my life meant more to me that minute than hearing her say *Look at me when you come.* I told her that this is what making love to her had meant to me: not that she knew me from inside my head and that being known this way was precisely what I found so arousing every time I thought of our bodies together, but that when we stared at each other in the way she wanted and had taught me to want, she and I were one life, one voice, one big, timeless something broken up into two meaningless parts called people. Two trees grafted into each other by nature, by longing, by time itself.

E-mail does this to people. We fess up more and censor less, because what we say is blurted out and doesn't really count, like steamy words uttered during sex, spoken with an open heart and a forked tongue. "You are my life," I finally wrote to her once.

"I know," she replied.

"Do you really?"

"I do. Why else do you think we keep writing all day?"

So I told her how the very thought of being Englishmuffined when she lowered herself on me at her parents' table made me so hard when I was alone at night.

An unknown serum coursed between us on the web. There was an *us* on e-mail.

But e-mail was also our nightmare. "I cannot keep writing," she said. "It ruins everything else I have."

And why should this hold me back? I thought. I wanted everything else in her life ruined. I wanted it soiled, damaged, dismembered. She resented when I crossed the line and spilled into her private life. I resented that she held off spilling into mine. Within minutes of intense arousal, a misplaced word or an inflection not quite aligned to the other would suddenly flare between us, undoing the spell. There'd be something like a tacit sneer in her words or derision in mine, neither of us able to contain our bile or quell the other's. It would take days to recover the tremulous stirrings of desire. "See, I'm being nice," she'd write, fully conscious of the fleeting irony in her words. I didn't like her tart or caustic tone. It killed the passion of the one night I did not want to forget.

Weeks later we made up. But there were bruises everywhere. We tried to feed the fire with humor, tried oblique passes and implied apologies, but we could tell the embers were dying. We'd been riding on auxiliary all this time, always catching up to something that had probably never even been there or was simply locked down in all but some mythical vault of our invention. This should have stopped weeks earlier, she wrote. This should never have started, I replied. It never did, she shot back. It never stood a chance, did it? Nope! Thought so.

In her mouth truth had no use for velvet sheathes. It spoke serrated daggers. I learned to speak serrated too.

After three such flare-ups, we stopped writing. Neither wished to resume the correspondence, and if we did, neither knew how to work around the unavoidable scuffles lying ahead. Apology felt paltry, candor perfunctory. We let go.

"I just knew I'd find you here," she said when we met four years later at a book party on Park Avenue. She seemed ecstatic to run into me, and seeing she wasn't hiding it, I showed it too. She was with her author. Where is he? I asked. She pointed to a man in his early forties who looked more like a film star. He was talking to three women. "Looks very dashing and unmopey to me," I said, throwing in the old word to show I hadn't forgotten.

"Yes, and vain, you won't believe," she retorted, sarcasm dripping from all her features. We were back to normal, as though we'd had breakfast that very morning and dinner the night before. This was a six-to-eight party. Was I staying till the very end? she asked. Only if she was. We chuckled. "Are you and he . . . ?" I didn't finish the question.

"You're out of your mind," she replied. All that remained was for her to lose her author by eight and she was good to go.

"Good writer?" I asked.

"Between us?"

That said it all. She was in top form, sparkling and more frisky than ever, and I loved it. I asked if that small place across from her house was still there.

"The Italian kitchen with the nice waiter?"

"Yes."

"Bologna."

Why did I pretend to forget the name?

"Yes, as far as I know." But she didn't live downtown any longer. Where was she living now? Off Lexington Avenue, she said, basically a few blocks away from the book party. Is there a good place around here for dinner? Was this my way of asking her out to dinner? Yes, it was, I replied. There were plenty. "But I can whip something up real fast." She'd received a case of great Bordeaux from her author. "So stick around." I stuck around.

The years hadn't changed us. We walked to her home. She managed to cook something fast, using, she said, an already opened bottle of the same red for the veal, which was a crime, she said. Then we sat on the very same couch. Sill the same cat. Still the same wineglasses, still the same table she'd inherited from her parents. In Peter Cooper Village, right? I asked. In Peter Cooper Village, she repeated, to show she remembered that I remembered and was no longer impressed. Had anyone died? What a question! No, no one had died. What about the big black fan that looked like an indignant raven caught, scraped, and stuffed without ever having quite died? He had to go. And the latest boyfriend—*boyfriendz?* I corrected. None worth mentioning. What else was new? I asked. She smiled, I smiled. "Between us, you mean?" How I loved the way she zeroed in on the unspoken drift in what I didn't always dare to say. "I'm still the same—and you?" she asked, as if referring to an old acquaintance she wasn't sure I remembered. "Haven't changed one bit," I replied, "never have, never will." "Thought so," she said. "And I didn't mean my looks." "I know what you meant." Our awkward, tentative smiles spoke the rest. She was standing holding a wineglass by the kitchen door. Eventually I caved in, I wanted to cave in right away. It gave me an erotic, almost indecent, premature thrill to kiss her now without waiting for the perfect moment. She kissed me as passionately. Perhaps because it was easier to kiss than to speak. I wanted to say I'd been waiting years for this, that I couldn't hold out another four if this was to be our last time. We were too happy to speak.

Two days. Then we argued. I wanted to go to the movies on Saturday night; she preferred Sunday afternoon. Theaters were too crowded on Saturdays, she said. But that's why I liked theaters on Saturday nights. I liked a crowd. Sunday afternoons were depressing. Besides, I hated stepping out of the theater into an overcast twilit Sunday lurching to its unavoidable death. Neither of us budged. It would have been so easy to give in, but we didn't, and the more we dug in our heels, the more difficult was yielding. To prove my point that night, I went to the movies alone, then headed back to my place and didn't call her. The next day, she went to see the same film and didn't call me. Our hasty explanations by e-mail Monday morning lasted no more than two minutes. Then e-mail blackout.

When we spoke again, neither remembered which movie we'd argued about on that faraway weekend of four years earlier. We laughed. Obviously we had issues, I said, trying to gloss over the episode and make light of how absurdly we'd behaved—*I behaved*, I corrected. She could think of better words than "issues." Stupidity? Definitely. Yours or mine? I asked, once again trying to spin mischief into our conversation all the while allowing her to fire the first shot. "Yours, of course." Then, having scored, "But maybe mine as well," she said. Or just our usual tiff in a teapot.

The room in the Upper West Side apartment thronged with people and was extremely loud. She wanted to introduce me to her husband, who was in another, equally crowded room. You? she asked, clearly meaning had I come with someone? I was with Manfred. He's here too? She smiled, I smiled back. Then we looked at each other and, because of the polite silence hovering between us, we burst out laughing. It wasn't life with Manfred that made us laugh, though maybe laughter was as good a way as any of putting the subject on the table. We laughed because it was instantly obvious that each of us had been keeping distant tabs on the other's life. I knew about her husband, she knew about Manfred. Maybe we laughed simply because of the ease with which we could now be on such good terms tonight after the way we'd parted the last time. "I knew I'd find you here," she said.

"How?"

"I had them invite you."

We laughed.

"But then you probably figured I was behind the invitation, which is why you came."

She was in my head again, and I loved it.

"How is it?" she finally asked. I knew exactly what she meant. But seeing I was apparently drawing a blank, she added, "I mean with Manfred." "Ordinary. Domestic. Sundays, we fold the laun-dry," I said. "And your husband?" I asked as we threaded our way through the crowd. "The type I always end up with: bigheaded, blustery, and when we're alone together insufferably mopey. All men are mopey, I've decided, or didn't you know?"

"I was always mopey. Since senior year," I said, trying to blunt her barb.

"Since forever," she corrected.

"Actually, he's too macho to be mopey in public." She looked in the direction of her husband. "It hasn't been easy," she finally said. I could sense something unsettling coming.

"You didn't ask," she said, as though uncertain how to proceed.

"But—?" I threw in, urging her on with the obviously miss-ing word.

"But I'll tell you all the same, because you're the only one on this fucking planet who'll understand. I may love him. But I've never been in love with him, not once, not ever."

"So you have the perfect marriage," I said. It was meant to keep things light and flippant. Perhaps because I didn't wish to hear more, or didn't want her prodding into my own life to pull the rug from under it as well. But she ignored my comment.

"Don't be cruel," she snapped. "I'm telling you this because you and I are the exact opposite. We'll stay in love until every-thing about us rots, down to our teeth, our fingernails, our hair. Which means nothing, of course, since we couldn't survive a weekend together."

"And you're telling me this because . . . ?"

She stared at me starkly as if she couldn't believe I hadn't guessed already.

"Because I'm always thinking of you. Because I think of you

every day, all the time. As I know you think of me every day, all the time. Don't bother denying it. I just know. Which is why I'm so happy to find you here tonight. Maybe because I needed to see you again and just spill it all out for once. And the irony is"—she caught her breath—"there's nothing either I or you can do about it. So there. And please don't pretend you're any different—with or without *your* Manfred."

I didn't know that this was how she felt about me or about her husband or, for that matter, about poor Manfred whom she'd just cut down with a blunt *your*. But at the book party, with all the noise and the speechifying and the brouhaha over the rave review in the coming Sunday paper, all I wanted was to leave the apartment, race downstairs, and stand outside on the curb with the cold wind fanning my face and drown everything she'd just told me.

She was right. We'd always been in love, she and I. But what had we done with our love? Nothing. Perhaps because the model for such love didn't exist, and neither of us had either the faith, the courage, or the will to come up with one. We loved without conviction, without purpose, without tomorrow. On spec, as she'd said once.

Faking love was easy enough; thinking I wasn't faking, easier yet. But neither she nor I was fooled. So we bickered with our love the way we bickered with each other—but at what cost? I couldn't undo or tear it out, but by dint of swatting it down like an insect that wouldn't die, I could harm it, damage it, till whatever there was between us had all but addled. Nothing killed it. But was it ever alive? And when you looked up close, was ours even love? And if not love, then what? Broken, battered, blighted, wasted love shuddering in a cold alley like an injured pet that had lost its owner and scarcely survived a run-in with a bad dog, was this really love?—without heart, without kindness, without

charity, without love, even. Our love was like stagnant water
behind locked sluices. Nothing lived in it.

In the crowded room with the view of the Hudson, the realiza-
tion that ours was a stillborn love began to cramp something in
me. It wasn't going to kill me, but I wanted to find a corner somewhere in this large apartment where I could be alone and hate
myself. I tried to open one of the windows, but it was painted
shut. Typical, I thought, casting a blistering verdict on people
who never let a gust of fresh air into their homes.

"This is Eric, my husband," she said.

We shook hands.

"Great speech," I said.

"Did you really think so?"

"Terrific!"

More party talk.

When the party was over and everyone else had left, the four
of us thanked the host and, on impulse, decided to have dinner
together. We had no reservations, and after a few hurried phone
calls in the cold, Manfred eventually found a table at a small place
in TriBeCa. We hailed a cab, the husband gallantly offering to
sit in front next to the driver while the three of us snuggled tightly
in the back, with me cramped in the middle. As we raced down
the West Side Highway, I remember thinking, *I could hold both
their hands*, I could hold his hand and I could hold her hand, and
neither might care what I did with the other's so long as I didn't
let go. She must have felt something very similar, for she rested
a docile, inattentive open palm on her knee in a manner so trusting and acquiescent that it was almost asking me to do something with it, which is why I couldn't help but reach out to her
gloved hand and press it in mine before releasing it. The letting
go of it so soon was meant to suggest friendship, only friendship,
but it wasn't friendship only, and seeing that the hand was lying

still on her thigh where I'd just left it, I reached out for it again and slipped my fingers between hers. She seemed grateful and returned the pressure. Manfred's face wasn't moving at all, which told me he had seen and was trying to show that he hadn't. I reached for his hand, he let me hold it. He was humoring me. He'd heard about her many times and was probably struggling not to let it faze him.

As soon as we were seated in the restaurant, we ordered a bottle of red wine. It arrived with chunks of Parmesan cheese— old-world style. I could live off just these two, she said, meaning wine and cheese. And bread, I said. And bread of course. We complained about the weather. Plans for the summer? Manfred asked. They liked to travel. As far as possible, explained the husband. We preferred the Cape. They had a two-year-old daughter. We had cats. We had talked of adoption, and an old girlfriend had even offered. But in the end cats were easier. We liked action movies and TV series from Scandinavia. They liked to play Scrabble.

"You really want to know?" she said when I finally asked how life was with a child. Her worst time of the day was winter afternoons at the office on the forty-seventh floor, when the world started closing in on you with one crisis after another, plus, of course, panicked phone calls from her babysitter and, let's not forget, her aging parents in Florida. You stop belonging to yourself, she said. "I belong to my child, my husband, my home, my work, my babysitter, my cleaning lady. The time that remains, like after-tax dollars, doesn't last longer than a two-minute sonata by Scarlatti."

"And you don't even like Scarlatti," I said.

"How did you know?" she asked.

I remembered.

"At night, I don't fall asleep. I crash," she added, capping her complaints with a smile. "It would never have occurred to me when we were back in college spending all those nights translating *Animal Farm* into ancient Greek for Ole Brit that I'd hear myself whining like this." She was toying with a long bread stick but wasn't eating it.

"How do you two know each other?" her husband interrupted. It was his way of breaking the silence but also of deflecting the sudden melancholic drift in his wife's speech. His question told me that she had either never mentioned me or that he had never paid attention. "We meet every four years," I said. "Bissextilely," she added. But then, not knowing whether Manfred might take the word the wrong way, I could see her trying to backpedal. "Every four years," she repeated. I liked how she'd done this. "We exchange notes, catch up, argue," she continued, injecting a touch of levity in the word "argue" to blot out its more somber implication. Then we disappear, I added. But never a hard feeling, she said. No, never a hard feeling. "These two!" exclaimed Manfred. "They've known each other for ages," he added to sum up and move things along. Her husband couldn't resist quoting Hartley: "The past is a foreign country; they do things differently there." It was his little dig and postscript to our brief exchange. Either he had guessed everything or figured there was nothing worth guessing.

But his words summarized everything about us. "Yes, the past is a foreign country," I said, "but some of us are full-fledged citizens, others occasional tourists, and some floating itinerants, itching to get out yet always aching to return.

"There's a life that takes place in ordinary time," I said, "and another that bursts in but just as suddenly fizzles out. And then there's the life we may never reach but that could so easily be ours if only we knew how to find it. It doesn't necessarily happen on our planet, but is just as real as the one we live by—call it our 'star life.' Nietzsche wrote that estranged friends may become declared enemies but in some mysterious way continue to remain friends, though on a totally different sphere. He called these 'star friendships.'"

I regretted this as soon as I'd spoken.

Chloe immediately seized on my unintended reference to our own friendship, and so tried to divert the subject by saying that Nietzsche had written this in *The Gay Science*. But fearing that Manfred might once again take this the wrong way, she quickly reminded everyone that she had not only bought me the book but forced me to read it. When? I asked, pretending to have forgotten. Senior year, for Christ's sake.

We each gave the short version of our college days. Husband and Manfred had great memories. I offered a lapidary sketch. Then, because she had brought up Ole Brit, we ended up talking about the course. "Our senior seminars on Tuesday evenings in the winter with the twelve of us—*his disciples,* as he'd call us—were unforgettable," she said. "We sat cross-legged around his coffee table on his Persian rug, sipping his wife's mulled cider, some of us smoking, I forever chewing on a cinnamon stick, and good Ole Brit—whose real name was Rault Wilkinson—declaiming, or rather, conducting his words with the point of his curved pipe in his left hand." "Magical hours," I said. "Totally," she agreed.

"I learned to love commas from the rise and fall of his voice," I said. "Unforgettable voice when he read aloud to us. Four years of college and the very best I took with me was a love for commas."

I knew she'd agree about the commas. I had heard her say this years ago and was repeating it to her now, hoping it might draw us closer in case she forgot it was really her observation. I wanted her to miss those days with me, wanted her to think, *He always thinks as I do, he's never stopped loving me.*

Then I told them about one night years ago when we'd been discussing *Ethan Frome*, and after passing around the two pumpkin pies his wife had cut up in large wedges with a generous helping of crème anglaise on each, Ole Brit finally spoke about the author herself and said the book was started not in English but in French. Did any of us know why? he had asked. No one knew why. Because she wanted to master French, he explained. She was living in Paris at the time and had hired a young tutor. We still have his markings on the pages. So here she was, he said, writing a courtly, seventeenth-century French tale peopled with rugged, tobacco-chewing lumberjack types who are forever browbeaten by their wives and sledding away to their local saloon to drown their torment in rye and beef jerky.

"I forget the plot," I said, but I remembered the snow and I remembered the tremulous love of Ethan and Mattie as they sat at the kitchen table nervously struggling to avoid touching hands. I particularly remembered the golden bowl.

"You mean the pickle dish," her husband corrected.

I thanked him. "Edith Wharton," I continued, "had lived in New England a great portion of her life and yet suddenly, because of an affair with someone who was not her husband, at the age of forty-six she penned these nine words in her diary: *l have drunk the wine of life at last.* Ole Brit loved that sentence. 'Think of the courage it takes to say such a thing to yourself at an age when most people have long drunk and sobered up from the wine of life. And think of the despair in her last two words—*at last*—as though she had all but given up and was ever grateful to this man who appeared in her life in the nick of time.'

"After mulling over his own words, Ole Brit asked how many of us had actually drunk from the wine of life.

"Most in that room raised their hands, thoroughly persuaded they'd experienced life-changing bliss. Only two failed to raise their hands."

"Me and you," she said, after a moment of silence, as though that said it all, had always said it all. Silence hovered over our table.

"Actually, a third hand didn't go up that evening," I finally said.

"I don't remember a third hand."

"Ole Brit himself. Happily married, father, venerated dean, scholar, writer, wealthy world traveler—and there he was, not raising his hand either, yet not unwilling to let us see that he hadn't, all the while pretending to be busy replenishing his pipe so as not to seem too obvious in abstaining from the count of hands. It struck me. It made me think that he was living the wrong life, not his own. I saw a man crushed by one big, undying string of regrets. All the honors in the world, but not the wine. I felt sorry for him. He was, we sort of gathered from a remark he'd once borrowed from Lawrence Durrell, 'wounded in his sex.' We all fell in love with the expression, because it meant everything and nothing. *I can't on Thursday, because I'm wounded in my sex. Margaret finally realized she'd been wounded in her sex. The report from the committee members wounded him in his sex. I couldn't hand in my paper on time 'cause I was wounded in my sex.*

"One night the lights in his house went out. They frequently did on stormy nights, and they would go out everywhere in our college town. It was very spooky but also amazingly snug. We drew closer and bonded better in the dark. Even with the lights out, we continued to talk, some as always seated on the rug, others on two sofas, he with his pipe in his armchair. We loved his voice in the dark. Soon after the lamp failed, his wife walked in with an old kerosene light. 'I looked but we had no candles,' she apologized. He thanked her, as he always did, very sweetly. In the end, one of the girls in our group couldn't help it. 'You have the perfect life,' she said, 'perfect house, perfect wife, perfect family, perfect job, perfect children.' I don't know how, but without hesitating he trounced the remark: 'Learn to see what's not always there to be seen and maybe then you'll become someone.' That sentence stayed with me forever.

"Three years later, I came back and lived in their house for around ten days. I wasn't a student, but it was easy to slip back into the old mold, sit in on his evening seminar with a new cohort of *disciples*, leaf through the same books again, then, when everyone had left, help him clear the dishes and stack them in the dishwasher. It wasn't long afterward, while I was helping him dry the glasses, that he confided his name was not Rault Wilkinson at all, but Raúl Rubinstayn. Despite his Oxonian credentials, he wasn't even a Brit. Born in Czernowitz and raised in, of all places, Peru."

"Is he still alive?" the husband asked, interrupting my short idyll.

"He is," I replied. "What was strange that night is that after discussing *Ethan Frome* as he'd done three years earlier with us, he raised the same question about the wine of life. This time only two hands did not go up. And then I knew, I just knew. And when he shot me a quick glance, he knew that I knew.

"We joked about the wine of life as we were drinking wine after his seminar. 'It doesn't exist,' he finally said. 'I'm not sure it doesn't,' I replied, trying not to disagree with him. 'You're still young. And because you're young, you may be the one who's right.' It occurred to me then that he, past his fifties, was perhaps younger than I was."

No one said anything, perhaps I had bored them going on about my college days. In the silence of the moment, I thought back to that winter when I stepped out of Ole Brit's house by my-self one night and remembered how Chloe and I used to cross the quadrangle together and count its nine lampposts, naming each after one of the nine Muses as a joke, using the mnemonic TUM PECCET. Thalia, Urania, Melpomene, Polyhymnia, Erato, Clio, Calliope, Euterpe, Terpsichore. His courses had defined our lives that year, as though his dimly lit living room in that large house on the sloping road off the quadrangle could shut out the real world and open up quite another. Suddenly, every-thing seemed lodged in the past, and I missed those days.

I remembered another evening, when I caught him standing outside on the porch staring out at the deserted quadrangle. It had just snowed and the place couldn't have looked more peace-ful or more timeless. I told him not to worry and promised I'd shovel the snow in the morning. "It's not that," he said. I knew it wasn't. He put his arm on my shoulder, which he never did, because he wasn't the touchy-feely sort. "I'm looking at all this and I'm thinking that one day I won't be here to see it and I know I'll miss it, even if I won't have a heartbeat to miss anything. I miss it now for the-days-when, the way I miss places I've never traveled to or things I've never done." "What things that you've never done?" "You're young and you're very handsome—how could you possibly understand?" He removed his arm. He lived in a future that wouldn't be his to live in and longed for a past that hadn't been his either. There was no turning back and no going forward. I felt for him.

The past may or may not be a foreign country. It may morph or lie still, but its capital is always Regret, and what flushes through it is the grand canal of unfledged desires that feed into an archipelago of tiny might-have-beens that never really hap-pened but aren't unreal for not happening and might still happen

though we fear they never will. And I thought of Ole Brit holding back so much, as we all do when we look back to see that
the roads we've left behind or not taken have all but vanished.
Regret is how we hope to back into our real lives once we find
the will, the blind drive and courage, to trade in the life we're
given for the life that bears our name and ours only. Regret is
how we look forward to things we've long lost yet never really
had. Regret is hope without conviction, I said. We're torn between
regret, which is the price to pay for things not done, and remorse, which is the cost for having done them. Between one and
the other, time plays all its cozy little tricks.

"The Greeks never had a god for regret," came the husband's
peremptory remark, either to show off or to sidetrack a conversation that was clearly not just about Ole Brit.

"The Greeks were brilliant. They used one word both for
regret and remorse. As did Machiavelli."

"My point exactly."

I didn't know what was his *point exactly*, but he seemed fond
of having the last word.

When we left the restaurant, she and I walked ahead together, while Manfred and her husband followed. "But are you
happy?" I asked. She shrugged her shoulders—either to mean
that the question was moot or that she didn't even know what the
word meant, didn't care, didn't want to go there. Happiness, *qu'est-
ce que c'est*? How about you, though? she asked. Her spontaneous
"though" told me she was expecting a completely different report.
But I shrugged my shoulders as well, perhaps to echo her own
gesture and leave it at that. "Happiness is a foreign country." I was
making fun of hubby, which I could tell didn't displease her.
"With Manfred there's lots of goodwill, and never a word out of
turn, but as for the thing itself—" I shook my head, meaning

Don't get me started. "Can I call you?" she said. I looked at her. "Yes." But even I could hear the tired, humbled, vanquished inflection in our voices, both when she asked and when I answered. I regretted it as soon as I heard it and once again tried to whip up the buoyancy of dinner talk. Perhaps I was trying to affect the tenor of those who have apathy in their hearts but feign not wanting to show it. Or perhaps I was trying to show how much I wished she'd call. I felt the cold, and I could feel myself shivering. But it wasn't from cold.

I just wished the two of us could stay together this way and weren't about to say goodbye, that saying goodbye was still twenty, thirty blocks, thirty minutes, thirty years away. When it came time to part at the street corner, I caught myself saying, "This is unusual." "What's unusual?" asked the husband. "Yes, very unusual," she echoed. We didn't bother to explain, because neither of us was entirely sure the other had caught the drift. Then we all shook hands. His handshake was firm. We promised to have dinner again soon. "Yes," he said, "real soon." We walked away. Manfred put his arm around me, saying, *"Courage."*

She called me not the following week, not even the next day, but later that same night. Could I talk? Yes, I could talk. My voice was once again bruised and beaten, as if I'd uttered a listless *It's your quarter.*

"I wish it were you."

What on earth did she mean?

"You know exactly."

What?

"I told you already! I wish it were you *instead.*" She sounded angry at me—for not getting it right away, for making her say it.

Like someone roused from a very deep sleep by a sudden demolition blast, I needed to make sure I'd heard right, needed a few moments to pull my thoughts together.

"What—have I upset you that much?" she finally asked, angry again.

"Yes."

It was her turn to be taken aback.

"Why should you be upset?"

I didn't know why I was upset. "Because my heart is racing right now and it's been so long. All those years, and it won't go away," I said. Her words about loving someone without being in love with him were coming back to me. I felt their lure in my body. I just loved her, I loved her with heartbreak and resentment, because we'd wasted so many years, because there is no love without desire, diffidence, defeat. And the more I thought about it, the more it tore me up. We've misspent years of our lives, I wanted to say. And then I said it. "We've misspent our lives—we're both living the wrong life, you and I. Everything about us is wrong."

"Not fair. We were never wrong. You and I are the only thing right in our lives—it's everything else that's wrong."

I didn't know what had come over me or what all this was leading up to, but I was floored by a tsunami of sorrow I hadn't felt since childhood, when sorrow seemed so immediate, so overwhelming, that without even the merest warning from my body, I caught myself sobbing, or at least trying not to sob so Manfred wouldn't hear. "It's been such a long time and—" I was fumbling for words, struggling with the tightness in my throat, not knowing whether I was speaking to her or to myself.

"Say it—go ahead, whatever it is, say it." What she really meant was, *Cry if it helps—it might help us both.*

But I took her at her word. "No, you say it for me," which also meant *You cry first,* which was another way of saying *I'll take sympathy, compassion, even friendship, just don't go away again, don't go away.*

I had never been this honest with anyone before, which is why I felt I might be dissembling even as I was sobbing, because thinking I was dissembling was the only way left to dodge the overpowering wave of sorrow that had just hit me. Perhaps in this, finally, lay the leanest proof of love: the hope, the belief, the conviction that she knew more about me than I did myself, that she, not I, held the key to everything I felt. I didn't need to know anything; she'd be the one to know. "You say it for me," I said. I had nothing else to add.

She thought awhile.

"I can't do this," she broke in.

"And I can? What's wrong with us?"

"I don't know."

"Are we going to hide for another four years now until the next party—is that it?"

She hesitated. "I don't know."

"Why did you call me, then?"

"Because I couldn't stand the way we said goodbye. We keep meeting at these parties but are less together when we meet than when we've forgotten who the other is. One day I'll die and you won't even know it—and then what?"

That choked me, and it took me a moment to recover.

"I can't live with who I become each time we split," I said. "Right now I dread the thought of who I'll be when this phone call ends. And," I added with a forced giggle in my voice, "I can't believe I'm crying now. I need to see you."

"This is why I called."

We arranged to meet sometime the following week.

A few hours later, "Sorry, can't do it," she texted when I sent her an e-mail suggesting a time and place.

"Can't do it next week," I texted back, "or can't do it *ever*?"

"Ever!"

Perhaps I had given her an excuse she didn't even know she was looking for.

I didn't reply. By now she'd know. Part of me wished she'd follow up with a text asking if I'd received her text. But we both knew the other knew this game.

I was right about one thing. After receiving her text I felt rotten all day Saturday. This was the only word that made sense. *Rotten.* I had gone to bed thrilled, had tried to seek ways to dampen my excitement with all manner of mental tricks, if only to think I wasn't being carried away and wouldn't get hurt in the event she canceled. I'd even thought of Manfred. In his arms, I might put off thinking of her, or even shut the door on her, or leave it marginally ajar, because I'd always left my doors ajar in life, which is what she and I had always feared from each other: that one was no sooner in the room than the other was already headed out. In midsleep I began to think of margins and sidelines, wondering whether she'd always be moored to the margins of my life without being part of it, that my life was filled with marginal beings who sit and wait like vacant ships on abandoned wharves. Then I realized that that the metaphor was all wrong, and that I myself was nothing more than a collection of marginal selves who sit out their time like unpaid stevedores on an unfinished pier where no boats ever dock. I was unfinished. I wasn't even born yet but had already misspent my time. I was no better than a collection of incipient beings lined up like nine milk bottles in a carnival booth.

That night, feeling Manfred's body against mine, I dreamt I was holding her and pressed myself against him. "Don't stop," he said, which is when I awoke but continued what I'd started so he wouldn't know. And he found joy with me in midsleep and spoke his love when he turned around and held my face and kissed me.

Her text buzzed me awake the next morning.

I spent that whole Saturday in a sort of stupor. I was grateful to Manfred for not saying anything about last night's dinner. At lunchtime, in my study, he brought me a plate with a ham-and-cheese sandwich and a handful of potato chips. Did I want iced tea or a Diet Coke? A Diet Coke, I replied. A Diet Coke it is, he said as he stepped out of the room, shutting the door behind him ever so quietly. He knew.

When he returned, he asked if I wanted a back rub. No, I was fine. "Then let's go to the movies tonight, it'll change you." So we went to the movies that night. It was another Danish film. Afterward, we took a walk around the area in front of Lincoln Center. I had always liked the place at night, especially when it is filled with people doing exactly what we were doing, mostly nothing, looking for a place to have a late bite, a drink perhaps, hope to bump into people we knew, no matter who. I didn't want to go home, but I knew that if we walked around the neighborhood, we'd end up running into the two of them. I just knew. Life works that way. I said I was tired and we hopped on a bus.

A few years before I had desperately longed to go to the movies with him on a Saturday night. If we cannot sleep together, I used to think, then I'll settle for a movie on a Saturday night. Dinner, drinks, movies. I wanted to hold his hand in the movie theater. Better yet, I wanted to be seen with him. I couldn't explain why wanting to be seen with him meant so much to me, but I knew it made me want him all the more. Now, outside the theater, I dreaded running into the two of them.

As I looked around the square before boarding the bus, I remembered planning in my own mind a late lunch with her. Then, since neither of us knew of a place to go, we were probably going to do the obvious, tacky thing, which I'd never done in my life: rent a hotel room. I had already thought of a hotel, which happened to be close to tonight's theater. Yes, a late lunch, hotel, and sex. Champagne? Champagne, before or after? Let's not get ahead of ourselves, I thought, injecting a dose of sobering realism to our fantasy date. I saw the two of us, the jack of hearts and the queen of spades, sitting on the edge of our bed, putting our shoes back on, talking once again of our defunctive love.

But now, facing that very hotel with Manfred, I felt rotten for another reason. Worse than being disappointed by how the day had turned out, and worse yet than hurting Manfred, I was disappointed in myself, in the person I'd always been and might never change. It shamed me, because despite aching for her and thinking back on her thighs when years ago she'd sat naked on my lap at her parents' table and asked me to look straight in her eyes and not let go of her, I saw something bleak and ugly in myself that I'd been begging for all night but then was sorry to see granted and clumsily gift wrapped. Relief. And with relief, its terrible partner, indifference, which is the impulse to let go before we've even begun reaching for what we crave.

Her surly *Ever!* had relieved me. I wouldn't have to plan anything, or test the passion, wouldn't even need to hide our meeting or where I'd been that afternoon. The hotel, the champagne, the clothes we were putting back on, the lies on being asked and forced to explain—thank God! Perhaps I didn't even want to sleep with her. Any more than she did with me.

This was all in the head. And that's where it stays.

MONTHS LATER I went to see a doctor after experiencing a persistent pain in my shoulder. I was sure it was acute bursitis brought on by a bad move I'd made playing tennis. But after two visits I was told that perhaps a CAT scan was in order—just to make sure, added the doctor in that typically hurried, offhand manner with which doctors brush off the merest inflection of alarm. "How much time?" I asked after a short pause, to show I was cutting to the chase. "We're not there," he said. But I could tell, even before he'd asked me to take a seat, that he was once again trying to skirt the subject.

My mind was spinning out of control. If I had a tumor, then I'd be dead before the year was out, and if I were dead, then there'd be nothing left, no second chances, no leap-year parties, and all this waiting for the right time would have been for nothing. I will die having lived the wrong life. No, not lived: waited. Two weeks later the diagnosis dispelled my fears. Bursitis.

Part of me was convinced that my brush with death had taught me a lesson. Time to act.

So, scarcely an hour after discovering that I wasn't dying, I did something I'd never done before. I called her. I had rehearsed everything I was going to say: lunch, just a quiet, ordinary, un-encumbered lunch somewhere—I knew of a good place—no, nothing like that!—she'd be back at the office for all the afternoon meetings she complained so much about. And if she asked why now, I'd simply say because something almost happened, but then didn't, and I wanted to tell her about it. Instead, when she grabbed her phone at the office after the first ring, I felt I had caught her at the worst possible moment and found myself asking if she could spare a sec. "Of course," she said, "but I'm really out the door to a meeting." When I said I'd call her another time, she said, "No, tell me right away."

I liked that she wanted it now and didn't want to wait. In her place, I'd have done the same. But the haste in her voice threw me off and made me forget the tepid little speech I'd been rehearsing about our lunch in some snug little corner bistro somewhere. Instead, I heard myself saying something totally different: "I need to see you now."

And suddenly, I knew that if I met any resistance or hostility, I'd lie and say that I had just come from the doctor's office with terrible news and that she needed to hear me now.

She must have picked up the remnants of urgency in my voice.

"Where are you?"

"I'm walking."

"Yes, but where?"

"I'm on Madison."

"Madison and what?"

"Sixty-third."

I named a store I had just passed.

I heard her holler at one of her assistants to get her a car *as in now!*

"Stay where you are. Don't move," she cried.

Without meaning to, I had spoken on two registers, as if the thought of dying, which two hours earlier had made me look back on my life and find desiccated craters everywhere, hadn't been dispelled yet and spurred the urgency in my call.

Less than ten minutes later she was getting out of a black SUV.

"Let's eat, I'm famished. But so we're clear . . . what's all this about?"

We entered Renzo & Lucia's. They sat us at one of the tables on the sidewalk that was bathed in glorious early midafternoon sun. The two tables next to ours were empty, and the sun-basked sidewalk was unusually quiet.

"Why?" she asked.

I knew exactly what she meant.

"Because until a few hours ago I thought I had two months to live."

"And?"

"And nothing. False alarm. But it made me think."

"I'm sure it did," she said, trying to throw in her usual dose of sarcasm.

"What I meant was, it made me think of you."

"Why me?"

"Not to sound presumptuous, but I kept wondering what would happen to you when I was gone."

She hadn't expected this at all. Her chin began to quiver. Her eyes glistened.

"If you die before me?"

I nodded.

"If you die, there'll be nothing left, nothing at all. But you know this."

She was silent.

"If you're not there, it would be as if a huge zero suddenly fell on top of me."

"But we're never even there for each other."

"Means nothing. You're always there."

A moment later: "And what if I should die?" she asked.

"If you die there'll be nothing too, just nothing."

"Even if we almost never see each other?"

"As you said, makes no difference. Now we know."

"Now we know." Looking down to avoid her eyes, I began fondling the hexagonal salt and pepper shakers and bringing them close together so that the two were touching head to toe. *This is me and this is you*, I wanted to say. *Look how we fit together*, I kept thinking, watching how the bevels of the two glass shakers seemed perfectly aligned. "You're the closest I've ever been to anyone," I said.

She looked at the shakers with something verging on sorrow and compassion for their sad, ill-fated love. At the end of each day, they either fall and shatter or are taken away and paired with another, and then another, and another, and it doesn't matter whether it's a salt or a pepper shaker, because all they are in the end are fungible little vials with holes in their heads.

Once again, she cast a silent gaze at me.

"So what now?"

She seemed as helpless as I was. We had said everything and yet we had said nothing. I wanted to reach out and touch her face, but this felt out of place. I had stopped trusting my impulses. How would we ever bring ourselves to make love again, I thought, if we can speak of our love only by oblique reference to death? We can't even look each other in the eye, much less get naked. What had happened to us? Years ago we sat naked having breakfast, and in the middle of it all, I was hard and she lowered herself on me and Englishmuffined me till we both came. Nothing felt natural now. If I showed any passion, or tenderness, or let myself go, she'd laugh in my face. "I want to tell you something, but promise not to laugh."

"I promise." But she was already laughing.

"I want to spend time with you away from everything and everyone. Let's go away somewhere for a couple of days."

When had I decided this?

Now. What I really wanted from our imaginary champagne in some make-believe room away from everyone was for her to kneel next to me naked and, reaching out to her champagne flute, suddenly crack it against the nightstand, and with a shard held decisively between her fingers, make an incision ever so slowly on my left arm and, with the palm of her hand, rub my blood on the wound, on my face, on her body, and then beg me and beg me again to do the same to her. This is what we had come to. If there'd ever been kindness and charity in our love, it was the kindness and charity of Huns. We loved with every organ but the heart. Which is why we stayed away from each other. I couldn't even find it in me to tell her how much I loved her—scanty, meager, scorched love that I had. To get a reaction now we needed to spill blood. Your blood into my blood, my fluids, your fluids, your muck all mine. Let the snake that bit you bite me back. Let it bite me on the lip. Die with me.

"I know why you called me," she said.

"Tell me, because I still don't know and I'm dying to find out." I couldn't have been more candid.

"You called to see if I'm willing to give everything up to be with you. And either way I'm damned. If I decide to go with you, you'll refuse, fearing I'll never forgive you. But if I say no, you'll hold it against me and never forgive me either. So, for once in your life, you're going to have to tell me what you want me to do, because I, for once, am clueless."

"All I ask is one weekend," I finally said. We never could do better than a weekend. Or maybe not even a weekend, just two weekdays, what could be more modest than a measly Monday and Tuesday?

She smiled, seemed amused by the idea. But she wasn't laughing. She was accepting.

"Where to?" She did not wait for my answer. "Let's go back," she said.

I knew where she meant. "People never go back."

"We're not people. We're another species."

I leaned toward her and kissed her on the mouth. With both hands, she cupped my face and kissed me back. When we left the restaurant, we couldn't let go of our hands and walked hand in hand on Madison Avenue. Neither said anything. We didn't care. It was one of the most beautiful moments in my life.

"What will you tell Manfred?" she asked, pronouncing his name the German way without the least trace of irony.

"Manfred is Manfred." Then on second thought, "He already knows, he's always known. And your husband?"

"Says we're basically kids." Then after a pause, "Maybe he's right. Either way, he'll live."

We'd tell them very little. Just something about a boring talk I had to give. She had to meet an author outside Boston who was homebound after an accident. But if they persisted, we'd tell them the truth.

The magic of that afternoon left us feeling so happy that without planning it, toward noon the next day I called her. Same place, same time? Of course. We met at exactly the same restaurant and ordered the exact same lunch. Then, seeing lunch ended the same way, we met the next day as well. "We've been three days together. Think this ends it?" I asked.

I was being a jerk, she said. She held my hand and did not let go. I walked her back to her office.

"Did you tell Manfred?" she asked.

"Not today, not yesterday." I was thrilled that she wanted to know. "Did you?" I asked.

"I haven't said anything."

"We could, if we want, do this for the rest of our lives."

"Rituals," she said. Meaning, *Yes, we could*.

"Not rituals. Rituals are when we wish to repeat what has already happened, rehearsals when we repeat what has yet to occur. Where do we fit?"

Nowhere, I would have added. And she'd have agreed.

"Star time, my love."

"Star time indeed," I said.

MONTHS LATER WE arrived by plane, not train. The train would have taken five hours, and in those hours, anything could have happened between us to spoil the trip. The flight lasted slightly under an hour. While flying, we did not speak about the trip, nor did we exchange more than a few casual remarks on the long cab ride from the airport in Boston to our small college town. We wanted to express neither excitement nor apprehension, for fear of saying the wrong thing. Two misplaced words, even if spoken in sparring jest, and the trip would be ruined; one mawkish comment and we'd snuff out the tiny flame we were desperately trying to coddle between us like a lighted candle in a stalled car on a snowbound highway.

Now in the cab I forgot why we'd decided to come back. To run away from our lives and be alone together in a town where no one knew us? To turn back the clock? To recover the other, perhaps truer, unspent itinerary of our lives?

The closer we approached our school, the quieter we grew, each scared to trip the mood or wrong-foot the other, though equally downplaying the kitschy thrill of all return trips. We wanted our arrival plain and ordinary. She kept looking at the lake, while I scanned the fleeting mansions on the other side, both of us silent and partly oblivious, as though our return after so many years were a mindless, uninspired errand. For all the cabbie knew, we were another tight-lipped couple from New York who'd had a terrible row at dawn and couldn't wait to get away from each other. If pushed, either of us would gladly have asked the driver to turn around and head back to the airport.

We'd made a point of arriving early on Monday. We wanted to be there just as classes were about to start, not when the day was under way. Perhaps I wanted to step back in time and walk down the same old cobbled alleys on my way to my first class of the day. She had her own habits and haunts she'd meant to revisit, spots of time she held dear and that probably did not include me. Perhaps I wanted our paths to cross at some meaningful point. Which is why, during our first few hours, we walked around town but kept trying to avoid every curb of shared memory. We walked about campus exactly the way jaded, jet-lagged tourists do: without memory or anticipation. There were a few *Do you remember this?* and *Look at the monstrosity they've put up where so-and-so used to stand!* But these were muted moments. At some point she held my hand, and I held hers. We took pictures with our iPhones. Of her, of me, a selfie of the two of us. She texted it to me on the spot. Behind us rose the ubiquitous steeple. It was only by seeing Yarrow Church and Van Speer Observatory looming in the distance that I realized we had indeed returned and were together here, that all this was real, and that from the look on our faces in our photos, we were actually happy.

By midafternoon, we gave in. We turned left on the quadrangle and took the sloping road downhill until we spotted the house. The large green sign on one of its glass windows heralded a stark warning of what awaited us at Ole Brit's home. His house had become a Starbucks. No use arguing, I thought. We stepped in, looked around what was once the foyer, and peeked into the back room where scattered students were typing away on their laptops. In that room we'd all sat on the faded Persian rug and drunk mulled cider. The new setup made us feel odd, like strangers who'd time-traveled and landed home in the wrong century. The stairway to the upper bedrooms had vanished. Looking at all the students sitting around, some chatting by the door, others rushing in and out of the store on their way to class, neither of us could forget we were not one of them.

We ordered two coffees. I paid with the app on my iPhone. She was impressed.

"Get with the times," I said ironically, realizing how thoroughly out of sync both of us were in this house.

"Do you feel old?" she asked.

"No. Should I?"

"I do."

Then she remembered Ole Brit's remarks about Edith Wharton. "She was not ten years older than I am today—kind of late for the wine of life, don't you think?"

"Why, haven't you drunk from the wine by now?"

It took her by surprise.

"You're fishing. Why, have *you*?"

"Happens. Maybe. Or so I'd like to think. But I'm no longer sure. Maybe not, actually."

She looked at me as I was putting sugar in my cup, and in her usual manner of fessing up to the very thing she'd been needling me about, she said, "I'm not sure I have either. Or maybe just a few sips here and there."

"*Sips* and *maybes* is not how one gorges on the wine of life."

"Touché."

We spoke about Ethan Frome's love for Mattie, wondering if a love so chaste could exist in today's world. "No one is that inhibited these days," I said.

"Are you so sure?" She was needling me again.

I looked at her as if I'd been caught fibbing and whispered, "Touché."

By the time we threw our empty paper cups in one of the bins along the downhill road toward the town's Main Street, it was already twilight. I liked the town by twilight. We were just in time to visit the school's dining commons at dinnertime. Students were flocking in from the cold and standing in line. No one stopped us, no one even noticed that we had almost queued up with the others for dinner. We stood back for a few minutes, just to watch what kind of food they served. Definitely gourmet compared with what they'd dished out in our day. Even vegan, she said, pointing to a sign. But the old wooden tables hadn't changed, the chairs were the same, the smell of the dining hall—you'd know it in an instant if they blindfolded you, spun you around, and dropped you in Mongolia. Old, filthy, musty, woody smell, adorable just the same.

Back in the courtyard we finally did the unmentionable. We looked upstairs. Her lighted window was on the third floor. After studying in the library at night, I'd drop her at her dorm's main entrance, and walking away toward my own dorm, I would look back a minute or two later to catch when she turned on her light upstairs.

We did not utter a word. We just stood there, not moving. She remembered everything. "In a minute you'll open the main door, walk up three flights, knock at my door, and say it's time for dinner. Any idea how I counted the minutes for you to come upstairs? I grew to recognize your footsteps, down to the mood you were in when you reached my door."

"I didn't know," I said.

"You didn't know shit."

In the emptied courtyard, we were still gazing up at her window, speechless, each wondering what would have happened had things turned out differently between us—Where would we be? Who would we be?—both equally aware, though, that absolutely nothing might have turned out differently, which made us stare all the more. Perhaps we stared to understand why we kept staring.

"The joy of shutting my books as soon as I heard the door slam behind you downstairs. I can feel it still tonight, especially now when it's as chilly as it was on those evenings just before dinner."

There was nothing to say, so I kept quiet. We simply looked

at each other. We both remembered falling asleep on her sofa the night we stayed up translating the last pages of Orwell. "We woke up curled into each other. Like two lizards," she said.

"Like a human pretzel."

"Here's what I find unbearable," she said as we were starting to leave. She was slackening her pace, as though part of her didn't want to leave yet. I had never seen her so pensive and hesitant before, almost humbled. "The thought that I could have lived through all the years in between to arrive at this moment on this courtyard with you and still feel I haven't budged an inch undoes me totally. I'd give anything not to know that the girl who was twenty at the time and who waited for you to come upstairs in the evening would end up having to live through so much nonsense only to find herself back where she started, almost eager to see it happen all over again. It's as if a part of me had dug its heels in, never left, and simply waited for me to come back."

We took a few steps. "My marriage never happened to me. I'm not a mother. For all I know I'm still just a student translating Orwell into Greek."

I told her she couldn't possibly be serious. Her husband, her daughter, her home, and the amazing authors she'd published and made famous—were they nothing?

"They belong to one itinerary. I'm talking about the other, the one we stumble in and out of every four years. The life both of us get distant, dimly lit peeks at when all else is dark, the life that almost doesn't belong to us but is closer to us than our shadows. Our star life, yours with mine. As someone said over dinner once, each of us is given at least nine versions of our lives, some we guzzle, others we take tiny, timid sips from, and some our lips never touch."

Neither of us asked which was our life. We didn't want to know.

Quantum theory is more resilient, I thought. For every life we live, there are at least eight others we can't begin to touch, much less know the first thing about. Maybe there is no true life or false life—just rehearsals for parts we might never be lucky enough to play.

On our way through the quadrangle, I spotted our bench. We stopped and stared at it. "If it could speak," she said.

"You wanted my spit."

She was about to pretend to have forgotten, but then, "Yes, I did."

My real life stopped here.

"WHICH REMINDS ME," she said after we left the courtyard and were seated in the restaurant where we'd made a reservation earlier that day, "are we sleeping in the same bed tonight?"

That was a strange way to phrase it.

"I thought this was the plan," I said.

"*The plan.*" She echoed the words with a pinch of irony. "Yes, *the plan*, of course," she repeated, as though she too had found the wording just vague enough to justify the humor.

We were sitting in what was still the best restaurant in town. This was where visiting parents took their college kids. I had dinner with my father here once, she with her parents. One day you'll have dinner with your daughter here, I said. She almost made a motion to dismiss the comment for the maudlin thing it was. "Yes, one day I may have dinner with her here," she said. But then, as though not wishing to dispel the sentiment this stirred, "On that day I'll wish it was the three of us."

Why had she said this?

"Because it's the truth."

I tried to divert her comment with something light and spurious.

"Wouldn't she think it was weird?"

"*She* might. But you wouldn't and I certainly wouldn't."

She had caught me totally off guard.

I reached out and touched her face. We didn't speak. She let my palm linger on her face and touch her lips. With both hands she held my other hand on the table.

"Two days," I said.

"Two days."

What we meant, though neither of us was going to say it, was, a whole lifetime in two days.

The meal was no good. But we didn't care. We stared out the window, had dessert, skipped coffee, lingered. Afterward, sensing that not a speck of tension had risen between us, yet always fearing it could, I suggested we take our time walking back to our tiny hotel, finally stopping in a small, picturesque bar that had been a deli in our day. The place was not full. Monday nights were never big with the drinking crowd here. We sat by a window overlooking the moonlit lake. But without ordering, we changed our minds and left. She wanted to walk along the frozen bank of the lake. Why not? I said, spotting a group of college kids scampering across, while farther out, two girls were skating. She wished she'd brought her skates. Did I mind walking to Van Speer to have a look? No, I didn't mind. Was she trying to step back in time? Or delay being alone in our bedroom?

But then, after walking along the edge of the lake and heading across on the ice, I felt a surge of emotion on spotting how her back curved ever so slightly. I stopped her, held her tight to me, and kissed her. I thought back to the moment when the owner of the hotel had first shown us to our bedroom. We hadn't

felt awkward then. We didn't feel awkward now. But I continued
to fear we might. We had come looking for the past; now, on the
lake, I couldn't have felt more indifferent to the past. This was
here and now.

Was she happy we had come?

"Very. Two days," she said, echoing what could become a
mantra of sorts: a gift from the two of us to the two of us. "We
belong here," she said, surveying the frozen lake.

"On ice?" I asked, careful not to emphasize the joke.

"All this is us, you know," she said, ignoring my comment.

She was right. This was us. The other us was in New York.
Manfred and I are watching TV. She and her husband are doing
whatever they're doing—Scrabble, for all I know.

This was our moment. All we'd done over the years was rehearse it, sensing now that it had waited no less faithfully than
Argos the dog waited for his master, Odysseus. We were like
people who return to their ancestral homestead two, three, four
generations later, slip the old key into the lock, and find that
the door still opens, that the house still belongs to them, that the
furniture still bears the scent of their great-grandparents. Time
had ransacked nothing. Van Speer, where we'd spent so many
late hours translating Orwell together, remembered us, seemed
to welcome us again.

I told her about Ole Brit. Almost four decades after having
been a student at Oxford, he returned from Peru with his twin
sons, who were planning to enroll soon. After giving them a
thorough tour of his old digs, out of curiosity, he took them
down a narrow lane and was surprised to find his old shoemaker
still open for business. The shop had been completely revamped
and the young salesclerk he'd once known there was long gone.
When Ole Brit told the new clerk that this was where he'd ordered his shoes decades before, the young man took down his

name and disappeared downstairs. Five minutes later, the sales-clerk came back upstairs with a pair of wooden lasts on which the name Raúl Rubinstayn was inscribed in indelible purple script. "Yes, we've kept them. The man who built these lasts was my grandfather. He left us three years ago."

At which the old gentleman from Peru couldn't help himself and burst into tears.

ON THE WAY to the hotel, she held my hand. "I'm happy."

She said it as though it had come to her as a complete sur-prise. Still, I needed to hear her say it.

I'd been wrong about us. We were not Huns. Just two persons who'd never found the confidence to go far enough or know where far enough was. We stopped again and kissed. I recalled my old fantasy. I wanted her naked with me, wanted to see her bare thighs straddle me and, as she'd lean toward me with all her hair in my face and me inside her, watch her pin both my arms down with her knees while she cracked my champagne glass with one hand and with the other cut me with a shard. I could picture my blood staining the ice and the snowbanks. I liked it.

"Tomorrow can't be our last day together," she said.

"Yes, but after tonight, I dread what you'll think of me."

"Wait until we hear what you'll say about me!"

"What do you mean?"

She shrugged her shoulders once, released them, then sec-onds later, as an afterthought, tensed them again. She did that thing with her back again, and once again it moved me. I should have suspected something sooner. She'd been uneasy since we'd left the lake. Now, nearing our hotel, I could sense she was al-most reluctant to stop walking. What made *me* nervous was that I wasn't feeling nervous at all. I had started wanting her at the

lake and didn't want to lose that impulse. I liked the idea of the
glass shard, and the bare knee, and of her mean, bruise-colored
lips almost smiling as she made her incision with me still inside
her. Would she remember *you of every man I've known*? Would she
ask to Englishmuffin me and then beg me to look her in the eyes
when we came together?

"The truth is, I'm a bit out of practice," she finally said, probably sensing where my thoughts were headed. We were sitting
on the same side of the bed with our clothes on. She was playing
with the cuff of her shirt that was sticking out under the sleeve
of her cardigan, which she gave no sign of wanting to remove.

"Out of practice how?" I asked, not sure I had seized her
meaning.

She shrugged her shoulders. "We don't sleep together. Well,
we sleep together but not really—you know . . ."

"Nothing?"

"Well, some, but not really."

She lifted her face and looked at me. "Sometimes I forget what
people do together. Or why they even do it. Plus I'm not sure I
may do it for you."

I couldn't help reaching out and holding her head between
my hands and kissing it again and again. I wanted to hold her,
and I wanted to hold her naked, I asked for nothing more. To
hug her in bed, to kiss her, and kiss her again and again, until
either we made love or fell asleep. She said nothing. Then, out of
the blue, "I feel as tense as a virgin—and with you of all people."

"If you're a virgin, what am I?" I said to show I had my own
reasons to feel uneasy.

"Are we so deeply wounded in our sex?" she asked, knowing
I'd remember the words we'd all laughed about over dinner
with Manfred and her husband and that had suddenly now acquired a darker meaning.

"I think everyone is wounded in their sex," I said. "I can't think of one person who isn't."

"Maybe. But not like me."

I stood up and pulled the blinds wide open to get a better view of the quadrangle. The hotel staff always assumes that people want the curtains shut at night. I liked the view. To see more of it, I turned off the two bedside lights. Whiteness everywhere, and beyond the whiteness, the gray outlines of the gabled houses. There was the lake, there the quadrangle, then the slope that led to that dear old house that had become a Starbucks, there the bar where we'd almost ordered two brandies before walking out, and farther away, Van Speer Observatory, with its quiet library, which stayed open all night and whose lights still glowed tonight as they'd done years before. We had spent our last winter together in that library, heading off to the observatory minutes after dinner, and coming back long after midnight, always becoming tentative as we reached her dorm, which is why we'd slacken our steps once we crossed the quadrangle, naming the nine lampposts after the Muses.

As I looked outside at the tranquil courtyard, it occurred to me that perhaps we had turned the clock further back than we should, for we seemed more timorous and more callow with ourselves, with our bodies, than we'd been back then. Had we become virgins? Or were we like people who have died before their time and are given a second chance by some minor deity, but with so many provisos that the new life feels like a deferred death?

"I think you should come and take a look," I said. She came next to me by the window. Then, staring out at the moonlit expanse of the snow-decked landscape, she repeated the word: "amazing, amazing, amazing," not just because the view was breathtaking, but because in that glowing *Ethan Frome* world nothing had changed in more than one hundred years, the way neither she nor I had really changed since we were here last. "Hold me," she said, "just hold me." I wrapped my arms around her. We stood stationary this way, until she put her arm around my waist. And as I held her closer to me, I wanted to feel her skin, and without thinking I began to unbutton my shirt. She did not help me, nor did she seem eager to unbutton her shirt. All she said was "I've always loved the way you smell." I removed my shirt and was about to help her undress. "Just help me forget I'm nervous," she said. "Look at this, I'm shaking all over." She asked me to switch off the light in the bathroom, the small nightlight as well. When I asked her about birth control, she told me she'd had an operation less than two years earlier and couldn't have more children. She hadn't breathed a word of it to me. She could have died and I would never have known. I began making love to her thinking of the child we were never going to have together. She didn't ask me to look at her, didn't ask me to stay with her, yet she held my face almost as though she were desperately trying to believe we were actually making love together, waiting for our eyes to lock before she could let herself go and shed habits acquired with someone else. "I'm awkward, I know," she said. "I need a moment, my love."

We were not sleepy afterward. We almost laughed when we realized that neither had completely undressed. While taking some of her clothes off to see her naked by the window, I had felt I wasn't undressing a woman but a child who was reluctant to go to bed but wasn't putting up a fight because she'd been promised one more story. "It's been so long since a man took off my clothes," she said.

"And it's been ages since I touched a woman."

"When *was* the last time?" she asked as she stood up, then went to the bathroom and came out tying her bathrobe.

"Claire, I think."

"Claire who never says anything?" she exclaimed, totally bewildered. "But why Claire?"

"It just happened."

I sat down naked on the undone bed, picked up my sweater from the floor, and slipped it back on. She was already sitting cross-legged on the bed. I did the same. I loved that we were talking like this, partly naked.

"So let me ask you this," she said, as though she were still deliberating the question and hadn't quite formulated the words. It thrilled me, because something in the way she said *So let me ask you this* warned me that she had read the answer long, long before putting the question to me. Part of me felt arousal course through my body. How I loved this. She wanted the truth from me, and the truth came with arousal.

"Maybe that drink at the bar wouldn't have been such a bad idea," I said.

"Try el minibar."

I stood up and headed for the minibar, where I found exactly what I was looking for.

"The shag carpeting is," I said as soon as I hopped back in bed, "questionable."

"You don't say."

"I'm sure there are things buried underfoot—nail clippings, crusts of all species."

We both grimaced as soon as we spotted each nested plastic cup sealed in its own antiseptic plastic bag, meant to make up for the scuzzy red carpeting. I emptied a brandy nip in each glass, then tried to clink our soft, wobbly plastic glasses.

"Why didn't you make love to me that night? The night after we came back from Van Speer and fell asleep on the sofa."

I knew it.

"Was there someone else? Not attracted? Not in love?" she asked.

"Wrong," I said. "It was always you. And God knows I was attracted. The things I told you when I was alone in my bed at night but didn't have the guts to tell you in person, and the number of times I got hard just thinking of being naked with you—you've no idea. But I had become so nervous, so tentative, that the closer we drew together, the more difficult it was to confide anything. But the truth is," and here I stopped a second, "there was something."

She gave me a quizzical look. "*Something?*"

So she wasn't going to let it slide or make it easy for me.

"My body had two agendas. You were the first. But on the very evening I came back to Van Speer after you'd shut your door on me, I discovered the second. It was outside the men's bathroom in the stacks of Van Speer. Everyone knew what went on there at night. I'd been trying to disown what I wanted for so long that still today I can't recognize it without first going through motions of disowning it. Manfred has learned to live with this, but I don't envy him. I wanted to know once and for all before turning to you, but I couldn't turn to you because I couldn't know about me."

She said nothing. But before she could ask again, I decided to take it a step further. "He was a chemistry student. A freshman. We met, or rather we bumped into each other, in the stacks upstairs. I was beyond aroused that night, especially after kissing you for so long. Part of me wanted to head back to our table as though hoping to find you still there so that we might close our books together and replay the walk to your dorm. But I also knew what I was after: I wanted warmth, I wanted it quick, and I wanted it clear, strong, and dirty. He and I didn't have to say a single word, barely a glance, we just fell into it, almost by accident, but not by accident, and in the unlit sections of the stacks our bodies lurched and leaned into each other. Before we knew it, our hands had already started undoing each other's belts. There was no shame, no guilt, it happened so fast that nothing felt easier or more natural. Unlike us, no hesitation, no deferrals, no thinking. All he asked afterward was 'I'll see you again?' I nodded but naturally forswore the whole thing as soon as I left the stacks. I wanted you even more after him than I did earlier that evening. I wanted to tell you what I'd done but I also felt restored somehow, almost purged, vindicated. I was even happy. After Christmas he was back in the stacks and so was I. You and I had made up by then and were working feverishly on our translation. Eventually, I'd say that I was going upstairs to the bathroom. Knowing you were waiting for me downstairs stirred something rakish and new in me. But I knew that sleeping with you, the way you slept with so many, would resolve nothing about me or about us—and the last thing I wanted was to wake up in the same bed with you, staring at the same question I wished to bury every night in the stacks. I also knew that if things stayed unresolved between us, I could claim I was still trying to figure out who I was and what I wanted. I was like an ellipse, with two competing foci but no center. In the words of the poet, my heart was in the east with you, but my body was out west."

Silence.

"Now you know," I finally said.

"Now I know what? That you liked men? Everyone knew."

I had expected her to snap back with something like "Nice work! All the weeks and months that I had your heart, your cock was someone else's." But she was more perceptive and, in the end, more forbearing.

"I was your front. That's all."

"No, not a front. Nothing made me happier than coming downstairs to find you waiting to walk back to your dorm, and nothing was worse than your placing a hasty goodbye peck on my cheek and shutting the door behind you because I had yet again failed to stick my foot in."

But I was still cloaking the truth. And I knew she knew it and was candid enough to dismiss my piece of sophistry before it could harden into yet another subterfuge. Yes, in those days, Chloe was my screen, my alibi, and thinking of her and being with her was a sure way of keeping the pilot light of desire kindled all day before it caught fire later every night in the stacks. If I did not think of him during the day and preferred to keep a lid on Van Speer, it was not to deny what I craved but to starve before feasting. She kept things in check. On the one night she was unable to come with me to Van Speer, I'd not only rushed upstairs to meet my freshman by the stacks but less than an hour later raced back up again to the same corner by the men's room where I found someone else, and it didn't matter who.

But perhaps the screen woman was herself less of a front than I'd allowed myself to believe. I could have been using him as a cover, and not the other way around. With him I was making minor and easier admissions about myself to avoid facing the state of a relationship that seemed to be so rudderless and slumping down a gorge. He didn't blunt my desire for her but stoked it and made me want her even more. All he did, though, was dull the urgency.

But that reasoning perhaps was as much a mask as the others. In the end, and without ever admitting it to myself, I'd grown to love serving two masters—perhaps so as never truly to answer to either one.

I did not say anything more.

"Did you think of him when we stopped by Van Speer tonight?"

She had to ask.

"Yes," I said.

"Would you have gone upstairs to take a look if I weren't with you?"

"Probably. But then, had I come with him tonight and walked about Van Speer, I would have thought of you, taken out the big Greek lexicon, and sat at our desk for a while."

Then I told her: "I like telling you the truth. It arouses me. The body never lies."

"I can see."

I had thought it was the memory of those nights at Van Speer that was exciting me now. But, no, it was avowal—and the unspoken tinge of indecency in every avowal—that thrilled and stirred me and made me hard again.

"Stay with me, and don't let go," she said.

OUTSIDE IT HAD begun snowing, and I thought of *Ethan Frome* again and of the suicidal ride that left the two lovers permanently damaged because neither had the courage to pick up and leave the suffocating rural town of Starkfield. It made me think of us. Would we have the courage to change anything? Did we have it back then? Did we have it now? Had being runaways for two puny weekdays put us in the camp of the brave? Or had our love been punctuated by so many regrets that we couldn't conceive of life without them? We had never taken things to the next step. We didn't even know what the next step was.

Snow. As ever the silent snow. It hems you in, lifts your spirit, and as you soar awhile it lets you down for being the meaningless ashen powder that it is. Was this a fantasy, then? A man and a woman dying to be snowbound so they wouldn't have to plan for tomorrow?

"You still haven't answered my question," she said. "So why didn't you make love to me that night?"

She wasn't going to let this slide.

"Because I was scared of you. Because I wanted to make love to you but feared you wanted it slam-dunk. Because I wanted you forever, and I knew you'd laugh if I told you. You and I were both quick and easy with men, and quick and easy was the last thing I wanted with you. So I waited. Then I got used to waiting. Eventually, waiting was more real than what we had."

"Are you happy, though?" she asked.

"Yes, very."

"Same here. The wine of life?" she asked, already poised for irony.

"The moonshine of life. Well . . ."

"Exactly!" she said, as though dismissing my feeble attempt to embellish our lovemaking.

And then she said something I would never have expected: "I think you'll go back to Manfred. It's what you want. It's who you are."

"You really think so?"

"I think so. But with you, who's to know? For all we've done tonight and all we've ever felt, I know one thing: you want me, and I know you love me, as I love you, but I don't think you ever craved me in your gut. You want something from me, but you don't know what it is. Perhaps all I am is an idea with a body. There was always something missing. Your hell—and it's mine too—is that even when you're with Manfred, you'll want to be with me again. You and I don't love the way others do—we run on empty." She touched my face, my forehead. "I could tell you to be happy that you have him, but it won't help. I could tell you to be happy we've got two days, but that won't help either. You're alone, as I'm alone, and the cruelest thing is that finding each other and saying *let us be alone together* won't solve a thing."

I loved her more than ever now.

"How do you know me so well?"

"Because you and I are one and the same person. Everything I said about you is true about me. In a month from now, but not now, we'll wake up and realize that this here was the wine of life."

We looked out at the quadrangle and the sliding hill, and at the scatter of lampposts standing in their gleaming pools of light on the snow. "Thalia, Urania, Melpomene," she said as we smiled at ourselves, happy that the saltire pattern of the quad had not forgotten the imprint of our old footsteps here. I liked holding her.

"What else are you thinking?" she asked.

"I was thinking that Ole Brit probably stood by a window like this at a hotel in Oxford after leaving his two sons in their hotel room and stared out alone at the old spires and the medieval quadrangle, trying to understand the tricks that time plays. He had once been in love with a young shoemaker in Oxford but had never had the courage to follow up on the hints and passes the shoemaker kept making. He'd been going to the shop for months, ordering pair after pair of shoes and getting all worked up when the cobbler touched his ankle with his bare hands or, as happened once, held his toes. But the whole thing didn't go anywhere—though it never went away either. It just sat there, no past, no future, like a glass of wine filled to the rim but never drunk from. In his view it was like a bad debt that keeps accruing interest and that you realize one day you'll never repay because it's eaten up all your life savings, so that when you turn your face to the wall to gather all the pieces on your last half hour on planet Earth you'll find neither closure nor redemption, for the pieces will have been scattered long, long before they scatter your ashes. I don't want to end up like the old gentleman from Peru who comes back to realize he's led the wrong life all these years."

"When did he tell you all this?"

I looked at her, and without hesitating, said, "When I stayed at his house as a guest for three years after graduating. It happened one night after his seminar when we were alone in the house. His students had gone home, and his wife was away in the city, and we were sitting downstairs drinking whiskey. We had just finished washing and drying the dishes. He was sitting next to me on the sofa and I could tell something was bothering him but was reluctant to guess what it was. 'Do you believe in fate?' he asked. 'Are we still discussing Wharton?' I replied, almost saucily, to show I was fully aware of his attempt to dispel the uneasy silence between us and to derail what I sensed was on both our minds. Perhaps I was trying to put him on the spot. 'Are we still talking books? Is that it?' 'We could if you wish,' he replied, evasive and cordial as ever. Then, I've no idea why, I reached over to him and held his hand. And because I wanted to make it easy, and because the wine helped, I said, 'I think you should sleep with me.' 'That's an idea,' he said, startled yet placid as ever, 'and when should this be?' he asked in his typical way of giving a humorous spin to things. But I wasn't going to let him off the hook. 'Tonight.' I'd never in my life been so certain of myself or so peremptory. 'Are you so sure?' he asked. Once again he tried to put me off. I found the right words to reassure him: 'Yes, tonight. I'll take care of everything, I promise.' And because a dead silence fell between us, I still remember repeating *I promise*. He reached over to me and held my face with both his hands and brought it close to his. 'I've thought of this from the very first time I met you. Paul.' 'I didn't know,' I said. I was more baffled by this admission than by anything I had said to him. 'Changed your mind?' he asked, putting a smile on his face. 'Not at all,' I said, more scared than I thought I'd be, because I suddenly realized that, despite the hasty, untrammeled sex I'd known, I had never made love to a man before and that this was what he was offering. When I led him upstairs to my room, he didn't enter right away. I thought he was nervous, but now I think he was giving me a chance to change my mind. I didn't turn on the light and began taking off my sweater. But he was naked before I was; he embraced me and started to remove everything I was wearing. I lost track of what we were doing. I was far more nervous than he. He ended up taking care of me.

"The next morning at my place at the breakfast table, he had left an envelope. *I think you were sent to me. Yours forever, Raúl.* No one had ever said this to me—that I was sent to him.

"His wife returned from the city that same afternoon. At the dinner table he could not look me in the eye. But late that evening, before going to bed, he caught me on the way upstairs. 'I bought you this,' he said, handing me a small wrapped package. 'I have one just like it. I wanted you to have the same pen.'"

THAT NIGHT, WRAPPED tight together in one thick quilt, we looked out at the glaring lampposts dotting the empty quadrangle, and in that quiet hour of the night, all nine of them seemed to have converged to stand outside our window. They understood so many, many things about me and in ways that I might never fathom. And for a moment I thought that they were not just lampposts but a collection of blazing selves shifting about in the cold, no different from nine headlit skittles, my nine lives, my unborn, unlived, unfinished nine selves asking whether they might be invited too or what to do with themselves if their time hadn't come.

"Why have we waited so long?"

I didn't know the answer. "Maybe because what we want hasn't been invented yet."

"Maybe because it doesn't exist."

"Which is why I dread how this ends."

"Good night," she said, turning her back to me, while I wrapped my arms around her.

"I know one thing, though," she said without turning around.

"What?"

"This doesn't end, whatever happens. Never, never ends." I tightened my arms around her. "Star love, my love, star love. It may not live but it never dies. It's the only thing I'm taking with me, and you will too, when the time comes."

ABINGDON
SQUARE

Her e-mails, when I look back, still show how fragile every-thing was. Brisk and lightly crafted, they were no different from everyone else's, except for that one overly effusive word that burst on my screen and aroused me every time. *Dearest.* It's what she called me, how she started every e-mail, how she said good night. *Dearest.*

For a second I'd forget how disappointingly brief each of her e-mails was, and how deceptive straight talk can sometimes be. In her attempt to reach out and say something real and close to the heart, she was simultaneously eliding the one thing I craved to hear the most. She wasn't curt, or shifty, or chatty—that wasn't her style—nor was there anything bland or tame in her e-mails. Her style was bold. But there never was a hint of *something else* in what she wrote, no subtext, no allusion, no Freudian slip asking to be mulled over and dissected, no nickel inadvertently dropped on the table for you to raise in what could have been a long-standing game of e-mail poker. Perhaps her tone wasn't troubled, wasn't needy or awkward enough. Perhaps she really was the happy, untrammeled sort who dropped into your life as easily as she sprang out of it, no baggage, no promises, no hard feelings. And perhaps the normal mix of anxiety and irony, which trips so many of us when we meet someone new, was so thoroughly airbrushed that her e-mails had the breezy good cheer of summer-camp letters to distant relatives who like to receive letters in the mail but seldom read them closely enough to notice that the unusually large script is there not to help with their failing eyesight but to fill the gaping blank spots in otherwise perfunctory bulletins.

Her e-mails looked like letters but were really text messages running out of breath. She respected capitals, punctuated with fussy correctness, and never used abbreviations—yet everything had an unmistakable air of suppressed haste, meaning *I could say more, much more, but why bore you with details*, the flip side of which was *I have to run but for you I'll always make time*, the whole thing capped and fluffed with a heady *Dearest* to keep me from seeing that the *something else* I kept waiting for was not coming this time either. Because there was *nothing else*.

I had read one of her articles and knew how complicated her mind was; I loved her complicated mind. Her prose reminded me of a warren of arcane, sporadic lanes in the West Village that take sudden turns and are perennially ahead of you. On e-mail, however, she spoke the polished language of the tree-lined *grands boulevards* of Paris, all clarity and transparency, no hidden corners, no false trails, no dead ends. You could always choose to overinterpret the meaning of so much clarity, but then you'd be reading your own pulse, not hers.

I liked the Lower Manhattan in her. I liked the way she'd sit with me over coffee and confide the intricate patterns in her life and then on impulse change her mind, turn the tables on herself, and say that patterns made for good stories but rarely meant anything—there were no patterns, we shouldn't look for patterns, patterns were for regular people, not for us, we're different, you and I, aren't we? Then, as if she'd taken a wrong alley, she'd back up and say that her analyst disagreed with her. Perhaps he'd figured her out long before she could, she said. I'm totally off track about myself, she'd add, throwing in unexpected zingers of self-deprecation that made me like her even more each time she took herself down, because it made her more vulnerable. I loved the way she'd say one thing, then sidle up to its opposite, because this unabashed tossing and turning with herself promised spellbinding fireside chats in some beloved, cozy corner of our invention.

We divided the world into two camps, Main Street people, who were all grids and cross streets, and us, pedestrian lanes and frisky passageways in the Meatpacking District. Everyone else was Robert Moses. We were Walter Benjamin. Us against them, I thought.

Heidi was a young writer whose article on opera I had turned down months earlier. Yet I had picked up an inflection in her prose that was at once wry and brooding and, in my two-page, single-spaced rejection letter, had outlined the strengths and weaknesses of her piece. She shot back an e-mail, saying she needed to see me right away. I replied just as quickly that I wasn't in the habit of meeting people simply because I had turned down their work; in any event, I'd have very little to add to what I'd already written in my letter. All right, thank you. I wished her luck. Many thanks. Our tit-for-tat was over in a fraction of a minute.

Two months later, she wrote back to tell me that her piece

had been accepted by a major magazine. She'd used all my edits. Now would I see her? Yes . . . Would I see her this week? Yes . . . She bought me coffee in a place on Abingdon Square, *just across from the little park*, she said, *and not too far from your office*. Both of us sat with our winter coats on. It had started to rain, and we ended up staying much longer than we'd planned, talking for almost two hours about Maria Malibran, the nineteenth-century mezzo-soprano. As we were saying goodbye and she was getting ready to light a cigarette, she said we should do this again, maybe very soon.

We should do this again, maybe very soon stayed with me as I rode the train home that evening: bold and feisty yet unambiguously sweet. Was she asking me, *Maybe very soon?* Or was it just a deft, roundabout way of saying, *No need to wait two months to meet over coffee next time?* I felt like someone who'd been promised a Christmas present in June.

I tried to nip the flurry of joy by reminding myself that her *maybe very soon* might easily be one of those open-ended deferrals thrown in to cover up an awkward leave-taking between people who already know they probably have no reason to meet again.

Or was it trickier than I thought? Was there perhaps a touch of affected diffidence in her implied *next time?* Had she already guessed that I'd say *Absolutely!* the moment she asked but wanted me to think she wasn't sure I would?

I never asked why I spent so much time mulling over her sentence on the train. Nor did I ask why I reread her piece first thing the next morning at the office or why I kept catching myself thinking of Maria Malibran that night. But I knew I'd been one hundred percent right about her: a woman with that sort of a pen, spirited and glum in the same breath, just had to be very,

very beautiful. I knew where this was going. I'd known it the moment I'd spotted her in the café.

ON THE SAME evening after we met, an e-mail arrived. *Dearest*, it started. Not *Dear*. No one had called me *dearest* in years. I loved it though I knew I wasn't her dearest. The line of men her age or a few years older with a better claim to the title was surely very long. Everything about her told me she was well aware of this. *Dearest* was also her way of thanking me for meeting her on such short notice, for helping her with her piece, for coffee, for talking to her about her next article on Malibran. *Dearest* for being such a dear. There was something so practiced and easy, so surefire in her gratitude that I couldn't avoid thinking that many had helped her in exactly the same way and become *dearest* because they'd given so selflessly—at first to draw her closer, later when they were up to their knees in friendship and couldn't step back to ask for anything else. *Dearest* was how she spelled the terms of your induction, how she kept you in tow.

In her e-mail that evening she told me it thrilled her to think that only .0000001 percent of humanity knew who Maria Malibran was, and yet the two of us got to meet in this unlikely café in, of all places, Abingdon Square—and with our coats on for two whole hours, she added.

I was smitten. I loved *and with our coats on for two whole hours* thrown in as an afterthought. So she too had noticed that awkward detail. Perhaps neither of us had wished to show we wanted coffee to last longer than fifteen minutes, which is why we sat with our coats on, not daring to alter anything for fear of reminding the other that time was flying. Perhaps we'd kept them on so as not to show we were actually enjoying this or that we hoped it might last a little longer, provided we behaved as though it might at any moment come to an end. Or was this her way of telling me that we'd both noticed the same thing and that we ordered two refills each because we were still wearing our winter coats, which gave us an alleged out in case we'd overstayed our time?

Dearest. It instantly brought back how she looked at me and returned my gaze as though nothing else mattered in that small café. *Dearest*: how she made no secret of having read up on me. *Dearest*: the flattering barrage of questions—what was I working on, what were my hopes, where did I see myself in five years, what next, why, how, since when, how come—questions I'd stopped asking myself but that were being now hammered with the reckless, searching whimsy of youth, tying knots in my stomach each time she drew closer to the truth, which I loved. Then there was her smile, her lips, her skin. I remembered watching the skin of her wrists, of her hands—it glistened in the early evening light. Even her fingers glistened. When was the last time I'd had coffee with someone so beautiful who had things to say that I loved hearing about and who seemed equally riveted by what I had to say? The answer scared me: not in years.

Not to be easily taken in, I forced myself to reconsider *Dearest*. It probably signified zero interest. It was the kind of over-the-top formula she would never have used on someone her age, and certainly not immediately after meeting him the first time. One used it with friends of one's parents, or with the parents of one's friends when they became quasi-avuncular figures—an endearment, not a come-on.

From Germany early the next morning came Manfred's e-mail: *Stop it. Learn to take things at face value. You're always looking for what's not there.* He knew me so well. This was his response to my e-mail in which I'd managed to wring every conceivable twisted reading of what *Dearest* could mean. With no one to confide in,

I'd reached out to someone who was still close but far away enough not to ask more questions than I was eager to ask myself.

That morning I wrote to her and said we should meet exactly a week later.

Where? flashed her speedy reply. Same place, I said. Same place, same time it is, then—Abingdon Square. Abingdon Square, I repeated.

She arrived before me again and had already ordered tea for herself and, for me, the same double cappuccino I had the last time. I stared at the cup waiting for me on my side of the same table by the window. What if I'd arrived late or had to cancel? "You didn't and you wouldn't have." "How could you tell?" "It's so good to see you,"' she said, standing to kiss me on both cheeks, nipping the senseless banter I'd attempted.

Coffee lasted longer than either of us expected. Outside, she took out a cigarette. Obviously two-plus hours without smoking was difficult for her. On the way to where we had separated the first time, we were stopped by two individuals speaking into walkie-talkies. They were part of a film crew. They asked everyone on our side of the sidewalk to wait and remain very quiet. I liked the pretext of hanging out together awhile longer in this kind of induced suspension. It gave our walk a dreamlike quality, as though we too belonged in a film. I asked one of the crew what they were filming. Something from a 1940s novel. Old hotel sign blinking away—THE MIRAMAR—middle-aged couple arguing on the deserted sidewalk, vintage Citroën parked aslant on the gleaming slate curb. At a given signal, there was a sudden downpour. All of us stepped back. Applause seemed called for, but no one dared.

The director wasn't pleased. They were going to have to shoot the scene all over again. *Thank you for your cooperation.* We were allowed to cross the street and go on our way.

Did I want to go? she asked. Not really. Did she? No, not yet. Watching them shoot the scene again was just another way of staying together awhile longer. So we stood and waited for the cameraman to start filming again. Blinking Miramar sign, arguing couple, old black Citroën with its passenger door flung open, everyone waiting for the sudden downpour in this twilit setting that made me feel we'd stepped into John Sloan's portraits of Greenwich Village. Ours was not an incidental, throwaway encounter. There was a script to what was happening, and it wasn't so difficult to read.

When we separated, it was almost eight o'clock. Next time we'll have drinks instead, I said. You're right; it's way too late for coffee. We kissed goodbye, then she turned around. "Do I get a hug?" she said.

DEAREST, SHE WROTE. She had started work on her essay on Malibran. I told her I'd once seen a long-out-of-print volume containing Da Ponte's letters to the young Malibran. She should try to find it. Mozart's beloved librettist, the much older Da Ponte, living in New York in the early years of the nineteenth century, had helped launch the operatic career of the young Maria García. In New York, Maria would marry the banker François Eugène Malibran, twenty-eight years her senior. She kept his name but then left him to find fame in Paris. The parallel didn't escape me. It thrilled me.

Our third meeting was no different. She was waiting at the same table by the window with my double cappuccino. So no drinks, I thought. "I like repeats," she said, as though she'd read my mind, "and I know you do too." We watched the snow begin to fall on Abingdon Square. This was a gift, I kept telling myself. *Learn to be grateful and avoid asking so many questions.* Part of me, though, couldn't help but take sneak peeks at what was waiting around the corner. "Maybe, if the weather changes, we'll pick a day and visit Da Ponte's grave in Queens," I finally said.

Fancy Mozart's librettist buried in Queens, she said.

And in a Christian cemetery too, I replied. He was born Jewish but later converted. Maria García's family was not really of Gypsy origin either but more than likely of Converso descent, I said.

She knew a woman who claimed to be of Converso descent.

Out came the story of an old, rather pious Catholic woman she knew who, on the Jewish High Holidays each year, made sure all the Christian images and icons in her house were turned to face the wall. "When do you think we should go?"

"Go where?" I asked.

"To the cemetery!" meaning, *Where else?*

Could things be so easy, I thought, or was I missing something?

I'd let her know, I said. I'd meant to say, *Not all of us are free-lancers,* but suppressed it. *Maybe early next week*—but I avoided saying this too. I would have had to check my cell phone's calendar and I didn't want the formality of the gesture to cool what had all the makings of a spontaneous outing to Maspeth.

But the silence and the time it took to say *I'll let you know* had already cast a chill. The unasked, the unspoken, sat between us. Her bewildered look was the question, my silence the answer.

When she continued to stare at me with that bold, inquisitive gaze that lingered on me as though she had more warmth in her heart than she wished to show, I knew that what had rippled between was a disquieting instant of awkwardness and of opportunity lost. Perhaps we should have talked about it right then and there. Perhaps it needed bringing up. But neither of us said anything.

When we separated, I gave her a kiss and then hugged her.

She walked away, but then turned around. "I want a real hug," she said.

WE HAD MET three times already and never once spoken or inquired about the other's life. Ours were the cobbled lanes; major arteries we steered clear of. On Abingdon Square the snow kept piling up and made me wish we could spend endless hours together in our coffee shop, do nothing but sit there and hope that neither made the slightest effort to lift the spell. Provided we stayed put, and provided it snowed, we could manage to meet just like this next week, and the week after, and the week after that as well—she and I together at this same corner table by the window, with our coats bunched up on a third chair.

Tread softly. Do nothing. Spoil nothing.

Two days later I decided to push things a bit. Did she want to have drinks?

My dearest, I'd love to. Just let me get a couple of things out of the way. I'll let you know.

Early the next morning: *I'm free tonight.*

Yes, but tonight I may not be, I e-mailed back. *I can do drinks but then I have a dinner to go to. How about six?*

Let's make it five thirty. Gives us more time together.

Fine, I wrote back, *there's a bar off Abingdon, not far from our café. So it's ours now?*

On Bethune. All right? I said, overlooking her humor but hoping my hasty reply told her that the tiny lilt in "ours" wasn't lost on me and that it pleased me.

On Bethune it is, my dear.

Seldom had anyone been so willful and acquiescent at the same time. Was this a sign? Or was she just the accommodating sort?

When we met again a week later, we ordered two Hendrick's

gins. "The rest of this week is not going to be good for me," she said. "Actually, it's going to be pretty awful."

Well, I thought, finally something's coming out.

The week wasn't so hot for me either. I alleged a dinner in Brooklyn and cocktail parties that were excruciatingly boring, give or take a few people.

"Give or take?"

I shrugged my shoulders. Was she teasing me? Why was her week going to be so dreadful?

"I'm going to have to break up with my boyfriend."

I looked at her, trying not to show how startled I was. Most people throw in *boyfriend* to tell you they're taken.

I hadn't known she had a boyfriend. Was he that terrible?

"No, not terrible. We've just outgrown each other, that's all," she said. "I met him at a writers' colony last summer, we did what everyone does in those places. But once we were back in the city, it just dragged—we fell into a rut."

"Is it that hopeless?" I asked.

Why was I playing friend-analyst? And why the disappointed inflection in the word "hopeless," as though the news pained me?

"Let's say it's just me. Plus—"

She hesitated.

Plus?

"Plus I've met someone else."

I thought for a moment.

"Well, in that case, maybe you should break up and clear the air. Does he know?"

"Actually, neither of them knows."

She leveled her eyes at me with a confiding, semi-rueful shrug of the shoulder that meant something like *Life. You know how it is.*

Why wasn't I asking more prodding questions? Why was I refusing to pick up the hint? What hint? Why let her drop this bombshell and pretend I wasn't even fazed? All I ended up saying was "I am sure things will work themselves out."

"I know. They always do," she replied, at once grateful that I'd left things vague enough yet sorry, perhaps, that I'd dropped the matter a bit sooner than she might have wished.

At seven she reminded me I had to be at a dinner party to dine with my *give-or-take* friends in Brooklyn. She remembered the wording. I liked it.

I wished I could bring her along to such dinner parties. She'd have them eating out of her hand, women included. As we stood outside the bar, I stared at her hoping she'd see how sorry I was that we were separating so early in the evening. She reached over to kiss me as she always did, on both cheeks. Without thinking, I found myself kissing her forehead, then hugging her. I felt the spur of arousal. This was not just in my head. And she had hugged me back, tightly too.

As I walked her to what had become the undeclared spot where we'd say goodbye, something told me she should have asked about the dinner party. I had railed too much against dinner parties for her not to have made a passing comment. But she had shown no interest even in asking where it was being held—for the same reason, perhaps, that I hadn't asked a single question about the new boyfriend. Perhaps, like me, she didn't want to appear interested. On Abingdon Square, we took everything that had anything to do with the rest of our lives and turned its face to the wall. My life, her life, like everything that didn't bear on why we kept meeting here, we simply staved off, never brought up, put a padlock on. On Abingdon Square we led a spare, hypothetical life, a life apart, between Hudson and Bleecker, between five thirty and seven.

After saying goodbye, I watched her walk downtown and, for a few moments, lingered on the square, thinking that I could easily stop taking the train, move in somewhere not far from here, start a new life right next to the bar, take her to the movies on weekday evenings, find other things to do, and, if this worked, watch her become famous, more beautiful, have children, until the day she'd step into my study and say we'd outgrown each other and fallen into a rut. *Life. Can't be helped. You know how it is*, she'd say, and, FYI, I'm moving to Paris. Even this didn't scare me. The vision of this alternate life was outlined on the large glass pane of the bar where she and I could easily spend so many more hours together. When she looked back at me after crossing the street, I liked being caught just standing there, watching her go her way. I liked that she had turned around and then, without being prompted, waved. I liked the sudden arousal when I hugged her, and for the first time since we'd met, I thought of her naked. It had come unbidden.

That Saturday evening, in a crowded movie theater, I watched a young couple ask those seated in our row to move one seat over. You could tell they were on their first date by the tentative way they took their seats and then hesitated on how to go about sharing their bag of popcorn. I envied them, envied their awkwardness, envied their back-and-forth questions and answers. I wished she and I were together in this very same movie theater. With a bag of popcorn. Or waiting on line outside with our coats on, eager for our show to begin. I wanted to see *Last Year at Marienbad* with her, take her to hear *The Art of the Fugue*, listen to the Shostakovich Piano and Trumpet Concerto together and wonder who of us was the piano and who the trumpet, she or I, trumpet and piano as we'd sit and read the lays of Marie de France on quiet Sundays and hear her say things I'd never known about Maria Malibran, and then, on impulse, throw on a few layers and head out together to see something really stupid, because a stupid movie with super moronic special effects can work wonders on drab Sunday evenings. The vision grew and began to touch the other corners of my life: new friends, new places, new rituals, a new life whose contours I could almost begin to touch.

There was a moment while I helped her with her coat when I could have said something. The unspoken, the untold, the unasked, just a few words, and everything would have gone up in smoke. But I knew, as I watched her make her way through the crowd, that she was as grateful for my silence as I was for hers. I asked her once which she'd like to be in the Shostakovich concerto, the piano or the trumpet. The piano is blithe and spirited, she told me; the trumpet wails. Which did I think I was?

FROM GERMANY CAME a short e-mail from Manfred: *You're back to stalking. What you need is less skepticism and more courage.* Courage, he said, comes from what we want, which is why we take; skepticism from the price we'll pay, which is why we fail. *What you need is to spend some time with her, not in a café, not in a bar or a movie theater. She's not sixteen. If it doesn't work, you'll be disappointed, but you'll move on, and that'll be the end of that.* When I told him that my skepticism was hardly misplaced, considering she had already told me there was someone waiting in the wings, his reply couldn't have been more heartening: *That someone could be you. And if it's not, just thinking it might be can move mountains. This woman is real. You are real.*

I tried to find a way to pry open the block between us. But the more I realized how much I wanted her, the more the idea of her new beau began to muddy my thinking, the more her blandishing *dearests* began to irk me. Everything I liked about her, everything she wrote and said had the ring of hollow appeasements thrown around to prevent me from drawing closer. There was nothing up front about her. I became guarded and oblique.

Twenty-four hours after our gins, I wrote saying I wished I'd stayed and had dinner with her in *our neighborhood* rather than gone to that dumb dinner party.

Dearest, did you have as terrible a time as all that? What about the give-or-take friends you like so much?

I liked sarcasm. *Wish I had brought you along with me—would have livened the company, thawed winter, dusted the old bookcases still in place after Duncan's death—and it would have made me so happy.*

Would it have made you that happy?

So very, very happy.

I wanted to tell her about dinner in my friends' carpeted dining room overlooking Lower Manhattan's skyline with a scenic view of the East River, all of us talking about Diego, who was still cheating on Tamar but had chosen to stay with her because he couldn't think of life without her, or of Mark, who had left Maud for a much younger woman, claiming that all he wanted was *just another go*. One complicit glance from her across the table, had she been present that night, and we would have burst out laughing together, repeating *just another go* on the sidewalk as we were heading back to Abingdon Square.

We were neither friends, nor strangers, nor lovers, just wavering, as I wavered, as I wished to think she wavered, each grateful for the other's silence as we watched the evening drift into night on this tiny park that was neither on Hudson, nor on Bleecker, nor on Eighth Avenue, but a tangent to all three, as we ourselves were, perhaps, nothing more than tangents in each other's life. In a blizzard, we'd be the first to go, we'd have nowhere to go. Ours, I began to fear, was a script without parts.

TWO DAYS LATER, past midnight: *My dearest, I haven't been happy once this week. It's been very rough. And the worst isn't over. I want you to think of me.*

Think of you? I'm always thinking of you, I wrote as soon as I was up at five thirty the next morning. *Why do you think I'm up so early?*

Later that same day: *My dearest, let's have drinks soon.*

Done.

"I wish I could do something to help. Have you told him where he stands?" was my tentative foot forward.

"I've told him everything. I'm not afraid of telling people the truth."

I wish I knew how to tell people the truth.

I wanted her to say something like *But I thought you did tell the truth. You turned down my article when you didn't like it, didn't you? You've always told me the truth.*

I wasn't talking about that kind of truth.

Then, what kind? she'd have asked, and I'd have told her. All I needed was an opening.

I could just hear Manfred: *Find the opening. Make the opening. Life throws thousands of them—you just don't see them. It took two years with me. Don't make the same mistake.*

"Truth is difficult sometimes, and I don't always like being straightforward," she said, "but I always tell the truth when it matters." She had sidestepped my flimsy little trap, deftly.

A few days later she wrote saying a family emergency was taking her to DC. Meanwhile she had finished her piece on Malibran.

How many words?

Too many.

I'd love to see it.

But you know I can't publish it with you.

I know that. I don't care who runs your story. But I care about everything you do, write, think, say, eat, drink, everything, can't you tell?

This was as straightforward as I could be. If my meaning wasn't clear, then obviously she wasn't eager to know it.

Dearest, your feelings for me touch me deeply. I do listen to everything you say. Surely, you know this. I just hope I'm worthy of you. I'll e-mail the manuscript as soon as I've revised it for the nth time. Your loyal and devoted me.

Manfred: *Stop talking shop with her. This is not about work.*

What he didn't see was that as she and I continued to write to each other, my e-mails were becoming ever more cryptic: too many smoke signals and plenty of allusions to the point where I no longer knew what I kept hinting at; what mattered was for her to know I was hinting, that hinting had become my only language, that I wasn't saying what needed to be said.

Peeved by her inability to respond in a manner less oblique than mine, I didn't write for three days.

Dearest, what's wrong?

I could almost feel the smooch you give grumpy granddaddy when he wants to seem hurt.

Manfred: *You've been seeing each other far too many times to assume she doesn't already know. She wouldn't have met you a second, certainly not a third time if she didn't already want what you want. No man I've ever known—you included—spends more than a minute with another man without knowing they both want the same thing. She likes you, she doesn't like the twenty- or thirtysomething idiots who surround her. If anything, she probably feels no less puzzled or hampered than you are. Just cut the coffee face-to-face interviews and sleep with her. Get drunk if you have to and tell her what you told me the first time.*

The following Friday we decided to have dinner. I'd found a restaurant on West 4th Street and made reservations for six thirty. *That early?* she quipped. I knew exactly why she was smiling and what she was asking. The place gets overcrowded, I explained. "Overcrowded," she replied, echoing my own word, to mean *Understood*. Tart and snide. At least this much is clear between us, I thought. Knowing that she saw through everything was an irresistible turn-on. A woman who knows what you're thinking must think what you're thinking.

If the weather didn't change, it might snow again, and the snow would slow things down and put a halo on an ordinary dinner date and give our evening the luster and magic that snow always casts on otherwise drab evenings in this part of the city.

On my way to the restaurant I already knew I'd never forget the sequence of streets as I took my time on West 4th Street. First Horatio, then Jane, then West 12th, then Bethune, Bank Street, West 11th, Perry, Charles, West 10th. The picturesque buildings with their tiny, picturesque high-end stores, the people heading home in the cold, the cold lampposts shedding their scant light on the glinting slate sidewalks. I caught myself envying all young lovers living in their tiny apartments here, all the while reminding myself, *You do know what you're doing, you know where this is likely to go tonight.* I loved every minute of the walk. Manfred: *She knows what this is about. She knows and she's telling you she knows.* The worst that could happen at this point was being invited upstairs after dinner and explaining that I could stay but couldn't spend the night. No, I corrected myself, the worst was walking back along these same streets a few hours from now after making love to her and wondering whether I was any happier than I'd been before dinner, now that I had left her and was crossing Charles, Perry, Bank, in reverse order.

Then it hit me. The very worst would be walking back these same streets without having spoken or come close to speaking. The worst was watching nothing change. This is when I'd feel the cruel stab of delayed irony as I'd recall rehearsing my clever little exit line about sleeping with her but not spending the night. It would have to sound unrehearsed, a tad fumbled even, if only to dull the awkwardness. Fumble if you must, said my inner Manfred.

SHE SHOWED UP wearing a short black dress and high-heeled boots, looking much taller than I remembered. She had dressed up and was wearing jewelry. When she came to our table after negotiating her way through the crowded bar area, I told her she looked ravishing. We kissed on both cheeks and I on her forehead, as I always did. Any doubts about what we meant to each other were instantly dismissed. This moment of sudden clarity in my incipient new life thrilled me and dispelled my inhibitions. How silly of me to have even considered taking my time getting here.

I ordered two Hendrick's martinis. Did she like the place? "Feels decadent but quite, quite wonderful," she said. She removed her shawl, and for the first time I saw her arms—same glistening skin, same tone as her hands, slim but not delicate; the merest sight of her underarms stirred me and reminded me that none of this was a mistake, that I wasn't making any of it up, that if I couldn't find it in me to make a pass, just the sight of her underarms at the table when she sat and stared at me would dispel all my inhibitions.

The menu seemed to confuse her. She didn't feel like order-ing. "Order for me."

I didn't quite believe her. But I loved what she was doing and couldn't resist: "I know exactly what you'll like."

She seemed relieved. She immediately put the menu down and continued staring at me. I loved that she was staring. I reached out and held her hand.

She let me order the wine too.

The way she scooped her oysters off their shells made me hope she'd take her time and keep eating and finish none of it, ever. You're staring at me, she said. I'm staring at you, I said. She smiled. I smiled back.

Of course, there was no way to avoid Maria Malibran. I asked if she knew that Pauline Viardot, Maria's sister, was an opera singer as well. Yes, she knew that Maria's sister was an op-era singer. Somehow, it didn't seem to interest her any longer. Did she know that Turgenev was madly in love with Maria's sister for years? A lifelong love, she said, yes, she knew about Turgenev too . . . "Now tell me about you. You never say any-thing about you."

It was true. I seldom spoke about me. "Everything there is to say is more or less already out there." A moment of silence.

"Well, then tell me what's in there." She pointed to her chest to mean mine.

"Do you really want me to answer this now?" I didn't mean it to sound wistful or cryptic. What I meant was: I'll answer this question later, once we leave the restaurant and are on our way to your place. I want you to ask me again what's going on *in there* when we're past the film crew, which I hope will be out there tonight and which I pray will stop us from crossing the street as fake rain pours down. Let the gofers manning their cell phones and eating donuts tell us to be very, very quiet, because I want to

walk and talk and be very quiet and walk till we reach your
door, where you'll ask me to come upstairs, and we'll go upstairs,
and you'll open the door and say, *This is my place.* I want to see
where you live, how you live, how you look when you take your
clothes off. I want to see your cat spring on you and snuggle in
your bare arms, I want to see the table where you sit to write
and hear how you came to own the things you own, I want to
know everything. That's what's happening *in there.*

Instead, I ended up saying, "A restaurant may not be the best
place."

The girl who had written about Maria Malibran, and who
knew all about crypto-Jews who for centuries had been living
with their identities hidden, would easily have read what I was
saying in my crypto-lover's speech. *If she picks up on it, she's telling
you something. If she lets it slide, she is telling you something too.*

Manfred: *You're giving her an out.*

Me: *Yes, I am.*

Manfred: *Not fair. Not fair to you. Not fair to her.*

I remembered his latest e-mail after I'd told him of our plan
for dinner tonight. *If she invites you home, don't hesitate, don't ever,
ever let her think you're rejecting her. And send her flowers before you
see her tonight. Your problem is not that you misread signs; all you see
are signs. You're blind, amigo.*

I know when to put the moves on, thankyouverymuch.

I'm not sure, was his reply.

But I heeded his advice and sent flowers.

No sooner had my flowers arrived than she wrote back: I
love lilies.

And yet, as we lapsed into a moment of silence during dinner,
how very, very far from sleeping together all this seemed. Dinner began to feel like a concession I'd wrenched from her. There
was even tension in our silence. One more second of this and

she'll say something that could dispel even the illusion of perfect harmony between us. I could even tell that what she was about to say was not what I wanted, that her arms, her hand, her fingers, which seemed to beg me to reach out across the table and touch them once more, would, within seconds of what she'd say, turn into stone and take back the dream and the godsend. But she chose silence instead.

"We should plan to see the Da Ponte tombstone," I finally said. Shoptalk better than no talk.

"Maybe this weekend," she said.

Her comeback was too hasty to sound like a real yes.

"This weekend is difficult."

She stared at me.

"Dinner and things?"

What a sharp and twisted mind she had.

"Dinner and things," I replied.

Any other woman would have scorned *dinner and things* and held it against me. Instead, she let it slide. In anyone else this silence would have meant *I don't want to cause trouble.* In her it felt different. *Dinner and things* worked for her too—which is why I began to feel something rise within me akin to anger, though it might have been despair or, worse, sorrow. I couldn't tell them apart.

More shoptalk then. "Pauline Viardot became friends with everyone who was anyone: Chopin, Tchaikovsky, Liszt, Sand, Gounod, Berlioz, Saint-Saëns, Brahms." But, not knowing what else to add, I couldn't help myself. "So tell me about this new man in your life." Was I acting jealous? Or was I trying to show that I wasn't? Or was I trying ever so delicately to give her the chance to tell me that the new man in her life was none other than I?

"The new man?" she said, musing for a moment. "I don't want to talk about him yet."

"Doesn't want to talk about him," I echoed, trying to be jovial.

"Doesn't."

Her mood had changed. I couldn't tell why. Our conversation was losing its footing. We were both groping for strings.

Toward the end of dinner, I said I knew of a small place nearby for dessert and coffee. I was hoping she'd counter with an offer of coffee at her place. "Sounds like a good idea," she said.

We walked out. This, I knew, was the moment when years earlier I'd have put a hand on her cheek and kissed her there, on the sidewalk, in full view of the other diners. I took my time putting on my coat while she was looking for her cigarettes. In the end she produced one out of her pocket but, considering its bent shape, called it a cripple. I said I used to smoke two packs a day. How long ago had I quit? she asked.

"I'm not going to answer this."

"Why? Because you cheat, or because you are afraid to claim that you've actually quit?"

"Do you really want me to answer?"

"I asked, didn't I? You're dying to tell me, anyway." She had regained her spirited tone, it seemed.

My answer, after so much hesitation, might cast a shadow and betray why I was stalling with the answer. So I told her the truth.

"I quit the year you were born. Does that tell you enough?"

She looked at the ground as though taking her time to examine her boots. She had lit her cigarette and was either deep in thought or was inhaling for the first time in more than two hours.

"Do you still miss them?"

"Cigarettes? Are we still talking about cigarettes?"

"I thought we were"—she paused—"but I guess we're not."

"I don't miss cigarettes, but I miss who I was before quitting."

This was by way of both compromise and evasion.

She must have sensed, from my hardscrabble confession, why I wasn't comfortable being clearer.

"Has this been bothering you?"

Was she speaking about cigarettes? Or about us?

I wanted to scream. When I'm with you, I feel I can take what others call my life and turn its face away from the wall. My entire life faces the wall except when I'm with you. I stare at my life and want to undo every mistake, every deceit, turn a new leaf, turn the table, turn the clock. I want to put a real face on my life, not the drab front I've been wearing since forever. So why can't I speak to you now?

All I said was that no one liked watching time go by. That was abstract and safe enough, perhaps too abstract and safe for the likes of her or Manfred.

She made light of the whole thing. "So, while I'm kicking about in my mommy's tummy, you're smoking away in some nameless café in Paris. Is that what's been bothering you, dear?"

"There's more to it than just that," I said, "as I'm sure you know."

"I do know." She said nothing more.

"My dearest." Even I expected she'd come out and throw in a *dearest*. But then she surprised me. "You shouldn't hate yourself."

I did not answer, did not object. She looked at the ground again and began shaking her head ever so slightly. At first I thought she meant, *This never bothered me, but you'll never let yourself go, and what a pity that is.* Then I thought she meant something a touch more hopeful, even exasperated, as in: *What am I*

ever going to do with you, Paul? Finally I made out what the shaking was about: *I don't want to hurt you.*

"What?" I asked.

She continued to shake her head in silence. Then she looked
up and I could feel the tension almost explode in my temples.
"Walk me to my building?" she asked.

"I'll walk you to your building."

We were, I assumed, nixing the idea of coffee and dessert. A
good sign. Or a very bad sign. I did not say anything. I was trying
to keep pace with her as we made our way down Bleecker. Why
was she walking fast, why the sudden chill between us, why
the mounting fear of saying goodbye the closer we got to her
building?

Suddenly, before I knew it, there we were. She stopped at
the street corner, not even at her stoop. She was actually going
to say goodbye. She kissed me on one cheek, I kissed her back,
and she turned to go away but then came back and gave me a
hug. I didn't have time to hold her, nor did she give me time to
perform what had become my ritual kiss on her forehead. I
watched her walk away toward her house. I thought she looked
downcast and deep in thought, dejected, almost. She did not look
back this time.

Why hadn't we spoken? Had I perhaps rejected her as Manfred had warned me not to? Had I missed my cue?

There was never a cue.

As I walked away toward the West 4th Street station, I had an
image of her entering her apartment, dropping her keys on her
table, and giving out a yelp of relief. She'd acquitted herself of
dinner, it wasn't even nine o'clock, and she was free to do as she
pleased, take off her clothes, lounge in jeans, call her beau. Yes,
dinner's over, thank God he's gone, it's the weekend, let's go out
and see something really stupid tonight!

Bold and rakish, like the piano, while I, the trumpet, felt plangent and lost.

I HAD MEANT to take her to my favorite pastry shop after dinner. I'd known happiness there once, or maybe not happiness, but the vision of it. I wanted to see whether the place had changed at all, or whether I had changed, or whether, just by sitting with her I could make up for old loves I'd gotten so close to but had never been bold enough to seize. Always got so very close, and always turned my back when the time came. Manfred and I had dessert here so many times, especially after the movies, and before Manfred, Maud and I, because it was so hot on summer nights that we'd stop to drink fizzy lemonades here, night after night, happy to be together drinking nothing stronger. And Chloe, of course, on those cold afternoons on Rivington Street so many years ago. My life, my real life, had not even happened yet, and all of this was rehearsal still. Tonight, I thought, relishing Joyce's words and feeling exquisitely sorry for myself, the time has come for me to set out on my journey westward. Then I thought of Saint Augustine's words: *"Sero te amavi!* Late have I loved you!"

So here I was, making my way back through the streets just as I had feared a few hours before, remembering now with a cruel chuckle that I'd even gone so far as to rehearse an exit line. But I recognized the walking home. This was not the first time. It took me back to my childhood when one evening, after desperately wanting to be undressed and held naked in a man's arms, I was told to go home, behave and go home, he'd said, while I thought, this was home, you're my home, it's you I want to grow up with, you I want to grow old with. *I want to live with you* is what I should have said years ago. It's what I should have said tonight as well.

As soon as I stepped into my study, I opened my e-mail and started typing something very short: *We'll have dessert another time.* I had just pressed Send when her e-mail arrived: *Dearest, I forgot to thank you for the wonderful conversation, a great meal, a truly lovely evening.* A few seconds later, another e-mail from her: *I'd love that.*

She was thinking of me.

No, she was just scrambling to say something nice.

No, she was thinking of me. She was trying to stay in touch and not break the evening's spell. Perhaps she was trying to tease something out of me, get me to say those extra few words that I'd been trying to coax out of her and have frequently blamed her for not saying, or myself for not helping her say them. Perhaps she was reopening a window I thought she'd closed the moment we'd said goodbye.

So I ventured something light. *Have coffee with me tomorrow.* She did not reply.

On Monday she wrote back. She'd been out with friends all day Saturday and Sunday. And Sunday night, dearest, was just too horrific for words. *But let's definitely have coffee soon.*

Monday evening I couldn't resist. I wrote what I considered a layered e-mail about Maria Malibran and her sister. *It turns out that Casanova had known Da Ponte in Venice and he too, like Maria's father, is alleged to have had Gypsy origins. Could it be, do you think, that Casanova too . . . ?* Then, as though it had occurred to me right then and there: *We should go out for dinner again. It was good to be with you. But I don't mean to crowd you. I'm leaving things in your hands.*

Not crowding me in the slightest, she replied, eventually.

In the days that followed I didn't know how to reach out to her without sounding either desperate or peevish. In discussing Turgenev's hopeless love for Maria's sister Pauline, I finally let myself go: *I understand him completely, I'm there myself.* I had nothing to lose, and like all those who know they've lost already, I was firing my last salvo, no ammunition left, no backup, no water in my gourd. The feckless sputters in my sentence said I had shot my wad.

The silence that followed was more than a simple omission to respond, crueler than a gloved rebuke. She had lost interest, and I had lost her.

I would wait another half a day, maybe a day or two, but a week was certainly pushing it. Still, I'd have to struggle to avoid drowning in this. I'd never allowed myself to sink in too deeply for her—that much was good—though I did like her, liked her very much. Liked her on the day she ordered coffee for me. Liked her when I sent her my two-page, single-spaced rejection letter. Liked the sheen on her skin. I even liked the spot of eczema under her right elbow that she showed me on that night at the restaurant after she'd removed her shawl and knew I was admiring every inch of her. "See this?" she said, pointing at her elbow. "It's new. Do you think it could be cancer? I've always had good skin."

"I know," I said. She knew I knew, every man knew. "Probably eczema," I replied. "Nothing but dry skin. Do you have a dermatologist?" I asked.

"Nope." As if to mean, *Why should I? At my age?*

"Want the name of one?"

"Nope. Don't like doctors."

"Want me to go with you?"

"Maybe. No. Yes."

"Maybe. No. Yes?" I asked.

"Yes," she replied.

There was nothing I wanted more at that very moment than to put my arms around her, or reach over and hold her hand and say, "Put on your coat, I'm taking you to the dermatologist. He's a . . . give-or-take friend, he'll see you if I ask him." No sooner said than once we'd stepped outside on the curb I would have changed plans, taken matters in my own hands, and said, "We're going to your place instead."

I opened the window of my study and let in the cold air. *We're going to your place instead.* My unspoken words rang like a promise of bliss that I'd almost uttered and that continued to resonate throughout the day like a good dream long after we've woken up and had coffee.

I liked the cold air. A few nights ago, I'd faced the same street, the same view, the same neighbors' lights across from my building, and asked myself whether I'd ever miss this street once I was off to my new life. I remembered the young couple I'd seen at the movie theater a month earlier; they couldn't even eat popcorn together. Yet they were going to see plays together, have children, hang out on rainy Sundays and listen to Shostakovich and hold their breath when the bold piano and the soulful trumpet sang to each other of old sorrows and newborn hopes. Later, they'd head out to eat somewhere in the neighborhood and then loiter their way into one of those large bookstores where people always end up buying books, even when they don't mean to, the way I'd bought her a book one Saturday night after a movie, not sure whether I was buying it for her or for me, yet almost certain it would make her happy. "I need a hug," she'd say. Now, how far away did Abingdon Square feel, as though it and she and the restaurant, and Maria Malibran, and the sudden false rainfall by the flickering lights of the Miramar hotel sign belonged to another life, a life unlived, a life I knew had turned its back to me and was being nailed to the wall.

I would survive this easily enough, of course, and grow indifferent, and soon learn to squelch every access of regret. For heartache, like love, like low-grade fevers, like the longing to reach out and touch a hand across the table, is easy enough to live down. There were sure to be more e-mails with more *dearests*—I knew this—and my heart would skip a beat and catch itself hoping each time her name floated across my screen, which meant I was still going to be vulnerable, which meant I could still feel these things, which was a good thing—even losing and aching was a good thing.

What was sad was knowing she was most likely the last reminder that there might never be *another go*. We might still communicate, might still meet for coffee, but the dream was gone, the hand across the table was gone, the square itself was gone. And I knew this because for the first time, after shutting my window and turning off my computer, I walked into the living room and told my wife about a brilliant new piece that was soon to be published about a nineteenth-century diva called Maria Malibran. Had she ever heard of her? I asked.

No, she hadn't. "But obviously you're dying to tell me," said Claire.

ACKNOWLEDGMENTS

I wish to thank the Corporation of Yaddo and the American Academy in Rome for their gracious, generous, and ever-inspiring hospitality. I also want to thank my agent, Lynn Nesbit, who opened the world to me, and my editor, Jonathan Galassi, for all that is ever priceless in an editor who is also a friend.